THE KILLER SHE KNEW

NICHOLE SEVERN

Storm

Ebook ISBN: 978-1-80508-505-8
Paperback ISBN: 978-1-80508-507-2

Cover design: www.designbysim.com
Cover images: Shutterstock, Adobe Stock

Published by Storm Publishing.
For further information, visit:
www.stormpublishing.co

ALSO BY NICHOLE SEVERN

Leigh Brody FBI Mystery

The Girl Who Survived

The Vanishing Wife

Hunting Grounds

Run, Run, Seek

Over the Flames

Into the Veins

Bits and Pieces

View from Above

Study in Color

Art in Blood

Cold Grounds

Taken

New Mexico Guard Dogs

K-9 Security

K-9 Detection

K-9 Shield

Defenders of Battle Mountain

Grave Danger

Dead Giveaway

Dead On Arrival

Tactical Crime Division

Midnight Abduction

Heroes with Heat and Heart Anthology

Mountain Murder

For Kent and Marla. You've shown me what family truly means.

PROLOGUE

Monday, October 7
9:43 p.m.

No one ever said being a killer was easy.

He'd been hoping this day would come.

Eighteen years. Of planning. Of waiting. Of blending in for the right time to strike. He'd been patient. Waiting for her to make a mistake.

And this was his reward.

A quiet shuffle reached his ears from the other side of the room as he pinned the latest news article to the board. This one an interview from the *Gulf Shores News*. "Revengeful Mother of Teen Sentenced to Life Without Parole." He didn't care about the case. It was already losing its shiny-new-crisis appeal. But the FBI agent interviewed and pictured in the center of the front-page article did hold his attention. So damn perfect. But sad. Broken.

Dozens of faces stared back at him from the wall. Well, one

face. They all belonged to her. She'd kept herself out of the media well enough over the years, but she'd always been a star in his eyes.

The one who'd gotten away.

A weak sound filled the dark room. Exasperation killed the enthusiasm in his veins. Apparently his guest wasn't going to follow the rules after all. He turned to face the slumped woman coming to against the built-in shelves constructed of raw two-by-fours.

This small below-ground escape-from-the-real-world didn't meet his usual standards. He preferred not to have to get a tetanus shot each time he descended into the basement, but it would do for now. After all, this was all temporary.

She was pretty in an unremarkable kind of way. Curled blonde hair and flawlessly applied makeup. Smart, too, from what little conversation he'd overheard between her and her professor earlier. Something about positivist victimology, victim environment, non-random risk of violence. Blah, blah, blah. Ironic her understanding of criminal behavior wouldn't do her any good now. "You're wondering why you're here."

He crouched in front of her, reaching for a thick strand of hair as she blinked up at him. It was all she could do, thanks to padded binds around her wrists and ankles. Couldn't be leaving any bruises, after all. What was her name? Anne? Adrienne? He wasn't sure. They all started blending together after a while. And this one didn't have long. There was no point in trying to remember. Ten minutes, maybe less. "Would you believe it if I said you remind me of someone I used to know?"

"Please." Her begging had lost its meaning over the past couple of hours. It always did. If he was being honest with himself, this whole charade was starting to feel stale. Then again, pretty little Abigail hadn't been his original target. He'd had to adapt in the moment to get to her. Take advantage of an opportunity he hadn't considered before, and for the first time in years, he'd nearly dropped to his knees from the rush. But, in the end, Alison and the others who'd come before her were nothing more than place holders.

The one he wanted—needed—was still out there. Waiting for him.

ONE

Tuesday, October 8
11:16 p.m.

"You're not my mother!" The door slammed in her face, nearly breaking her nose. "I hate you!"

Leigh Brody tamped down the visceral inclination to shout something immature back, to stick out her tongue, and slam another door in response, but she was supposed to be the adult in this relationship. Were all fifteen-year-olds this impossible to live with, or had she been particularly lucky?

She'd known adopting a teenager would be hard, but nobody had warned her about the fact there was no return policy. Ava wasn't a random teen in need of a home. She was the beloved daughter of Leigh's best friend. Well, former best friend.

Murder and a life prison sentence had a way of adding distance to any relationship. Not to mention a heavy helping of resentment.

Ava had shown an incredible willingness to do just about anything to get as far from their new situation as possible over the past couple of weeks. Sneaking out in the middle of the night, stealing Leigh's credit card, refusing to tell anyone where she was going, who she was hanging out with. Leigh couldn't blame her. Neither of them wanted to accept the truth: They were all each other had.

"Dinner is on the table when you get hungry," she said through the door.

Ava didn't respond. In Leigh's experience, she wouldn't for a while. The silent treatment had become Ava's number one weapon, but it would be much harder for her adopted daughter to sneak out onto the balcony attached to her room with the new hardware Leigh had installed during tonight's escape attempt. She hoped no one reported the shiny new bolt lock to the landlord. Or the fire department.

Forcing herself to take a step back from the thin wood separating them, Leigh faced the dining room in the too-small two-bedroom apartment. Boxes lined the walls of the living room to her left. Mostly hers, some of them Ava's. Two lives coming together from an explosion of disaster and new beginnings. It was a mess they would have to systematically clean up together. But not tonight. "Thanks for bringing her home, Caine."

"Anytime, Agent Brody." The Quantico PD uniformed officer dipped his standard issue baseball cap with the touch of his index finger at the brim. Nice and polite. Leigh had the fortune to get to know most of the officers out of Quantico since relocating to Virginia earlier this year. Came with the territory as a criminologist in the FBI's Behavioral Analysis Unit Two, but Caine was starting to become a regular face. Thanks to Ava. "Teens this age don't know who they are. It's all about experimenting and pushing boundaries. They're not kids anymore but they're not adults either. And, from what you've said, she's been through a lot. I wouldn't go too hard on her."

Officer Caine had no idea how right he was. How much Ava had been through in the past few weeks alone. First losing her father to suicide, her childhood home to a blackmailer, then her mother to life behind bars for murder. Then being placed with a woman she didn't know in a city she'd never stepped foot in. Leigh wanted to escape, too.

"Can I offer you some orange chicken to go before you head back on shift?" Leigh stretched across the peeling circular dining table set for two, pulling Ava's plate to the edge in offering. Heat crested her neck and into her face as she realized she'd given Officer Caine a direct view down her sweater with the movement, and he'd taken the opportunity to catch a glimpse. Great. She pulled back sharply, adjusting her neckline, and tried to think of a reason for her embarrassment. She wasn't married. Hadn't even had a boyfriend in... She didn't want to think about how long. "I have a feeling it's going to go cold."

Officer Caine was classically handsome. Chiseled jawline, long, straight nose, which had obviously never been broken. Usually clean shaven with a hint of beard growth, his unkept appearance told her he'd had an equally as long day as she had. They were around the same age. He might've been a couple years younger than her thirty-seven. And it wasn't the first time she'd been a little more than embarrassed with him in the house.

The third night Officer Caine had brought Ava back, clawing and screaming about her human rights being violated, Leigh had dumped an entire mug of coffee on his crotch. Every interaction since got a little more pathetic and desperate to prove she wasn't holding a fifteen-year-old hostage against her will. Illegally. She was a good person with a good job and very little baggage. That last part was a lie. But, all things considered, she had to work with this man. And the thought of taking her and Officer Caine's relationship beyond fugitive hunter and "the actual devil," as Ava lovingly referred to Leigh, scared her more than facing down a killer. Acquaintances worked fine for her.

"You know I'll never turn down one of your home cooked meals." He took a step forward.

"Not sure you'd consider this home cooked since it came out of a box, but it might be better than the garbage you usually eat." The truth was she and Ava were living off boxed dinners as they figured out new school schedules and transitioning back from medical leave. Who knew mom guilt was transferrable?

"Hey, that garbage serves a purpose. Mostly." Officer Caine's smile cracked wide, and Leigh couldn't help but return it. Being in law enforcement put them both center stage to evil of the worst kind. Moments like this got her through. The... connection to another person that didn't come with a load of obscenities and slamming doors.

His radio crackled in interruption. A call down the street. He pinched the handheld and notched his head down to respond. "Sorry, Leigh. Raincheck?"

She didn't want to give too much attention to his use of her first name. He'd never called her Leigh before.

"Of course." She motioned to the door. He could let himself out as he had the few times he'd dragged Ava home before. And within a matter of seconds, she was alone again. Not in the most basic sense. Ava would calm down. She would venture into the common areas for food once her stomach got the best of her, as most feral animals did, but it wouldn't change the hollowness in Leigh's chest. She'd wanted this her entire life. Wanted Ava and a family and all the impossible things that came with it since losing her own mother. But why did it have to feel as if she was slogging through mud day after day with no finish line in sight?

Leigh secured the deadbolt on the door and cleared her dishes from the table.

Her phone vibrated from the peninsula counter jutting out

from the wall. She grabbed for it with a soapy hand and wedged it between her shoulder and ear. "Brody."

"Agen' Brody, time's up." Director Angelina Livingstone's thick Scottish accent cut through the line as sharp as the blade paramedics had pulled from Leigh's shoulder a month ago. "I have a case for you."

A knot physically released in her gut. As grateful as she'd been to have the time out of the field to recover from the hysterectomy and to get Ava situated in Quantico, not to mention overcoming a stab wound, a part of her had been waiting for this moment. Craving it. Consulting on serial investigations and scouring data for criminal patterns for over twenty years had become an obsession. Made violence part of her very being. Without it, she wasn't sure who she was supposed to be. Clearly not a stand-in mom to a teenager who kept trying to escape or even a sensible person who could attract a date. "What do you have?"

"You're going back to New Hampshire," the director said.

Gravity drained the blood from her face. Leigh forgot about the dishes, reaching to steady her phone against her ear. Not Lebanon. For crying out loud, please not Lebanon. She'd barely managed to make it out of her hometown alive the last time she'd visited. "You're going to have to be more specific."

"Durham." Livingstone let the word sink in. "University of New Hampshire. The US Marshals office is specifically asking for your collaboration, as you have relationships within the local police department and know the area well."

University of New Hampshire. Previously Granite State. Her alma mater. The hairs on the back of her neck stood on end. In her experience, law enforcement only asked for the FBI to consult after they'd already exhausted and run through potential leads. Or something came up pertaining to an old case. But Director Livingstone's assumption hit the target. She still had contacts at the university, however strained. "I'm trained to work serial crimes, which means the university has more than one victim on their hands, and police are concerned there may be a serial element."

That was how this job worked. Despite the violence and sadness and desperation for answers tacked onto this job, Leigh had made patterns her entire life. From the moment her brother had been abducted twenty years ago, they'd consumed and driven her to become one of the FBI's most nationally recognized assets. She found the connections—between evidence, victimology, and unsubs—most experts ignored in favor of physical proof. Solved some of the country's coldest cases through personal interactions, body language, and relationships. She read people. Probably better than she read herself.

"I need you on scene as soon as possible," Livingstone said. "A storm is approaching the east coast. The crime scene is at risk."

Leigh's gaze flicked to the closed bedroom door on the other side of the dining room. There'd been a time she wouldn't have hesitated to jump into the next investigation. The promise of a shiny new puzzle kept her from spiraling into the crushing weight of the past. But a lot had changed in the last month. Now she had a teenager—a flight risk—to worry about. "There are far more qualified officials in and around Durham to handle this investigation than someone who hasn't been back for almost twenty years. Let one of them have this one."

Unless there was a reason Livingstone had offered her up.

A reason Leigh hadn't let herself think about since she was a college freshman.

"One victim, Agen' Brody. Alice Dietz. Twenty-one years old. Blonde, athletic build, brown eyes." Livingstone's accent went neutral but still managed to reach a couple of levels above deadpan. There was enough life in her voice to give her away. The director knew exactly what Leigh was thinking. She wouldn't be able to turn this investigation over to some other agent. "According to the officials on scene, the body smells as though it was recently bathed in a mixture of bleach, and she was left in front of Thompson Hall. Sound familiar?"

Leigh found herself sagging against the counter to keep herself on her feet.

"Let me guess. Poisoning?" The pieces were starting to line up. The familiarity knotted her gut tighter. She'd moved on. She'd left the black hole of her college days behind. They weren't supposed to catch up with her until she was ready. Or never. "The medical examiner likely found she was poisoned with an equal mixture of arsenic and cyanide that will be traced back to the university biomedical lab. The killer also cleaned under the victim's fingernails to ensure there was no trace of DNA to connect back to him."

"It seems you're already quite familiar with the investigation," Livingstone said. It wasn't a question, but no. Leigh wasn't just familiar with this potential case. She'd lived it. "There is no sign of a puncture wound anywhere on the body, no burn evidence in the esophagus revealing the victim was forced to swallow the poison, and her stomach was empty of food that could've led to her death."

It was all adding up. Same MO. Different victim.

He was back. Taunting her. Daring her to give chase.

And she was going to take the bait.

"You and I both know why the US Marshals Service is asking me to consult, Director." Leigh tried to keep her voice even to avoid Ava overhearing the conversation through the thin wood door. The dread pooling at the base of her spine refused to relent. "Durham PD or campus police recognized the MO and connected me back to the original investigation. Considering my new popularity, I'm surprised it took them this long."

She'd managed to escape the media for most of her life. Up until she'd solved a twenty-year-old cold case. Her brother's. The attention was getting more suffocating now that she'd put her best friend behind bars for murder. And adopted the woman's daughter as her own. She'd managed to keep their new arrangement out of the news, but it was only a matter a time.

"When you get to Durham, your contact during the course of the investigation will be US Marshal Max Ford. He'll meet you at the crime scene tomorrow morning." An order. Livingstone took a beat. "Tell me, Agen' Brody. Will there be a day when you don't have a personal connection to one of our cases, or can I expect your past to keep my team employed for the foreseeable future?"

Leigh wished she could deny the possibility, but secrets had a funny way of coming back to life at the most inopportune times. "Lucky for us, I already know who's doing this."

TWO

Durham, New Hampshire

Wednesday, October 9
9:17 a.m.

It was one of those postcard towns made of traditional brick, too-narrow roads, and a city center that compelled families to take part in the festivities for major holidays. There was even a picturesque bay tourists could work into their vacation photos if they got the right angle. Similar to her hometown, Durham, New Hampshire had one additional draw: the University of New Hampshire. Students from all over the country brought their bad driving habits into twenty-two square miles of densely populated fall-colored trees and crumbling roads. One upon a time, Leigh had been one of them.

A combination of red and yellow leaves was strewn about her path. Fall had thrown up all over campus with an added bite in the air from whatever storm was moving in. Skulls, witches' hats, and blood-streaked handprints clung to campus doors and told her Halloween was around the corner. This would be her first official holiday with Ava. No better way to get in the mood than by investigating a real-life murder.

Leigh followed the familiar maze of sidewalks cutting across a perfectly manicured dying lawn, all dead-ending at the front door of Thompson Hall. The Romanesque Revival had been built on a knoll south of Main Street, structured with heavy massing, granite trim, and a tall clock tower bellowing its protest every hour on the hour. It was possibly the most recognizable building out of fifty others on campus.

And where a killer had chosen to make his point.

Keystone arches supported the extended overhang protecting the double glass doors, consuming her whole as she approached the yellow crime scene tape cutting off access to the building to academics and students alike. Fall had settled in the air with a nip capable of slithering beneath her coat. It hadn't gotten cold enough to form crystals at her mouth, but it was only a matter of time. A rogue gust of wind whipped her hair from her collar as she approached the perimeter of crime scene tape. Weather reports from the screen built into the back of the airline seat in front of her had shown the growing strength of the storm gathering off the coast, but hurricanes this far north weren't common. And they certainly couldn't touch the university this far inland.

Leigh pulled her credentials from her wool coat pocket as an officer moved to bar her from getting too close. Protect the scene. No matter the cost. "Agent Brody, FBI. Marshal Ford is expecting me." She took the sign-in clipboard from the officer posted as scene security and scribbled her initials, handing it back as he lifted the tape to see herself into an exclusive club of observers. The kind that made death and violence resemble an office job.

She'd been to near a hundred crime scenes, most of them death investigations, but coming back here? Standing in this exact spot? It was all starting to compound. She replaced her credentials and pulled her phone free. No update from Ava back at the hotel. Leigh had barely had time to toss her overnight bag on the bed before the fifteen-year-old had grabbed for the TV remote, thrown herself on the opposite bed, and put up the oh-so-recognizable wall teens were experts in building. She sent a check-in message. More to make herself feel better about leaving Ava alone in an unfamiliar hotel room in the middle of a random New England town while Leigh gave someone else her full attention. No response. Seemed Ava hadn't forgiven her for having her forcibly dragged back to the apartment last night.

"Bet you didn't expect to be back here of all places." The rough voice came from her left, slightly outside the target scene where controlled chaos buzzed. Local police, medicolegal investigators, photographers. All focused on the body at their feet. But the US marshal stepping to her side didn't want to be in the middle of the action. He'd been waiting. For her. "Victim's name is Alice Dietz."

Impossibly dark eyes landed on her in expectation. At over six feet tall, he could probably intimidate the hell out of anyone, and Leigh had to crane her head back to hold a gaze set in a too-handsome face free from violence. Perfectly styled hair with a few grays at his temples, the unbuttoned suit jacket, and shiny black shoes completed the Boy Scout look and lent a heavy dose of charisma Leigh was sure he unleashed on unsuspecting victims when needed. But it was the disarming half-smile and the wire-rimmed glasses that had the potential to lure the unwary into his web. A smile he hadn't used to hook a wife if his ringless finger was anything to go by. He stretched out one hand. "US Marshal Max Ford."

She took his offering, her hand immediately swallowed under his. Calluses gritted against her palm. A sign of hard labor. Max worked with his hands. No desk jockey here. "Leigh Brody."

"I know who you are, Agent Brody. You've made quite the name for yourself with your last few cases." His attention was still on her. Limited to this two-person bubble he'd created around them. It was honed and as sharp as a blade and told her he was a lot wiser beyond what she guessed were his forty or forty-one years. He knew it, too. He expected people to underestimate him. "From what I've read, you're exactly who we need on this case."

Leigh's skin grew hot under his touch. Leaving her... exposed. She'd never been a fan of attention, private or public, and Ford was giving too much of both. She slipped her hand free of his. "From what I understand, USMS hunts fugitives and manages seized assets of criminals. Can I ask why you're interested in the homicide of a university student?"

His smile was back in place, targeting the invisible crack he'd created in her professional armor. He rested his hands at his sides, giving her a view of the marshal's service badge clipped to the waistband. "I have reason to believe there is more than one victim in this investigation, Agent Brody."

More than one. Had Livingstone gotten the body count wrong? Highly unlikely considering the FBI had access to every law enforcement database in the country. Which meant Ford had made another connection to this case. "I'm assuming you're not counting the victim who was poisoned and left to be found on this campus eighteen years ago, but, if so, why would the Marshals office be interested? Any investigation that crosses state lines falls into FBI jurisdiction. Unless you already know who's behind this."

"I've been chasing a suspect across the country. Santa Ana, Glendale, Garland, Boston, and now Durham." Ford cast a glance back to the scene. "Every town this guy visits, there's always a body left behind."

"Let me guess. Murdered with a combination of arsenic and cyanide." A pit solidified in Leigh's gut. It was Teshia Elborne's case all over again. Poison wasn't a merciful way to kill a person. Abdominal pain and uncontrolled vomiting from arsenic poisoning took effect within thirty minutes while the cyanide burned the central nervous system from the inside out. The victim died slowly and painfully, unable to move. Unable to scream. MOs involving poison always led to the same motive: to inflict pain. Either of the poisons on their own would have the desired effect. Why use both unless to make a point? "How many in total?"

"Four, not counting this one." Concentration deepened the lines between Ford's brows. "But he's never killed a woman before."

Interesting.

"I'll need to see the investigation files for any previous victims." A change in victimology didn't come easy to veteran killers. There were rules to be followed. Needs to be met. Protocols couldn't be broken when chasing adrenaline and pleasure highs serial offenders craved. Leigh would take the change in victimology into consideration later. That, and the possible connection to the first homicide here at the university, but for now, they had a fresh body. One that might give them some answers if they moved fast enough. "And I'd like to see the body."

"I thought you might." Ford didn't hesitate in taking the lead through the semi-circle of investigators and photographers. The small crowd parted with his presence alone, revealing the pale blonde taking up all their attention. And now Leigh's.

She'd seen this crime scene before. Studied it until the images had burned into her brain. The location of the body, how the killer had arranged her as though taking great care not to blemish her skin, the blonde hair and wide staring eyes. Too familiar. The force of similarities threatened to unravel the little composure she'd managed to build since stepping foot back onto this campus. She could practically feel the burn of Ford's attention between her shoulder blades as she crouched beside the body. Trying to learn every secret the victim had ever kept, every lie she'd ever told.

"Meet Alice Dietz. Sophomore. Twenty-one years old. Campus police received a report filed by a roommate she'd been missing for two days before the president's executive assistant found her here last night around 6:45 p.m. Said she was working late to help organize the fall fundraiser. Was so focused on the files in her hand, she tripped right over the victim." Ford kept a respectable distance from the body. "I had the ME's office hold off on transporting her to the morgue until you could see her yourself. They've done a preliminary examination. Now they're chomping at the bit to bag her and tag her."

While humor had always been a tool for investigators to keep the demons they slayed on a daily basis at bay, Ford's attempt at lightening the mood struck Leigh oddly. Perhaps he really didn't have much experience with murder investigations? His request to keep the body on site, while beneficial, would have the medical examiner's office seething by now. Any change in temperature, weather conditions, and police activity could affect time of death estimation and the condition of the remains. He'd made the wrong call.

She had to work fast. Leigh crouched to get a better view of the body. Snapping a pair of gloves over both hands, she pried Alice's right eye open, then the left. Blonde hair and brown eyes weren't common genetic traits. Less than 1 percent of the country fell into both categories naturally, and the chances of two victims turning up dead with both were even smaller. Sharp cheekbones and a thin frame would've garnered plenty of attention. A thin layer of makeup accentuated full lips and drew attention where Alice had presumably wanted it. She'd clearly been fastidious in her appearance, in her choice of clothing if the tailored white dress was anything to go by. Almost... dressed to impress. And Leigh couldn't help but compare this victim with one found in this exact location eighteen years ago. Her stomach soured. "You believe this is the work of a killer you've been hunting?"

"Wouldn't you? It's not common victims are killed with two different poisons in their systems," Ford said. "Once I realized my suspect had deviated from his preferred victim, I reached out to the BAU, though I can't imagine what he would've wanted with Alice. Up until now, everything this guy has done has almost been... functional."

"What do you mean?" Leigh sat back on her heels. As much death as she'd seen should've hampered her ability to feel anything but pure focus on this case, but a heaviness she couldn't breathe through sat on her chest. Alice Dietz had barely scratched the surface of her potential at twenty-one. Had she been excited to graduate and step into the real world? Had she already fallen in love or made a bucket list of countries to visit? Were there people who cared she wouldn't be coming home for Thanksgiving in a few weeks?

"The men my guy has killed in all those towns—Santa Ana, Garland—he didn't just kill them. He took their identities. He lived their lives for weeks before moving on and leaving their bodies to be found." Ford pushed his glasses back into place with his index finger before going for a small notebook. "Sometimes it's for a couple of days. The last one was nearly a month."

Leigh had to think about that for a moment. What did any of this have to do with a college co-ed killed in the same manner and location as an eighteen-year-old cold case? "Quite the feat. Your victims most likely had friends, families, coworkers who would spot the differences. Why would he want to become them?"

The answer to her own question clawed to the front of her mind, but she pushed it away. Didn't want to consider how much death and violence and lies she'd intentionally ignored all these years.

"I don't know, but I have a feeling this victim wasn't chosen at random." Ford's gaze rose to meet hers, and she knew what he saw. How similar she must've looked to the woman at their feet. "I've read through the original investigation files, Agent Brody. Durham PD had a suspect in the death of a female student, Teshia Elborne, but he was never arrested. A witness alibied him for the night of the murder. His girlfriend at the time. Without any new leads, police had nothing, and the case went cold. The victim's family and friends never got the closure they needed to move on, and I have reason to believe that suspect is killing again."

"I'm already familiar with the case and the suspect you're talking about, Marshal Ford." Leigh straightened while studying the body in front of her. The same confusion pulsed now as it did then. She peeled her gloves off with too much force. "I'm the one who alibied him."

THREE

Durham, New Hampshire

Wednesday, August 23, 2006
10:14 a.m.

The box slipped off the stack she'd carried to the second floor.

Leigh braced for the impact.

A body plunged into her peripheral vision from the single door in the claustrophobic stairwell.

"I got it!" He did not, in fact, have it. The box hit the cement, one corner denting inward. A grumble of a laugh vibrated through her as her would-be rescuer set his gaze on her. Intensely dark. The color of a clear summer night in the middle of nowhere. Except there was a hint of warmth in his features. Near black hair and a clean-shaven face somehow brightened his smile, but she'd learned from experience that looks—even as handsome as his—were almost always deceiving. He was older, maybe twenty or twenty-one to her eighteen, but could still rely on a few boyish charms. She couldn't help but smile as he collected the box but didn't move to restack it. "Well, damn.

Guess speed isn't one of my superpowers. I'm Dean. One of the resident assistants for Christensen Hall."

He stretched out a hand, expecting her to somehow manage to keep hold of her possessions and meet him in the middle. Then laughed as he withdrew. "Sorry. Habit."

"I'm Leigh." She shifted the remaining boxes to one hip, arms already tired from the multiple trips she'd made up the stairs. Christensen Hall was one of the most competitive residence halls on campus with its proximity to Dimond Library and the campus bookstore, and the most crowded due to its first-year-student status. Didn't make it any easier to move into. The halls were too narrow, the dorms too small for more than a twin-sized bed and a desk, and the idea of a communal bathroom she had to share with the rest of the floor really made her want to start a "no shampoo" campaign.

Still, she'd made it all the way to college despite a depressing GPA her last year of high school. That was what happened when your father was convicted of murder, your mother barely spoke or left her bed, and you had to become a parent to your thirteen-year-old traumatized brother. Leigh tried to keep the thoughts of that last one from bleeding into her face. While she'd applied and been accepted to Granite State for the next four years, her brother couldn't go back home as long as his abductor was still on the hunt. So he was coming to Durham, too. Homeschooling from her dorm. Staying out of sight until she knew he'd be safe on his own. "If a single one of my pillows comes away damaged, I'll know who to blame."

"On your left!" a voice yelled a few steps back.

Leigh tried to maneuver out of the way of the guy coming up the stairs behind her. Managing to shove the corner of her box into Dean's gut. Heat flared up her neck and into her face. She managed to balance the last box in one hand, reaching for him with the other. "I'm so sorry!"

Dean lifted a hand in surrender, doubled over to catch his

breath. A too-wide nose with a slight bend in the middle domi-
nated his face but somehow managed to fit him perfectly and
accentuated the laugh lines leading down to his mouth. He was
handsome in a rough way. Obviously confident with his
muscular frame, and her eighteen-year-old brain automatically
jumped to wondering how many more muscles his T-shirt and
low-cut jeans tried to hide from inexperienced and clumsy girls
like her. "It's all good. Move-in day isn't for the faint of heart. I
needed the reminder."

"You should probably run while you still can." *Leigh*
couldn't get rid of the embarrassment working into her voice.
Her fingers ached as she clutched on to the box in her arms. What
the hell was wrong with her? She'd stood up to her entire home-
town in defense of her dad, but she couldn't manage a simple
conversation with a cute guy? "I'm new to all of this, and every
second you're with me is another chance you might break something important. Or worse. I could accidentally knock you over
the railing and send you plummeting to your death."

"I'm not the one who looks like they want to rabbit out of
here." *He straightened, his smile back in place, and the stairwell*
didn't seem so crowded anymore. As though there wasn't anyone
else in the building. "But who said I don't like a challenge?"

Durham, New Hampshire

Wednesday, October 9
9:45 a.m.

"Durham PD narrowed down their suspect pool during their
investigation eighteen years ago to one man. Dean Groves."
Leigh faced the stuffy office crowded with campus police,
Marshal Ford, a handful of Durham police, and the president of
the university himself. Most notably the should-be-retired
professor who'd wedged himself into the corner of the room

against an overstuffed shelf of books no one had ever read. Age
had been kind to him, merely adding a few patches of white
against his polished hair and beard. A few more lines had
carved around his mouth and across his forehead, but ultimately, he hadn't changed a bit. Time hadn't altered his preference for open button-down shirts and blazers with hand-sewn
patches in the elbows. He remained quiet, out of the way.
Waiting for her to notice him. Her heart rate picked up at his
lopsided smile. Meant for support. Alliance. Comfort. It was
the first stage of his trap. "At the time, Groves had ties to the
victim, Teshia Elborne, and access to the arsenic and cyanide
used to kill the victim through his research internship in the
biomedical lab."

The medical examiner had taken possession of the body
twenty minutes ago. If she looked out the massive window
behind the oak desk overrunning the bookshelf-lined walls, she
could see straight down to the crime scene outside. Whoever
had dumped this victim wanted to be noticed. To send a
message.

Question was, who was it meant for?

While it looked as though Alice Dietz had been killed in the
same manner as the victim during Leigh's freshman year, they
wouldn't have any solid connections until the results of the
autopsy came back. Her nerves took a backseat as she recalled
any detail she could about the man she'd considered a light-
house in the storm that was her life back then. Maybe that was
why arresting Ava's mother for murder hadn't hurt as much as
she'd expected. She'd already been through this all once before.

"Groves would be forty years old today. He's highly intelligent and strategic, and professionally intimate in biomedical
and toxicology. Investigators at the time were able to trace the
arsenic and cyanide used to poison a victim in 2006 back to the
biology lab where Groves spent a good amount of his nights.
The victim, Teshia Elborne, was his ex-girlfriend. From what

THE KILLER SHE KNEW   25

police had been able to put together, the breakup was anything but amicable when he discovered she'd been cheating on him for months before her death."

Leigh packed all those pieces—clues—she'd tried to ignore into a dark box at the back of her mind. She slid her hands into her slacks. All too aware she had nothing there to ground herself to in the moment.

"Groves was arrested for the crime, but no charges were brought against him as a fellow student alibied him for the night of Elborne's murder. Upon release, he disappeared off local, state, and federal agency radars."

"Disappeared to where?" one of the Durham PD officers asked.

Wouldn't she like to know? Finding him certainly hadn't consumed hours and hours of sleepless nights in the weeks following his disappearance. And he certainly hadn't invaded her dreams since.

"At the time, investigators believed Groves managed to secure himself a new identity and has been using the alias since. We don't know where he's been residing, where he works, or if he's even returned to Durham. He has no living family, and he's never bought property, registered a vehicle, or filed taxes under his own name. While suspecting Groves would be the easy route for this latest murder, it's possible whoever killed Alice Dietz may be trying to use the Teshia Elborne case to make a name for themselves or attract our attention."

"I think it's pretty damn clear there's a connection between Ms. Dietz and the poor girl who was killed under the watch of my predecessor, Ms. Brody." The president of the university sat forward in his over-cushioned leather chair, elbows on the edge of a desk that could swallow him whole. Pure gray hair swooped into the president's face as he set cold blue eyes on her. Compared to the professor positioned behind him, the university president held himself to a strict standard of appearance and control. "Groves was never caught. Now he's back to rub it in your faces, and one of my students paid the price."

Dread suctioned her stomach to her spine. "It's Agent Brody, sir. And it's too premature to make assumptions at this point. We won't know if there's a connection until the autopsy results are finalized by the ME, but the FBI, the Marshals Service, and Durham police are considering every possibility. Of course, our number one priority is the safety of your administration, staff, and student body during this investigation."

"How? How are you going to protect anyone on this campus? Police couldn't charge him back then because you, of all people, gave Groves an alibi." Tension radiated down the president's neck. He had to tip his head back to keep his hair out of his face. Thin, weathered skin told her his life was harsh, and sitting behind this desk hadn't been part of the plan or even close to a dream job. None of that was her problem, however. She was here to do a job. Not stroke his ego. "Are we supposed to believe you're here out of the goodness of your heart? Maybe you're here on Groves's agenda."

Heaviness shifted into her legs, pinning her in place. She was standing in front of the chief of police back in her hometown all over again. On display. Answering for crimes she hadn't committed.

"You realize you just accused a federal agent of aiding and abetting a fugitive." Ford's reaction gave voice to the shocked expressions pasted on everyone else's faces. The marshal shoved to stand, out of place with the academics in this room and barely in place with the officers. "Do you have any proof Agent Brody is guilty of misconduct, or are you projecting your fears on everyone else in the room? Because I will personally vouch for the work she and her team have done if anyone has a problem with her being here."

Her blood warmed at the defense. People weren't jumping at the opportunity to stand up for her considering her background, and she wasn't exactly sure how to respond. Ford was the kind of man who kept his word. In every regard. The weight of his attention grounded her from spiraling at the thought, and a thread of confidence returned. "What Marshal Ford means to say is I have a long history of consulting with law enforcement on cases similar to this. While I may have a personal connection to the Elborne case and this university, we are not certain Dean Groves is involved here. We will do whatever it takes to find the killer responsible for Alice Dietz's murder."

The president sank back in his chair. It was always the men at the top who couldn't handle confrontation. The ones who folded the quickest when the room didn't sway their way, and she couldn't help but nod gratitude toward Ford. "Marshal Ford."

She sidestepped to give the marshal room.

Ford raised his phone, screen bright. "Each agency will receive the incident reports of previous victims the USMS believes to have a connection to this latest murder. Four victims, not including Alice Dietz. Our suspect not only murders his victims, he becomes them by altering his appearance and manner of speaking, using their identification, embracing habits and routines, and integrating himself into their lives over a matter of weeks. If Alice Dietz's murder is connected to my investigation, there's a chance our killer has already become someone new. Someone we wouldn't suspect."

A tree limb slammed against the oversized window behind the president's desk in a burst of noise that brought the entire room to life.

Every nerve in Leigh's body fired at the impact. Her heart rate took longer than it should have to settle, and from the reach of several officers toward their sidearms, she hadn't been the only one. Trees swayed violently through the glass. The storm was picking up. Potentially destroying evidence in and around their crime scene.

"Campus police have been asked to conduct student and staff interviews concerning Ms. Dietz's whereabouts and movements over the past week leading up to her disappearance and report back. I want a timeline of where she went, which classes she attended, and any significant relationships in her life," Ford said. "Durham PD, the fact our killer used the university as his preferred location to dump a body makes me think he won't stray far. I want a grid pattern search up to three miles around campus while forensics pulls apart our crime scene."

"The storm is going to make that hard, Marshal," one of the officers said as rain started ticking against the window glass.

"I believe in you." Marshal Ford turned compelling dark eyes on Leigh. "Agent Brody, you're familiar with the Elborne case and the way serial offenders think. Any words of advice?"

Leigh raised her chin a fraction of an inch, memorizing the faces in this room, and settled her attention on one. The professor still watching her from the corner of the office. "Watch your backs. No one else will."

FOUR

Durham, New Hampshire

Wednesday, October 9
10:04 a.m.

She was going to suffocate.

Mauve paint darkened the already small dorm room. Builder-grade laminate floors attempted to add some lightness and color, but this place was still as depressing as Leigh remembered.

What was it about college dorms aiming to suck the life out of the residents inside them? Alice Dietz's room was identical to the hundred others in the building except Adams Tower West was slightly newer and catered solely to second-year students. Two loft-style bunkbeds took up each side of the room, dressers tucked underneath to save space. A single closet took up position across the room with a motel-style private bathroom off to the right. Two windows met in the middle of the far wall, each angled toward each other to create a false bump-out and the illusion of more space. Three mattresses. Three roommates.

But university police had only managed to find one. Well, other than Alice Dietz.

"I can't believe Alice is dead." Jeana Gray's perfectly shaped eyebrows met over a pair of dark brown eyes as she sniffled into a soaked tissue from the edge of her mattress. Once-tamed hair escaped the ponytail at the back of the young woman's head in frizzy wisps, accentuating the warm orange undertones of her black skin. A thick sweater hid a willowy frame. Dressed to repress. Schedules, calendars, and a printed syllabus on her desk said Jeana was the kind of student who colored inside the lines, followed the rules, and wouldn't dare make the first move with a guy she might find attractive. An overachiever of the highest order. "I knew something was wrong. Alice wouldn't just stop showing up, no matter how upset she was."

"You're the one who filed the missing persons report on Monday morning?" Leigh asked.

Jeana nodded, taking another swipe at her nose.

"How long have you and Ms. Dietz known each other?" The length of the roommates' relationship would help Leigh understand how well Jeana could interpret their victim's behaviors and moods leading up to her death. Leigh studied the personal effects of three distinct areas of the dorm.

Jeana had taken up position on her own bed, decorated with cutouts of books, a sticker showcasing a pink bubble font spelling "Word Nerd," and a book thrown haphazardly at the end of the thin mattress. The other two spaces weren't as organized. Clothes bunched on one bed. Highlighters and textbooks thrown across the other. There were few personal touches, but it could have something to do with the way the university assigned campus housing. Students never kept their dorm more than a year, relegated to moving from one building to the next at the start of each academic year.

"We don't. I mean, not really." Jeana sat straighter as if she had to remind herself about posture. "We were both assigned this room at the start of the semester. So, about six weeks, but we were becoming friends. Me, Alice, and Tamra. We hung out, got dinner together, and watched movies. Talked about guys and classes whenever we happened to be in the dorm at the same time, stuff like that."

Leigh directed her gaze to Marshal Ford, who'd hung back by the door, all too willing to let her take the lead. For a federal agent, he was remarkably aware of his presence when faced with a female witness. None of the overbearing, competitive alpha-male bullshit she'd faced from previous male colleagues too many times to count.

"Tamra Hopkins, the third roommate," Ford said.

"Let's check in with campus police on Tamra's where-abouts. Pull her out of class if necessary." She didn't wait for Ford's acknowledgment, trusting that he would follow through as he left quietly. Leigh crossed deeper into the room, memo-rizing everything she could about the space. It was the little things that shaped a victim's life. The brands they preferred told her a lot about financial mindset and likely debts. The type of devices they used determined whether their data was backed up to the cloud automatically. Personal photos and contacts established close relationships and potential leads. "Jeana, in the time you've known Alice, have you noticed anything unusual in her routines? Were you aware of any problems she was having in her personal or academic life?"

"Nothing she told me about, but as I said, we were just recently starting to get to know each other. As for her routines, I can't say if she really had any. At least, not outside of showing up for her classes. She didn't have a job. I don't know how she was paying for school. Honestly, Alice was the kind of person who played everything by ear. Kind of impulsive. It was one of the things we argued about the most. Especially when we had plans to meet up, and she'd just not show up. And now she's gone." A fresh wave of tears pooled in Jeana's eyes. "She was... moody at first. Like being here was some kind of punishment. It took a while before she made an effort to talk to me and Tamra, and even then, she liked her privacy. Looking at her, you get this cheerleader vibe and think she's gonna be bubbly and insist on making best friend bracelets, but I got the feeling she wasn't the kind of person interested in keeping in touch after graduation, you know?"

She did know. Had been that person herself. It'd been necessary. To protect her brother. But now, Leigh found herself inventorying the relationships in her life. Her father had spent the past twenty years behind bars, her brother couldn't admit his real identity without putting Leigh in the law's crosshairs, and her best friend was currently serving life without parole in Alabama. And Ava... Leigh didn't know how to be a mom. Least of all to a teen who wanted nothing to do with her, fought to run away any chance she got, and rarely said more than two words in a conversation. Nothing close to the relationship she'd had with her own mother.

Expectations: the real happiness killer.

"And which bunk is Alice's?" Leigh pointed to the one closest.

Jeana nodded. "That one with the clothes piled on it."

"When was the last time you saw Alice?" She visually searched the closet without touching anything.

"Saturday night." Three full days.

Leigh picked through a couple of T-shirts and a pair of jeans. Sliding her hand into the pants pockets, she pulled a tube of Chapstick free and dropped it on the bed. No phone. No laptop. No backpack. The only personal effects on Alice's body had been her wallet and keys. Without them, it would've taken DNA, fingerprints, and dentals to identify her remains and wasted precious hours. A few high-end cosmetics were scattered across the nearest dresser. Good quality and well-used.

The clothing, too, spoke of quality over quantity. Alice Dietz invested in key pieces. "Did you talk? Get a sense of her mood or where she planned on spending her time yesterday?"

"I know she had class at nine," Jeana said. "But we weren't exactly on speaking terms."

She'd come back to that.

"All right. What about anyone new in her life?" Leigh gave up on sifting through the items on the bed and moved on to the dresser stacked underneath the bunk. "Boyfriend, girlfriend?"

Jeana shook her head. "Not that she told us, but I got the impression she was seeing someone she didn't want me and Tamra to know about."

She searched the top dresser drawer, then moved on to the second. Nothing but underwear, bras, pajamas, and everyday essentials. Then again, people tended to get creative when it came to secrets they never wanted uncovered. Leigh noted the air returns and vents throughout the room. As of now, they had nothing to tell them what kind of woman ended up at the wrong end of a syringe of arsenic and cyanide. Nothing obvious to mark Alice Dietz as a victim. "What gave you that idea?"

Hesitation etched deep into Jeana's features. Burdened with betrayal for telling investigators this much. "She'd get messages in the middle of the night. Slip out after Tamra and I were already in bed. I'm not sure she realized I knew. She never said anything about it."

Ford slipped back through the door. Quiet. Reserved. Waiting.

"Do you know where she was going so late?" Instinct had Leigh ending her search prematurely. In her experience, everyone had secrets, but there was nothing here. At least nothing she would've left lying around with two roommates to find. No journal detailing the victim's life or raving over a secret affair. RAs patrolled the floors late into the night. Most universities, but more so the University of New Hampshire, enacted curfews for their students. Of course, there were always ways around them. She'd found a few herself during her years here. Had Alice done the same? Where had she been going in the middle of the night?

"No." Jeana seemed to curl in on herself, wrapping her arms around her middle with the tissue still clutched tight. "I asked. It didn't end well. That's why we weren't talking."

"Tell me more about that." Leigh flicked a glance to Ford.

"She got all defensive. Told me to mind my business," Jeana said. "That was about a week ago."

"What about close friends who she might confide in or people in her program? Could she have been sneaking out or seeing one of them?"

Jeana pulled the tissue in her hand apart, close to tearing it in half. "If she was, she didn't want me or Tamra to know. Now I wish I would've pushed. Maybe then she wouldn't have died."

Guilt settled heavy on the girl's shoulders. Something that would stick with her for the rest of her life in Leigh's experience.

"We recovered her keys and wallet with her remains, but there isn't any sign of her phone." Ford took a single step deeper into the dorm room, sucking all the air out of it with his size alone. "Did she usually keep in on her?"

"Alice never went anywhere without it." Jeana sunk back in on herself. The shock was setting in. They wouldn't get much more out of her.

"We'll see if we can locate it with GPS. Until then, it would help if you let us know if it and any other of her belongings turn up." Leigh's phone vibrated from her slacks pocket. She pulled it free, her lungs seizing as she read the caller ID. Ava. "Excuse me a moment. I have to take this."

Marshal Ford's eyebrows rose as he followed her out of the dorm into the narrow corridor. This entire place had been coated in an odor. Something wet, musty, and stale in the air.

She answered. "Ava? Everything okay?"

"When are you coming back? I'm sick of being in this room." Thunder resonated through Ava's side of the line. Deep and booming. "I mean, how many more episodes of *The Office* am I supposed to watch before you come back? Isn't there a law or something that says this is neglect?"

Funny. Ava usually went out of her way to avoid contact with other humans. Well, humans with Leigh's face anyway.

Leigh checked her watch. Three hours since she'd left the hotel. The trees jerked side-to-side through the window at the end of the hallway. The storm had picked up. Rain pitted against the glass, the sound pecking at her nerves even this far down the corridor. Damn. The crime scene was at serious risk. Mother Nature was fighting to wash away vital evidence every second the techs left it exposed. Tarps would help, but only for so long. "Yeah. I'm sorry. I wasn't expecting to have to go so long without checking in, but I'm almost finished here at the university. Did you get breakfast?"

"The menu here sucks. They don't have anything I want." Leigh swallowed back a laugh at the stroppy, hormonal answer. But, at the same time, Leigh couldn't blame Ava's hormones for their relationship. She'd been in Ava's position. Mad at the world. At her new reality. At the unfairness of it all. Rage was what got her to where she needed to be in life, and it wasn't until Leigh had faced the past that she'd been able to let go. To feel something more. Ava wasn't alone. But she hadn't realized it yet. "Can I at least go down to the lobby? I saw vending machines on the way in."

Yay for junk food. Just what growing bodies needed. "Sure. Give the front desk the room number, and they'll charge—"

The line went dead.

"Ava?" Leigh pulled the screen back. She'd been disconnected. Tapping her adopted daughter's name from her contacts list, she tried to get back through, but the call refused to connect.

The lights overhead cut out.

"That can't be good." Ford stared up at the ceiling, almost willing the power to surge back to life with a single look.

Light from the window at the end of the corridor barely reached her. Dorm room doors swung inward as second-year students poked their heads out. Groans and complaints competed with the *tick tick tick* of the rain pummeling the windows. No power, no Wi-Fi. Leigh headed for the single source of light and caught sight of a traffic light down the block. It was dead. Campus power was out, but the university generator should be kicking on to pick up the slack. Except it wasn't.

Ford closed in behind her, and her skin warmed at the proximity. What was it about him her body wanted to automatically accept? She'd never allowed people to hover in her personal space. But in just a couple hours, he'd managed to slide through her boundaries. "How are we going to review the surveillance footage from campus security without any power?"

"The school's generator should be kicking in." Why wasn't it? Leigh's heart rate pulsed at the bottom of her throat. She checked her phone again. The cell towers would each have their own backup generators in case of emergency, but she still wasn't getting any service. What the hell was happening out there? Another gust of wind ripped through the trees outside the dorms. An oversized branch twisted and broke before their eyes. It slammed into the ground with an impact that could've broken the sound wall.

Low murmurs from nearby students swarmed her. Some laced with disbelief. Some with fear.

Leigh backed up a step, reaching for Marshal Ford with the side of her hand against his chest. "Contact the university first-responder staff. We need to get everyone on lockdown and begin to shelter in place."

This wasn't just a storm.

This was something far worse.

And it was headed right for them.

Universities had emergency preparedness drills and proto-cols. But she never thought she'd be stuck in the middle of one during a murder investigation. Seemed Mother Nature herself was trying to aid their killer at this point.

Her thoughts went to Ava. How to get to her, how to assure herself she was safe. Leigh turned toward Ford, who looked as if he'd accidentally swallowed an insect, and shoved through the throng of students staring out the window. Jeana was one of them, her gaze wide and pupils dilated in a combination of fear and grief. "No one is leaving this campus."

Not even their killer.

FIVE

Durham, New Hampshire

Wednesday, October 9
10:39 a.m.

Monsters loved small towns.

It was the rush of familiarity. Of being able to easily read the rules and fit in. The ability to manipulate, dominate, and control came easily when people thought they knew you inside and out. Leigh had seen it back in her hometown. Then again in Gulf Shores last month and a dozen other places similar to Durham over the course of her career. No matter where she went, the monsters followed. Unwilling to let her go.

Was Dean Groves really one of them, or had he become the killer's personal role model? She'd been nothing more than a confused freshman at the time she'd alibied him for Teshia Elborne's murder eighteen years ago. Had 100 percent believed he hadn't been capable of lying to her. That the evidence had been wrong. That the police were wrong. She'd fought a losing battle to keep her father from going to prison and lost. She'd been primed and ready to make the same fight for Dean at the time.

Thoughts of Dean—of the mistakes she'd made—hounded her as she pulled her rental into Durham PD's parking lot. If there was a connection between Alice Dietz's murder and that of the UNH student, they needed inside information. Information she'd never been privy to as a student herself.

The station resembled countless others Leigh had visited. Drab cinderblock walls, scuffed tile flooring, and public service posters slapped across any available inch of the lobby, but she'd been here before. The building was smaller than most. The brick rambler had once been a single-family home and converted into a police station over the years. A ramp had been added for easy access to the front glass doors with a few windows overlooking the L-shaped parking lot surrounding the building. Trees blocked visual access to the properties on either side, each fighting for their lives as thunder and rain pummeled the town.

Winds had picked up over the past thirty minutes. Weather updates were few and far between with cell towers and power down across the city. According to campus police, the town's twenty-one full-time officers were short-handed due to downed trees blocking roads, flooding around Durham Town Landing, and more than a fair share of automobile accidents. The front desk phone rang unanswered as Leigh and Ford followed the remaining officer on staff to a conference room at the back of the building.

Emergency protocols were already beginning to take effect. University police had ordered all students on campus to shelter in their dorms. Those who lived off campus were being corralled in Thompson Hall with administration and professors while Durham PD strived to warn the public. Classes had been cancelled until the threat passed. But, at this point, Leigh wasn't sure which was worse. The impending hurricane or the fact that

Alice Dietz's killer might be mixed in with the displaced students.

Leigh rounded into the conference room to face Durham's chief of police handing out radios to the officers called in during the emergency. The trio dispersed, leaving their chief's expression stressed and exhausted. It wasn't every day a man in his position was faced with two impossible threats at the same time. "Chief, I'm Leigh Brody, FBI. This is US Marshal Ford."

"Marshal, good to see you again. I take it you're also here to work the homicide over at the university campus, Agent Brody." The chief—his voice more strained and gravelly than she'd expected—leaned back against the edge of the conference room table and folded his arms across his chest. Piercing blue eyes stood out from a weathered face touched by too much sun probably earned on weekends in a small fishing boat on the bay. Straw-colored hair swept in a perfect arc from one side of his thinning head to the other while a few areas of stubble had gone completely gray around his jaw. Wrinkles creased down the sleeves of his suit jacket. One he'd obviously been wearing for a while now. "Hard to believe something like this could happen in our own backyard. Twice."

"Were you on the force during the first campus homicide investigation eighteen years ago? Teshia Elborne's murder?" Ford clearly liked to take his chances. Test the boundaries of their partnership by taking the occasional lead. He'd done it back in Jeana's dorm room, too, and while she was the expert in serial offender behavior, Ford hunted fugitives for a living. He had as much right to be here as she did.

"Now, that's a name I haven't heard in a while. I was a detective at the time. I stayed in the loop, but that one wasn't my case. You want details, you'll have to read the investigation file. The detective who worked it passed away last year. All I can give you is his notes." The chief pulled his phone from his slacks, then a pen and notebook from the other pocket. "We don't get many homicides. That's the case number. You can requisition the file with the desk clerk out front."

"We'll do that." Leigh took the offering. While they'd gotten what they'd come for there was no way she and Ford could work this case without additional support. "Any units you could spare for the search for our unsub would also be greatly appreciated."

"Brody. I know the name." The chief notched his chin higher in her peripheral vision. "Chief Brent Maynor was a friend."

Dread settled low in her gut. An automatic reaction any time Maynor's name came into play, but the detective-turned-chief-of-police who'd gone out of his way to convince an entire town of her father's murderous guilt twenty years ago didn't deserve her emotion. He didn't deserve any consideration at all.

"Who's Brent Maynor?" Marshal Ford's attention ping-ponged between her and the chief.

The chief didn't waver. Wanted her to take credit for the downfall of a good man, a friend of his, someone who'd served his town selflessly and did his duty to the people he cared about. Forget about the corruption, the lies, the framing and arrest of an innocent man. This chief wasn't the first. He wouldn't be the last. No. He was waiting for her to give him a reason to deny them assistance during this investigation. To maybe get a little bit of revenge on Maynor's behalf.

Leigh wasn't going to take the bait. She needed him. His resources, his officers, and his access to the original case file. "Chief, as you know, the first twenty-four hours of a homicide investigation are critical. While campus police are good at their jobs, we simply don't have the resources to secure our primary crime scene, search for our unsub, and collect statements from friends, family, professors, and other students while enforcing the shelter in place order. It would be helpful if you could loan us some manpower."

He studied her a moment too long. Clearly disappointed she hadn't given him what he'd wanted. "I'm not sure you're aware, Agent Brody, but I'm shorthanded as it is. All of my officers are out there trying to get the people of this town to safety before the storm hits." The chief pointed toward the door to emphasize his point. Shoving to his full height, he tried to make himself the largest person in the room, but he'd never compare to Ford's lean, muscular build. The marshal might try to contain it all in a fancy suit, but the evidence of physical power was there in the careful, controlled way he moved. Certainly more so than the chief who'd accepted a career behind a desk. "But in the interest of cooperation, I think I can pull two officers to assist your investigation. I'll have them report to campus police within the hour."

"It's greatly appreciated." One obstacle in the way of this investigation down. A dozen more to go, and, frustratingly, she couldn't do anything about the most pressing one, the weather. "Would you also mind lending us a few radios? Seems the storm is playing havoc on cell towers." She wiggled her phone in one hand. The second service came back, she'd reach out to Ava. Until then, she'd need another way to get hold of the teenager.

The chief reached back to the box on the conference table, one his frame had blocked from her view until now. "Don't have many left, but what I do have is yours. Anything to help the FBI during these hard times."

Sure. Leigh divided the remaining two-way radios between her and Ford, testing the batteries and push-to-talk buttons. They weren't state of the art. Not compared to the ease of cell phones, but they worked, and she was grateful for that. And they'd wasted enough time in this ridiculous pissing contest. "Thank you."

She headed for the door.

"Agent Brody," the chief said from behind, and she pulled

up short a second time. "I want you to know I'll be taking a personal interest in this investigation while you're here."

Of course he would.

"I wouldn't expect anything less, Chief." Leigh rounded into the corridor and retraced her steps back to the station lobby. Every step released the vise around her ribcage, but it wouldn't disappear completely. She'd always hated police stations. Durham's was just one more added to the ever-growing list.

"That sounds ominous." Ford's attempt to lighten the mood hit wrong. His inexperience was all too obvious sometimes. At other times, it sounded as if he'd seen too much. Something she could relate to bone deep. It didn't matter what agency you worked for. Law enforcement wasn't for the weak of heart.

"I put his friend behind bars for abuse of power and a whole mess of other things earlier this year." As far as she knew, former chief of police Brent Maynor was serving five years, but there really was no point in revisiting the past. It had haunted her too much as it was. "The chief sees this as his opportunity to put me in my place."

"I have a feeling he doesn't know what he's getting himself into." A wisp of a smile played across the marshal's mouth.

She was beginning to like the marshal more and more.

"You think he's going to expect something in return for his help?" Ford braced himself against the door as it nearly ripped free of his hold. There was no chance they'd be able to get anything from Alice Dietz's death scene in this weather. The best they could do was protect it until the storm passed, but from the look of the clouds to the east, that wasn't happening anytime soon.

"More than likely." Wind whipped her hair free of the ponytail at the back of her head and into her face as she raced out into the rain. They needed to get back to campus, but road conditions weren't getting any better. Alice Dietz had been murdered at the most inopportune time. Part of her wanted to believe it hadn't been intentional. No one could predict the weather, despite all the technology and meteorologists claiming otherwise. No one had seen the incoming hurricane reaching Durham, of all places. But it was certainly paying off for their killer.

"I need to make a stop by my hotel on the way back." Leigh wrenched the car door to her rental open and dropped inside. Her clothes stuck to her skin, squeezing her in all the wrong places. "I've got to check in on someone."

"Boyfriend?" Ford whipped into the passenger seat with more grace than she'd owned in her life. He had the uncanny ability to throw his frame around like he weighed nothing. A solid presence she couldn't ignore.

Years of earned suspicion knifed through her, but Leigh kept her head down as she started the ignition. "Are you asking me if I'm romantically involved with someone? Because that's none of your business, Marshal Ford."

The windows fogged as humidity escaped from their wet clothing, casting them into another one of those bubbles where it was just the two of them. Blocking out the world, the chaos of their jobs.

"You're right." He ripped the seat belt across his frame as rain spit against the top of the car at an increasing rate. "But if it makes you feel any better, I was mainly asking for the purposes of the case."

"The case." She didn't give him more as she backed out of the space and maneuvered free of the lot. It took her a minute to let go of the smile tugged at the corner of her mouth. The wipers went full force, distracting her from the pull of Ford's attention as Leigh directed them to the hotel. "No. I'm not romantically involved with anyone. My work doesn't leave room for much of a personal life."

Okay, she'd never had much of a personal life to begin with, but Ava had sparked a need to try for one. To make them a real family with nightly dinners, boardgame Mondays, movie nights, and trips to the beach. Thus far, attempts to start these had been met with the same response as a bout of dysentery.

"I'll make a note of that. In case it becomes pertinent to this investigation." His glasses fogged with the difference in temperature inside the rental. Ford swiped at them with a tissue he'd kept in his windbreaker. A Boy Scout through and through. Cute.

"I'll be a minute." She pulled the vehicle into the hotel parking lot, grabbing for one of the radios provided by the chief. Furious winds ripped at vinyl siding along the hotel's exterior. A section dislodged, hurtling overhead and skimming down the street. Someone was going to lose a limb in these conditions.

Leigh pushed into the hotel lobby, leaving Ford to fend for himself, and jogged up three flights of stairs to her hotel room. Ava was still alive. Bored out of her mind without power. But alive.

"Take me with you." It was the first time her adopted daughter had asked to be in the same room with Leigh, let alone go anywhere with her voluntarily. "I'm losing my mind sitting here alone."

Leigh wavered. Despite the possibility of having to split her attention between the investigation and Ava, she wasn't sure how long she could trust Ava here alone. And if Leigh got stuck at the university overnight, was it fair to leave Ava to cope by herself? She could at least keep an eye on Ava on campus. Not have to worry if she was safe or getting through to check in. Within minutes, they were descending the stairs, shoving back through the hotel lobby, and heading for the car.

Ford studied them through the blotted windshield.

"Who's that?" Ava's face—a younger version of her mother's—scrunched up at the sight of the marshal in the front seat.

"A US marshal who knows how to chase down runaways better than Officer Caine. Do with that information what you will." Leigh collapsed behind the steering wheel as Ava climbed into the backseat. The fifteen-year-old remained quiet as Leigh navigated through town and pulled off the side of Main Street in front of Thompson Hall. The tarps the crime scene had put down struggled to stay put against the onslaught coming directly for Durham.

Leigh shouldered out of the vehicle. "I don't see any lights on inside."

They should've been able to get the generator up and running by now.

She steered clear of the scene perimeter with Ava and Ford on her heels and hiked up the steps to the front glass doors decorated with overly excited pumpkin decals. The president was already there in the lobby with what looked to be a maintenance worker and a university police officer. "What's going on?"

"Someone cut the power to the generator." The president held up a mess of severed cables. "Electricity, internet, phone lines—they're all dead. We have no way of reaching emergency services."

SIX

Wednesday, October 9
12:02 p.m.

Eighteen hours.

An entire lifetime since the killer had dumped Alice Dietz's body in front of Thompson Hall.

Leigh studied the bunch of wiring in her hand. Severed clean from the emergency generator. Intentional. She tossed the collection of cables beside Ava and scrubbed her hands down her slacks. The forensic techs hadn't found any fingerprints. Whoever had sabotaged the generator had most likely worn gloves. Marshal Ford had taken point in following maintenance and university police to the generator room in the basement. With any luck, their killer had left something of himself behind for them to follow. Without power, they no longer had access to surveillance footage taken from around campus. Had that been the intention? But why hadn't campus police or Marshal Ford tried to access it before now? Why wait? Damn it. This storm was pulling every lead out from under them without even trying.

"Agent Brody?" A soft-voiced, pale young woman penetrated Leigh's peripheral vision. She tightened her hold around her backpack straps at each shoulder as she approached, one of thirty-six stranded people in this building. Strawberry blonde hair. A dusting of freckles. No hint of nerves in her voice. Confidence bubbled from expertly done natural makeup to enhance blue eyes the color of the bay—nothing too heavy—and mid-label clothes meant to instill a sense of money. Most likely earned through her part-time job as a barista. Leigh could smell the coffee grounds from here. "I'm Tamra Hopkins. The police said you wanted to talk with me. About Alice."

"Tamra. Thanks for meeting with me." Leigh forced herself off the bench shoved against the lobby wall with an reassuring swipe at Ava's knee. The surgical sites across her midsection stretched tight. While there wasn't any pain left over from her last brush with the surgeon who'd stripped her of her uterus, her body clung to the phantom pain. Her blazer was still damp from the raging downpour, and she doubted there was any chance of it drying anytime soon as humidity worked through the main glass doors. "You and Alice were roommates."

"Jeana and I, yeah." The girl nodded, her mouth curling into a simple smile. "I can't believe something like this happened. I haven't stopped thinking about what I could've done better. If I could've stopped this from happening."

"It's natural to feel that way, especially when you lose someone close. Let's start small." Leigh motioned Tamra closer to the main doors the majority of students avoided to keep from getting wet for privacy. "Were you and Alice close?"

"No. Not like her and Jeana anyway," Tamra said. "We mostly avoided each other. You know how some people just don't get along?"

"Why didn't you two get along?" Leigh attempted to ease

Tamra's sudden nervousness by forcing the tension out of her shoulders. Mirroring. The brain's most powerful weapon during interviews and interrogations. "Did anything specific happen between you two?"

"It's stupid, really." Tamra laughed as if she couldn't believe the words coming out of her mouth. Then shook her head to jar the memories free. "I accidentally picked up her phone off the desk thinking it was mine while she was in the bathroom getting ready last week. We have the same case. The phone wasn't locked, and I shouldn't have, but I got a look at her messages. I think she was talking to a guy. I didn't even understand what I was seeing before she freaked out and started screaming at me about invading her privacy or some shit."

They hadn't recovered a phone on Alice's body or from her dorm room. Had the killer taken it? "Can I see your phone?"

Tamra handed it over without hesitation. The cover was simple, clear plastic. The killer might've taken it for himself, but without a way to a track it using GPS as long as the towers were down—with another of Alice's devices—they would have to use old-school techniques.

Leigh offered it back. "You said she was messaging a guy. Could you tell what kind of relationship the two had? Was he a family member, a boyfriend?"

They were still waiting on a list of acquaintances, professors, friends, and family names in Alice's life, but with the power down and the generator out of commission, it was going to take too long until they got what they needed.

"I didn't get a good look at more than a few words, but from the way she reacted, I could tell she was embarrassed." The corners of Tamra's mouth puckered as she squinted down between her feet. "Like it was some kind of secret."

"Did she ever talk to you about someone she was seeing?" Could this mystery man be their killer? It took a lot of strength to drag a dead body to the middle of the Thompson

Hall courtyard. The building itself was a good hundred feet from the main road with the nearest parking lot more than a block away. Whoever had dumped her body last night would've had to carry her in. Their unsub was most likely male. Much stronger than his victim. But without the location of where Alice Dietz had been killed, there were too many other variables to consider. "Or maybe any problems she was having?"

"No, but like I said, after I accidentally picked up her phone, she went out of her way to avoid me." Tamra hugged her backpack tighter, and the first real glimpse of grief stained her blue gaze. "I wanted to tell Jeana about what happened. When I saw Alice's messages. But she got so mad at me for even seeing them, I was scared of what she might do if she found out I talked to someone else about it."

Leigh didn't understand. "You said you didn't see more than a few words."

"I didn't, but the ones I saw... It sounded like a threat." Tamra's voice broke on the last word. A frozen lake cracking under pressure. "Whoever she was talking to threatened her if she said anything, he would find her. And make her regret it."

Pressure pooled at the base of Leigh's neck. Since arriving on the scene this morning, she and Ford had hit nothing but obstacle after obstacle, but this was a real lead. Something that could point them in the right direction and add more context to Alice Dietz's last days. "What didn't this person want her talking about?"

"I don't know." Tamra shook her head. "That was all I was able to make out in the few seconds I had her phone. Alice came out of the bathroom and started screaming at me after that."

"What about the person's contact information at the top of the message?" Leigh asked. "Do you remember a name or a phone number?"

"It had a 603 area code." The redhead cut her gaze to a

grouping of students near the stairs to the second story, and a flush of pink filled her face. "I don't remember anything else."

Durham, New Hampshire. Someone local? Most students kept their numbers from home, but without the exact number Alice was in contact with, they had nothing until the cell carrier responded to a warrant request. Which she couldn't submit without internet or cell service. A growing knot of frustration tightened in Leigh's gut. Eighteen hours in, and all they had was a dead girl's name. "When was the last time you saw Alice, Tamra?"

"Saturday night, though I don't think she knew I saw her." Tamra shifted between her feet, growing more agitated the longer her friends watched her from their circle across the lobby. "She was sneaking out again. I'm not even sure if Jeana knew."

The descending silence cut short as Marshal Ford came up from the basement into the lobby. Leigh attempted a smile to reassure Alice's roommate. "Thank you, Tamra. You've been a great help." She pulled a business card from her blazer, slightly damp, same as the rest of her. "I know cell towers aren't really reliable right now, but if you think of anything else that might help us find who did this to Alice, please let me know."

"I will." Tamra headed toward the back of the building into a gathering crowd of students, swallowed by the stranded masses.

Leigh forced her attention to Marshal Ford. "What's it looking like down there? Any chance they'll be able to repair the generator and get the power back up?"

"Not unless a whole new unit drops in their laps. It's a massacre." He swiped a line of sweat from his forehead with the back of his hand, but his wire-rimmed glasses still took a dive down his nose.

Damn it. The past month with a teenaged daughter had tested her patience to levels she'd never thought possible.

Leaving very little to rely on now. "Were the forensic techs able to pull prints?"

"No luck. Son of a bitch must've been wearing gloves when he hacked at that thing," Ford said. "I noticed the cameras down there were unplugged too. Even if we had power, I doubt there would be anything on the surveillance feeds."

Which meant whoever'd sabotaged the generator had known where the cameras were installed and how to navigate the basement to get to it in the first place. "This doesn't make sense. There is no way our unsub could've known a hurricane was heading in our direction and that it would knock out the power. Why go for the generator in the first place? And why are you and campus police only now trying to access them? It should've been one of the very first things you requested after Alice Dietz's body was discovered."

A flash of heat filtered into Ford's expression, and the Boy Scout front slipped. "I requested access to the feeds within the first thirty minutes of stepping onto the scene, Agent Brody. The university president told me I needed a court order. To protect student and faculty privacy rights. Campus police doesn't have the authorization to request warrants. We had to go through Durham PD to submit the request to the judge, and with everything being digital..."

Shit. Of course he'd already submitted the warrant request. And now they couldn't get to the feeds even with a judge's signature. Regret simmered under her skin and made her all the more uncomfortable in her own clothes. "I'm sorry. I shouldn't have assumed—"

"That I have no idea what I'm doing?" The notch of a smile was back. Ford finally removed his fogged glasses and stuffed them in his breast pocket. "It's a good assumption when it comes to this case."

"All right. So we have a body in the morgue that's been presumably cleaned and bleached of evidence, a crime scene under a hurricane warning, and no surveillance to determine the route the killer took on and off campus when dumping Alice Dietz's body." And an eighteen-year-old cold case that might connected to their victim. "What about witnesses?"

"University police are still in the process of collecting statements," Ford said. "As of right now, most people don't even recognize our victim. The few who do seemed to go out of their way to avoid her, especially in class. Apparently, Alice Dietz was very passionate about making her opinion known."

The University of New Hampshire was home to more than 15,000 students during any given semester. More in fall and spring than summer. It would be impossible to interview them all.

"Her roommates were under the impression she's been sneaking around with a boyfriend she didn't want anyone to know about," Leigh said. "From what Tamra has told me, it's possible he threatened her. Last either of them saw her was Saturday night, which means Alice disappeared between then and Monday morning when Jeana went to campus police." Leigh tried to ignore the sinking feeling in her gut. That left two days unaccounted for in their timeline. "The medical examiner's office should have a backup generator, but they will be using it sparingly. Autopsies won't be their priority. They'll turn their focus to protecting the building from flooding, so there's very little chance we'll have Alice Dietz's autopsy results soon."

Mere hours into this investigation, they were dead in the water. "Have you heard from Alice Dietz's parents?"

"Campus police notified them of her death last night." Ford slipped his hands into his pockets. "They're trying to get here as fast as they can from California, but with the storm it's likely it'll be a couple days before we hear from them."

The hairs on the back of her neck stood on end.

A warning signal telling her to move. To run.

That she was being watched.

"What do we do?" Ford's question was overrun by an increase in noise.

Leigh caught movement at the end of the corridor, over the heads of the group of students sheltering in place. A man. Standing perfectly still in the commotion of crisis. Intense, near-black eyes locked on hers. His close-cropped hair and height set him apart from every other person in the room. The angled jawline, the tendoned bunch of his shoulders. Familiar. Terrifying. Her chest constricted. One second. Two. A rush of confusion—and something more she didn't want to identify—had her taking a step forward. "Dean."

"Agent Brody?" Ford took position directly in front of her, cutting off her view. And broke the spell. "Leigh?"

She sidestepped the marshal and scoured the corridor. Blood drained from her upper body, cementing her in place. He was gone. Damn it. "Did you see him?"

Ford followed her gaze, twisting at the hips. "See who?"

"Dean Groves." She was sure of it. "He was standing there. Just... staring at me."

Challenging her.

"Groves is here?" Ford pulled his radio from his belt and pressed it to his jawline. "Possible suspect sighting in Thompson Hall, main floor. All units, suspect is Dean Groves, dark hair, approximately six foot four and forty years old. Be advised. He is potentially armed and dangerous."

Leigh didn't catch the rest of Ford's instructions. Hesitation loosened its stranglehold on her body. She turned back to Ava. "Don't go anywhere." Then she rushed toward the location she'd spotted Dean. Logic slammed into place as students clogged the corridor. Her heart rate spiked as adrenaline dumped into her veins.

She shoved through the congested hallway, nearly losing her footing from the resisting force of students. The main hallway ended in a T. Giving her two options. One mistake, and she'd lose him. Instinct had her carving left and picking up the pace. There weren't as many faculty and stranded students in this part of the building. They'd mostly kept to the lobby. Dean would've chosen it for the pure chance of getting away. "FBI! Move!"

Bystanders parted down the middle and flattened themselves along the walls on either side of her. Questions and shouts reached her ears from behind, but she didn't have the attention span to decipher them for anything other than surprise.

She wasn't going to let him get away this time.

She'd waited too long for this. For him.

Classrooms begged for her to take the time to search each individually as she passed, but Dean's need to escape would override his desire to stay hidden. He wouldn't risk getting pinned down by the storm of police closing in on this building. "Dean!"

She was in pursuit. Closing in. She could feel it.

The single glass door ahead slammed closed fifty feet in front of her. An exit on the west side of the building. It should've been locked when the shelter in place order had gone into effect. The backs of her thighs burned as she pushed herself to catch up with him.

"Brody, wait!" Ford was behind her. Trying to give her an advantage if faced with an armed suspect. But she wouldn't stop.

Not until Dean Groves was in handcuffs.

Until she made him pay for everything he'd put her through.

Leigh threw herself into the door's crossbar and shoved free of the building. It ricocheted off the brick as she ran straight out into the storm. Water spit against her face and drenched her all over again.

But there was no one there.

SEVEN

Wednesday, October 9
1:50 p.m.

He'd been real.

As real as the marshal on her left.

"Campus police doesn't have any reports of vehicles coming onto or leaving campus in the past hour other than the two officers the chief of police dispatched." Ford aimed his flashlight beneath the third row of stadium seat desks and moved down the aisle. "And they've searched the building. Twice. There's no sign of Dean Groves."

"He knows this campus as well as they do." There were any number of places he could've taken to hiding in. The university had an entire network of basements Dean had most likely taken advantage of. Leigh scrubbed at her face as the *pit pit pit* of rain continued against the window. There was no pattern in the rhythm, and it messed with her head. Her fingertips itched for something—anything—to pull her back into that calm space she needed to think through a case. To help her put the pieces together. They'd started searching classrooms twenty minutes ago, but they wouldn't find anything. Dean was too smart to hang around. "Maybe even better."

He'd been here. Something had drawn him back to this campus, and there were too many parallels between Teshia Elborne's death eighteen years ago and Alice Dietz's last night to be a coincidence. The location of the body, the scent of bleach on the victims' skin, the connection to this university, the similarity between the women's appearances—it was all right there. Waiting for her to pin him as their primary suspect.

She closed the door to the closet she'd been searching in one of the amphitheater classrooms. Nothing but a broken overhead projector, a fire extinguisher long past its last inspection date, and four stacks of textbooks which had gone out of print before she'd graduated. She'd taken introductory psychology in this very room. If she thought hard enough about it, she'd admit it'd been the class that had changed her life. Compelled her to understand human behavior and why some people wanted others to hurt. Why an entire town of people she'd once loved and trusted had turned on her family. Turned out, the answer was pretty simple. Fear.

"We can have university police do another sweep." Ford finished his search.

She turned to face him. At a loss. Everything that could've gone wrong in this investigation already had. How much worse would it get when storm winds peaked? Irritation spread fast and thoroughly, burning everything in its path. "It won't do any good. He's gone."

"I read through the investigation report we got from Durham PD while waiting for maintenance to assess the generator. That murder that took place here eighteen years ago.

Teshia Elborne had been a student here," Ford said. "You were a freshman, right?"

Something heavy and acidic settled in her throat. Leigh tried to focus on any other potential hiding spots in this room, but they both knew they were killing time until the storm let up. "I was."

"I can see it now." He cracked a smile, and she couldn't help but pay closer attention to the effect it had on his face. The escape it provided from the reality of their situation. "Fresh-faced and eager criminology student Leigh Brody with the whole country waiting for her to come solve their most heinous cases."

"Actually, I started out as a psych student. Ended up switching majors a few weeks into my first semester after one of my professors convinced me I had a talent for understanding the criminal side of human behavior." She pictured that same professor sitting in the corner of the president's office this morning, waiting for her to give him the attention he'd craved from her all these years. She climbed the stairs toward the classroom door at the top. While nearly two decades had passed, it felt like mere minutes since she'd been in this room. Ready to fix all the world's problems. Starting with her brother's. Then she'd realized no one would be coming to prove her father's innocence. That she and her brother had to be the ones to advocate for him.

Hell, she hadn't even thought about the fact her dad had probably tried to get a hold of her in the past few hours and couldn't. Knowing Joel Brody, he'd already called the director demanding to know where she was. She could imagine the conversation all too easily. Mainly because it'd already happened several times in the seven months he'd been released from prison. "For a long time, I was determined to become a therapist."

"I bet you would've been good at carving decorative wood bowls, if you'd put your mind to it." Ford followed her into the hallway as they moved on to the next classroom, this one smaller than the last. "You seem like the overachiever type. Good at everything you do. Making the rest of us look like losers."

She couldn't argue. Despite the inefficacy of birth order theory and characteristics assigned each child in a family, she was the oldest child, and she'd taken the role seriously in any capacity she could. High academic achievement, parental responsibility, and perfectionism to the extreme. It was one of the reasons she latched on to patterns so easily. Patterns didn't lie. They couldn't be manipulated. Not like people. "My fifteen-year-old might disagree with you. Seems nothing I do is good enough."

It'd been a slip. One she was regretting now. Letting Ford— a man she didn't even know—have a glimpse into her personal life. But if there was one thing she'd learned over the months since joining the BAU team, it was she couldn't do any of this alone. She was still standing here because she'd allowed people in. Her brother. Her father. Her best friend. Though, she wasn't sure that last one counted anymore. Murder charges tended to change relationships.

Ford let her little revelation sit between them for a beat. Almost taken aback. "I didn't realize you were a mother. Figured you were just kidnapping the teenager glowering behind you when you came out of the hotel."

"If you ask her, I'm sure she'd agree," Leigh said.

Ford's laugh tightened something in her chest. "In all the media coverage of you over the past few years, there wasn't any mention of kids. You would've been, what? Twenty, or twenty-one when you had her?"

He'd researched her?

"Something like that." She forced herself to clear the next classroom. Leigh couldn't put her finger on why she'd lied. Why she suddenly wanted to keep the specifics of her relationship with Ava to herself. It wasn't that she didn't trust Ford. But what she and Ava had was... hers. Forget the constant worrying, the attempted run-aways, the feeling she was doing everything wrong. Ava was... a bone-deep wish come true. The beginnings of the family she'd craved since she'd been seventeen years old and had lost everything and everyone she'd loved. She wanted the after-school snacks and shared secrets over popcorn her mom used to arrange for her and her brother. The family vacations that always ended up with someone having to pee by the side of the car with her mom holding up a blanket or towel to block other drivers' views. She wanted to be the kind of mom who brought out Ava's smile and courage, as her own mother had done for her. But Ava didn't owe her any of that. If she was being honest with herself, all she could guarantee was safety and security and support. "Nothing in here."

She and Ford moved through two more classrooms without luck. They'd almost reached the end of the corridor. They were running out of places to search, but Dean wasn't here. As they walked, the silence between her and the marshal turned physical but not uncomfortable. "Any word from the medical examiner?"

Ford kept his head down. Focused on his feet while the entire campus threatened to unravel at the slightest touch. "They sent one of their techs over for an update when the wind died down for a bit. Alice Dietz's autopsy is at the bottom of their priority list at the moment. Seems we're on our own for now. Chasing ghosts."

"She was hiding something from her roommates." Leigh faced the exit she'd shoved through when running after Dean. Rain pounded the glass and created rivulets of water pooling beneath the door and working its way inside. Had he really been there? Or had the connection to the past started playing tricks with her mind? Maybe she wanted him to be the one they were hunting. For closure. For the assurance she'd never gotten. Maybe the idea of him had slipped through her detachment to this place while she hadn't been paying attention. "Alice was sneaking out in the middle of the night when she thought they were asleep. Hiding private messages. Acting paranoid."

"Her phone wasn't with her when she was found," Ford said. "Fat chance of a judge signing off on a warrant for her phone records and financials until this storm passes. At this rate, we'll be lucky if we don't have a mutiny on our hands."

"What about her laptop?" There had to be something alluding to Alice's whereabouts since her disappearance. "Where's her backpack? Her purse? What about her textbooks?"

"Keys and wallet were recovered with the body. No one touched her until you were on the scene." Ford swept his flashlight toward the end of the corridor as the door threatened to come off its hinges. He lunged for the lock and secured it before it had a chance of ripping wide. "Killer must've taken her devices. If he's the one who's been texting her—threatening her as her roommate claims—he'd have good reason to make sure they're never recovered."

They weren't getting anywhere. Not with evidence. Not with the autopsy. And sure as hell not with their victimology. Alice Dietz had been a solid B student according to administration records. Perfectly average. Came from a well-off family, tuition paid for in full by her parents each semester. Full schedule of core classes. No real extracurricular activities or clubs. Every ounce the isolated, secretive type her roommates had described. At least on paper. From what little they'd been able to gather and without being able to speak to her parents or close friends, Alice Dietz had seemingly gone out of her way to remain invisible.

The complete opposite of Teshia Elborne.

What was the connection? Why kill Alice with the same MO of another co-ed after all these years?

"That fugitive you've been tracking." Leigh lost motivation

to keep up the search and let the tension in her shoulders drain. Dean Groves wasn't here. Always one step ahead. Just as he had been over the past eighteen years. Out of reach. "You said he assumed his victims' identities after killing them with a combination of cyanide and arsenic. That's what led you to Durham and to Alice Dietz's death scene, right? He lived their lives for weeks before moving on to the next target. Are there any connections between victims, or to this university?"

"Each victim was killed in a different city, but from what we can tell he started in California and has made his way to the east coast." Ford swiped his hands through his hair to contain the rigid style he must've spent hours to perfect. "If there's a connection between the four victims we've recovered, the US Marshals Service and local homicide detectives haven't been able to find it."

"Do you have a description, possible age, sightings?" she asked. "Anything to tell us who you've been chasing?"

"Nothing on age or description considering the only sightings we have of this guy are when he's in character. We've recovered boxes of store-bought hair dye, used prosthetics and putty to alter his facial features, colored contacts—all of it bleached to destroy evidence of DNA. This guy is thorough. He cleans up before moving on to the next city. No fingerprints left behind. Nothing to suggest he was even there until after the fact." Ford swept his attention down the length of the corridor. "Best we can determine is that each of the victims' bodies were discovered after he'd already moved on to the next city, sometimes days later when a coworker or neighbor reported not being able to contact the victim."

She arced her own flashlight to the opposite side of the hallway. They were outcast to the dark for now. On their own. "He would've had to watch his prey. Maybe even become part of their lives before killing them to ensure he had a reason for being in his victims' homes if evidence ever did turn up."

The marshal's dark gaze locked on hers. The soft planes of his jaw dissolved. Letting a hint of a too-familiar darkness investigators had to own to survive the realities of this evil they dealt with. "What makes you say that?"

"It's impossible to step into someone's shoes you haven't studied. How else would he have fooled the people in his victims' lives? We each have our own cadence when we speak, we use certain words more than others. Penmanship is different for everyone, the way we hold a pen or pencil. Apart from that, people are more aware than they give themselves credit for. Friends, family, co-workers. Sooner or later, they would've noticed something off, so the longer he retained an identity, the more risk he took," Leigh said. "Your fugitive would've had to learn their habits, routines, the way they spoke, visit their favorite restaurants. What better way to become an expert on your target than to slip into their life under normal circumstances? But to be honest, it all seems a little far-fetched."

"You'd be amazed at how often people refuse to acknowledge what's staring them right in the face." Ford spoke as though he had experience in that department.

She automatically wanted to swim in the mess of alternate theories Ford might not have considered in his chase across the country. To distract her from the growing feeling of guilt. Guilt for failing to see Dean Groves for who he really was. For allowing herself to be taken in by his charm and lies. Even after all this time, he was managing to get under her skin, and she hated it.

His disappearance told volumes about his guilt concerning the murder of his ex-girlfriend eighteen years ago. Question was: Had he killed Alice Dietz?

"We interviewed relatives, co-workers, and friends during each of the investigations." Ford kept pace with her all too easily at more than a head-and-a-half taller in height. "Between four victims, there weren't any crisis events or concerns for safety.

No significant others or intimate relationships other than a few past breakups. At least, nothing recent. None of them worked for the same company or donated to the same charities according to their financial statements. In fact, nearly all of them worked remote or owned their own businesses where they could vanish for days or weeks at a time. Something the unsub certainly took advantage of."

"Your killer has a type." Leigh forced herself back toward the building's lobby. "With as much detail as he would need to assume their identities, I would bet his victims weren't random. He chose them for a reason."

Ford rewarded her with a half-smile that could trigger a war if in the wrong hands. "Best we can put together, this guy chose victims around his same build with similar features to make the transition easier. No best friends or close family. That seems to have been important. He probably couldn't run the risk of being identified or having anyone looking into his victims' deaths until he was ready. Which means he sought out loners, victims who isolated themselves for one reason or another. The guy is a chameleon."

"Except he can't assume Alice Dietz's identity." The deaths Marshal Ford described seemed almost... calculated. Serving a purpose. What purpose did Alice Dietz serve? "You said it yourself. If your fugitive is connected to what happened on campus, he's never killed a woman before now. She's the outlier. She's the one we need to focus on."

Ford cut her off from reaching the lobby and gripped on to her arm, pulling her up short. "How? Our crime scene is being washed away as we speak, and the medical examiner can't perform the autopsy until the storm passes. We don't even have power or access to the internet."

Leigh swallowed through the heat branching up her arm from his touch. She hadn't realized how cold she'd gotten since stepping foot back in Durham. It shocked her system, and almost had her leaning in. Almost. Prying her forearm free, she cut her gaze to the university president surveying the student body crowded in the lobby. Her throat dried. "If we want to find Alice Dietz's killer, we need to look in the one place police gave up on. We need solve Teshia Elborne's cold case."

EIGHT

Durham, New Hampshire

Wednesday, September 6, 2006
8:19 p.m.

She didn't know how to be a girlfriend.

She'd never done it before.

But nerves and common sense had lost their hold over the past two weeks since Dean had helped her move into her dorm in Christensen Hall.

Leigh let her knees sink deeper into the beat-up couch on either side of his hips. His hands were on her, smoothing up her jean-clad thighs. His touch alone had the ability to make her lose her train of thought. It'd been this way from the very first time he'd brushed against her the night she'd met his friends at the beginning-of-the-semester party. She'd convinced herself his initial contact had been accidental, but the subsequent touches left her with little doubt and wanting more. He'd strode into that room with a freshman on his arm without a single care in the world. Him, a junior who had his entire life going for him. All the campus lab time he could possibly need, letters of recommendations from his toxicology professors, early offers from some of the best labs in the country pouring in. From law enforcement, pharmaceutical companies, even the federal government. He was older, had more... experience, but where she'd expected nothing but embarrassment on his part for his choice in bringing her—she was eighteen and knew nothing about college life or living on her own or having a job—nerves scattered whenever it was the two of them. Like this.

She wasn't even sure how she'd found herself in this position. One minute they'd been watching an old-school horror movie, and the next she'd climbed into his lap. His mouth was on hers, coaxing her heart rate higher. Sweat had built over her skin despite the frigid temperatures outside. Dramatic screams filled the small living room from the television behind her, but she wasn't paying attention to the movie. All she could feel was the trail of heat his kisses left behind.

It'd started out gentle—careful on her end—but now there was a wildness inside her clawing to get free. Made of curiosity and trauma and loneliness. A need to connect to someone and something completely and totally hers. Nothing tied to what'd happened to her dad or tied to her brother. Dean was... hers.

Salt spread across her tongue as he explored slowly, with patience and all the time in the world. Dean had mastered his self-control, but she needed more. More of him. Her senses ratcheted higher the closer she pressed against him. His hint of facial hair tickled across her jaw, those near-black eyes locking solely on her. For now, she was the center of his entire world, and she wasn't sure there was anywhere else she wanted to be.

"Leigh." Her name vibrated through his chest and into hers, a deep rumble that woke up nerve endings she didn't even know existed. Not a rejection. No hesitation. "Do you want to have sex?"

The self-consciousness attacked in full force. But on its tail a *blast of heat and adrenaline carved through her veins at the common decency of asking for her consent. Had anyone ever asked what she'd wanted before? Had anyone even bothered to put her desire ahead of their own? She couldn't remember. Those guys she'd kissed in high school—boys—had turned scoring into a game. One she wasn't too fond of playing again. She and all the other girls in her class had been nothing but pawns. Objects to use and discard on a whim. She'd been happy to play by the rules then, but Dean...*

He wasn't one of them. He'd never made the first move. Never pressured her to give in. He made her laugh with self-deprecating jokes and insisted on holding her hand when they ventured out of the dorms. He didn't mind having ramen for lunch any time they got together because that was what she could afford, or that there were times she had to choose studying over spending what little free time she had with him.

He was so different from the guys she'd kissed before. He was more. And she wanted more. In the end, he couldn't use her. This was her choice. "I've never..."

"I know." Dean gripped her hips then, setting her back on her feet. He shoved off the couch against the wall of his dorm room and offered his hand. Giving her the option to walk away. "I promise to take good care of you, little rabbit. Always."

Durham, New Hampshire

Wednesday, October 9
2:32 p.m.

How did you spot someone who went out of their way to become someone else?

Leigh's elbows dug into the tops of her knees as she made quick investigation notes on her phone from one of the few available benches in Thompson Hall's lobby. Everything Alice

Dietz's roommates had told her. The names and ranks of the officers searching campus for an idea of how their killer had stayed out of sight. The potential of having their unsub here on campus, as trapped as they were. She wasn't going to miss a single detail. Couldn't afford to.

Students clustered in packs to ride out the storm. Low conversations—even a few hints of laughter—had replaced the dregs of panic. It was easy to identify the cliques. Administration and staff in one corner, fraternities and sororities mixing in another. Older students, those coming back to school after a career change and families, kept to themselves while a few athletes floated from one group to another. Then there were the investigators. Forced to ride out the rain and wind.

"My battery's at six percent." Ava put her phone to sleep as she leaned against the wall at their backs and slumped as far as her spine would allow. Long dark hair bunched up around an impossibly adult face that reminded Leigh all too much of her former best friend. Clear brown eyes—the color of brandy— rolled toward the ceiling in a very Ava manner. Same full lips as her mother's. Same impatience, too. But this was where the similarities ended.

Ava had become more passive in their interactions since the adoption, more insecure in herself. Where Leigh had admired and respected the girl who'd lost her mother to murder charges and father to suicide a little more than two weeks ago—a position Leigh had more than enough experience in herself—Ava resembled a ghost. Entirely unreachable.

Something had happened back in Gulf Shores. Something Leigh had suspected for a while now. More than the sexual assault Ava had experienced at the hands of a man more than twice her age. More than losing her parents so close together or moving to an entirely new state with a woman she barely knew, but Leigh couldn't summon the courage to put what little relationship they had at risk. Evidence told a story, and right now, it said Ava had been there when her mother had murdered the man who'd assaulted her. Leigh just didn't know in what capacity.

"Doesn't anyone have a battery pack I can use?" Ava searched the corridors for someone—anyone—who might be able to help. "I thought police officers were supposed to be prepared for this kind of thing."

"First aid kits, latex gloves, batons, and tasers aren't going to help charge your phone." She watched as Ford played liaison, checking in with each department—campus police, administration, Durham PD—to keep communication lines open. He was handing out water bottles and packages of... fruit snacks? "I'm sorry to say that is not their first priority. We're going to have to be patient."

"I'm bored. There's no Wi-Fi." Ah, yes. Hungry Ava had arrived.

Leigh would have to find out where Ford was getting his stash of fruit snacks. Holloway Commons—the university's largest dining hall—was two buildings to the south of them and most likely inaccessible in the middle of a hurricane. A restlessness filtered through the small crowd of students and university staff and bored through her. Fruit snacks weren't going to cut it if this storm kept them isolated longer than a few more hours. "We could talk about where you've been going when you run away from home."

If looks could kill. The burn of Ava's gaze could raise the temperature of the room given enough time. "It's not home. And it's none of your business."

"Egg salad?" A cellophane-wrapped sandwich cut down the middle penetrated her ring of vision, and Leigh looked up at the sound of the familiar voice.

"Professor Morrow." She forced a weak smile as she stood to greet her former mentor. She offered her hand as the past rushed to fill in the gap of years since she'd seen him last in person. How long had it been? Sixteen, seventeen years? He smelled the same. Books and spice. His signature scent shoved her back into hours of reading and proofreading journal articles, pulling crime statistics, and bouncing ideas between the two of them in his office. There'd been a time in her studies when she'd looked forward to going back to her dorm with that scent on her clothes. The mark of hours dedicated to her craft had made her a better criminologist. "It's good to see you."

"Come now, Leigh. We dropped the formalities when you became a peer." Pierce Morrow exuded the professor aesthetic. It hadn't changed in all these years. He moved her to arm's length to get a better look at her, his sandwich still clutched in one hand. Straight white teeth smoothed over his English heritage, but there were still hints of an accent in a few stressed words. A wash of calm followed the head of the criminal justice department wherever he went, but she'd built up a tolerance over the past few years. "I almost couldn't believe my eyes when you showed up in the president's office this morning. You've made quite a name for yourself. I'll let you in on a little secret. I called in a few favors I have over at the FBI so I could get my hands on the case files you worked, and I have to say I couldn't be prouder. My star student."

The heat of embarrassment prickled at her skin. There'd been plenty of other students who'd earned the professor's attention in their program, but she'd been born with a knack for patterns and human behavior beyond a textbook education. Which he'd venomously taken advantage of multiple times over the course of her career. Emails, video calls, voicemail. The barrage of consultation requests had steadily increased in tandem with the decrease of his incoming opportunities. "You always believed I had what it took to solve my brother's case."

"And look at you now. Working for the Behavioral Analysis Unit, under Angelina Livingstone, no less. My protégée." Morrow slid his free hand into his slacks pocket, trying to achieve a casual stance he wasn't quite sure how to execute. "I know you're here on a case, but I'd love it if you could commit some time to talk to the program seniors when this messy business is all wrapped up."

All wrapped up. Because catching a killer should take no more than a few hours and certainly wasn't more important than answering questions from the current cohort of criminal justice majors. She couldn't ignore the hint of resentment in his request. For his protégée to put aside time for him. To give him some of the spotlight. The chasm of differences between her and her former mentor had long lost their influence until this moment. The reality was she'd taken his lessons and research skills and ability to identify with killers and gone out in the world to apply them. Morrow had the uncanny ability to know what any given person deeply desired despite personal histories, choices, routines, and relationships and had once in his career had too many job offers to count. Particularly in sales and marketing. But he'd fallen and gotten stuck in an endless cycle of trying to publish his research and teaching. His way of making a lasting impression on the world. To feed the egotistical gremlin under his pretty mask. "Actually, I'm afraid my daughter and I'll be heading back to Quantico as soon as the case is concluded."

"I'm not your daughter." Ava was back on her phone, her face bunched in opposition.

"The state says otherwise," Leigh said over her shoulder. "Perhaps we can schedule something when I'm between cases, and I can prepare a bit more."

"Of course. Perhaps until then I might be able to assist you during your current investigation." A light flickered behind his eyes. Morrow crossed his arms over his chest as he shifted his weight between both feet. Couldn't look too eager at the prospect to have his name attached to this case. "Anything you and the FBI need. I'm at your disposal."

Of course he was. "Did you know the victim, Alice Dietz? She's a psychology major, but according to her transcripts, she's taken two of your criminal justice classes in the last two semesters."

He shook his head. Almost too slow. Too... controlled. "No. I can't say that I did, but you know with more than two hundred students in my classes and even more online, it's nearly impossible for me to get to know them as more than a student number."

Leigh held herself back from turning this into an interrogation. For now. The problem with Pierce Morrow wasn't that he'd let his talents go to waste behind a desk and lost himself in unending hours of research. It was that he believed he was the only one who could truly read people. But he'd taught her well, even when he hadn't meant to. She withdrew a business card, the second of the day. "Well, if there are any papers or essays you can provide to help us get a better understanding of our victim's recent state of mind and background, that would be helpful. As you can imagine, we haven't been able to gather much since the phones and internet went down. If you could also let me know the last time she showed up on the rolls for your courses so we can get a better timeline of her final days, that would be appreciated."

"I'll see what I can do considering the circumstances." He nodded to Ava and handed off his egg salad sandwich. "Here. You two might need this more than I do."

"I appreciate it. Thank you." She watched him rejoin the group of staff hovering at the edge of the corridor. It was possible he'd been telling the truth. Between online courses and a massive increase of enrollment into functional programs like criminal justice and psychology, there was a chance Morrow hadn't had any interaction with their victim beyond that of professor and student.

So why didn't she believe him?

NINE

Durham, New Hampshire

Wednesday, October 9
3:53pm

They were losing their crime scene.

She watched as a corner of tarp protecting what little they had left came loose from her position at the lobby front doors. Within minutes, there wouldn't be anything physical connecting Alice Dietz's killer to her murder.

Ford handed off a bottle of water he'd produced from somewhere. The interruption to her brooding triggered her reactive defenses. Her heart rocketed into her throat, but she managed to limit it to a slight flinch.

"You okay?" he asked.

"Yeah. I just... didn't see you there." She did this. Disappeared into the dark corners of her mind to figure out the right angle, the right pattern, the right relationship to bring everything in a case together. To the detriment of her physical health. Eating, drinking, sleeping—none of it mattered in the course of an investigation. She wasn't sure how long she'd been staring out the glass doors separating her from the scene outside. At least long enough for Ava to be driven, albeit shyly, to go find entertainment with a group of students at the back of the corridor. "Thank you."

"Have you ever worked a case that didn't have a shred of evidence to support it?" He took a slug of his own bottled water, as lost in the rhythm of the storm as she'd been.

"No." Dozens of death scenes, countless man hours combing through investigation files, even more cataloging data into the federal databases for some hope of finding a connection —there'd always been something to go on. To lead her in the right direction. But this case... They were working blind. Having to rely solely on witness statements and character descriptions. That unnerved her. This was new territory. For both of them. But her instincts told her the killer had taken precautions with dumping Alice Dietz's body as he had with her remains. Ensuring there was nothing left to identify him or the location the victim had been killed. Whether they would've gotten anything from the scene before the storm hit remained unclear. "This is your first homicide."

"How can you tell?" A layer of exhaustion took residence under Ford's eyes, adding to the strain around his mouth. Up until this point, he'd taken the lead, kept his face of confidence, and held himself together. But she could see the cracks now. The sag in his shoulders and the way he'd socialized less and less over the past hour. The lack of progress was getting to him after a few hours. It was an impatience she understood, that she'd trained to overcome. "The people I hunt are responsible for some of the worst acts of violence in the country, but I'm always dispatched too late. After they've already committed their atrocities, and there's nothing but crime scene photos to study. The bodies are cleaned up and scrubbed down in the morgue, or the victims have already given their statements to police."

Ford filled his chest with a deep inhale. Preparing himself for something. He nodded toward the fluttering tarps outside, his Adam's apple shooting down his throat on a swallow. "I've never set foot on an active scene until last night."

"The first time I saw a body, I lost count of how many times I threw up." Leigh hadn't told anybody about that. Not even the detective who'd interviewed her afterward. She'd wanted to be strong for her parents, but finding the remains of a twelve-year-old kid in the crawl space of her childhood home had fractured something inside of her. "I want to say you get used to it the more cases you work, but I still have to take an acid blocker anytime I step onto a scene. Helps with the nausea."

"That strangely makes me feel better about throwing up in the bushes on the other side of the courtyard." Dark eyes cut to her. His smile made a reappearance, tugging on her insides in an uncomfortable and equally exciting balance.

"I won't tell anyone." Her laugh caught her by surprise. Genuine and a little too high-pitched. Damn it. A flush that had nothing to do with the humidity coated her body in an instant. She was a federal agent. She'd faced two serial killers and nearly died in the process, but apparently, embarrassment could still get the best of her. When she'd considered stepping back into the dating scene, she'd apparently forgotten how to interact with the opposite sex. She had to get it together.

"Is that the case file we requested from Durham PD?" He was trying to save her. "The Elborne case?"

"Yeah. I needed to read through it myself." Leigh locked down the urge to shake her head to reverse time and take another stab at this whole conversation. Handing over the manila file folder, she added a hefty amount of space between them to save him from the rush of sweat pooling beneath her blazer. Had someone turned on the heater?

Ford took the offered file and flipped through the first few pages despite the fact he'd already reviewed it all. He took a particular interest in the crime scene photos. "Anything stand out to you?"

"Nothing too enlightening. Teshia Elborne, nineteen years old, psychology major who made the Dean's List most semesters, high school popularity followed her to college. She was involved in a mass of student organizations. Biology club, rowing, student union. If Granite State had cheer, she would've been captain." Leigh had already known all of this before reading through the file. Memorized it, fed off of it eighteen years ago. Because there was no way someone could be so... perfect. "She was well liked. No disputes with roommates or fellow students. Professors had nothing but good things to say about her. Her parents told investigators she'd never had problems with her mental health or rebellion. On the surface, she was the picture of innocence."

"On the surface?" Ford's intensity focused on her between page flips. "You think she was hiding something?"

"Doesn't everyone?" She hadn't meant the words to sound so scathing. "Teshia Elborne and Dean Groves dated for about six months. Things ended... badly between them two months before her death."

A flurry of betrayal coated the inside of her mouth, acidic and bitter. Or maybe her stomach wasn't happy with the egg salad sandwich from Pierce Morrow, which she and Ava had shared. She had no allegiance to Dean Groves. And yet the part of her that'd failed to prove her father's innocence all those years ago wanted to pick up the fight for Dean all over again. To prove she hadn't misjudged him all those years ago. That he hadn't turned out to be one more person in her life who'd chosen violence over her.

"The report says he caught her cheating on him. An altercation ensued; campus police were called by a student in one of the neighboring dorms. She heard the fight through the walls and was worried it would turn physical if someone didn't intervene." Ford moved on from the photos, more focused on the statements taken from friends, family, and the dorm neighbor. "Is that what made him an initial suspect?"

The only suspect. It didn't matter Dean had moved on. Didn't matter that he'd sworn he didn't have feelings left for Teshia or in the short amount of time they'd been together he claimed to have fallen in love with Leigh. Looking back, she could see how his charm and her inexperience in a relationship had preyed on her past trauma. How he'd taken advantage of her feelings and used her to convince her to give him an alibi, despite the evidence staring her in the face. Ultimately, Durham PD had done their jobs and used the incident with Teshia to support Dean's guilt. "Teshia had been seeing a guy from back home on and off again since high school. He would come see her on campus whenever he could get away from his dad's farm. Police interviewed him, but they dismissed him as a suspect. Confirmed he hadn't been anywhere near campus the day she died. That left the most recent upset in her life."

"The shouting match with Dean Groves." Ford closed the file as a passing student careened a bit too close to the huddle they'd created. He craned his attention back through the glass doors. The tarp was gone now. Their crime scene was exposed, and there was nothing they could do to save it without putting their lives at risk. The marshal's energy had returned, reinvigorated in the past few minutes. He'd lost a bit of the detachment investigators had to keep between them and the victims they fought for. One wrong step and Ford would find himself personally taking responsibility for this case—for these victims —and there wouldn't be a damn thing Leigh could do to stop it. "Her body was left in the same location as our current vic. You think Groves is trying to make a statement?"

"I think whoever killed Alice Dietz is familiar with the

Elborne case and is using it to get our attention. Teshia Elborne's investigation was never closed. Groves fled before police could learn more. But there has to be a reason the killer chose to bring us here. Why they chose to kill her how they did." Was it coincidence Leigh had been drawn back to this university, that she'd been involved in the original investigation, or had that been the killer's intention from the beginning? "Which means there's a chance they've tried to replicate the investigation in more ways than leaving Dietz's body in the same location as the last victim and using an MO we've seen before."

"What do you mean?" Ford got that look again. He couldn't read her mind and connect the pieces as fast as she could, an outsider when it came to working active homicide investigations.

"The arsenic and cyanide used to kill Teshia Elborne was traced to the university's biomedical lab. In addition to the argument, police used that connection to narrow down their suspect pool to Dean Groves." Leigh was moving to the back of Thompson Hall's main floor, passing Ava and the group of students she'd joined to ride out the storm. She was safe for the time being. Leigh targeted the president's office at the rear of the building. "He was a toxicology major. His research focused on the effects of poisons and other compounds at a cellular level, and his professors and several students witnessed an increase in his hours spent in the lab around the time of Elborne's death. But the greatest predictor of violence is a history of violent behavior, and Dean was never violent. At least, not on record."

"You alibied him for the night of her death," Ford said. "Why?"

Leigh pulled up short of her destination. She wasn't sure how to answer. How to overcome the shame and the guilt holding her in a vise with letting a man get away with murder.

She'd tried. So many times. But that mistake had followed her into every case, onto every crime scene over her career. And she didn't have the energy to talk her way out of it. She wanted Ford to keep looking at her as though she had the answers, like she was the one who could solve this case. She needed him to believe in her. "In my experience, not everyone accused of murder is guilty."

Ford seemed to understand where they were headed. "But Groves had access to the arsenic and cyanide from the university lab used to kill Alice Dietz. Not to mention a relationship with the victim."

Both of which could've been used against him. Used to frame him. But then why disappear all this time? Why not fight to clear his own name?

Ford didn't have any trouble keeping up with her. Physically and mentally. He was more intuitive than he gave himself credit for considering this was his first homicide. Maybe one of these days he would get out of his own way and see he had more to offer in her arena rather than always responding too late, as he'd put it.

"The killer has recreated every other aspect of the Elborne case. The location of the body dump, the bleach used to clean the body, a victim who resembles Teshia Elborne. Why not this one?" Leigh ignored the executive secretary's protests as she charged straight into the university president's office. His outraged gaze locked on her as the president stood to confront them. "I need access to your biomedical lab."

TEN

Durham, New Hampshire

Wednesday, October 9
4:12 p.m.

The university's biomedical and bioengineering lab looked the same as she remembered.

A whole bunch of floating shelves stuffed with brightly labeled compounds, equipment and refrigerators she couldn't begin to identify, and samples that could blow up this entire campus if mishandled. Despite the recent ten-million-dollar National Institute of Health research grant and the size of the university, the lab itself was nothing more than a slim, claustrophobic galley students could stretch their arms across and brush the opposite wall with their fingertips. The little desk space available was crowded with empty Tupperware containers, scales, pens, colored tape, glass test tubes, with tables and data taped within view of two computer stations. The whole lab resembled a forgotten galley kitchen, only this one had the potential to change the world.

"Oh, I get it. This is where the meth heads come to do their cooks when the police run them out of their basements." Ford kept his arms by his sides as they navigated through the lab behind her, which was amusing in and of itself. His mass didn't belong in a place this tight, even when trying to make himself smaller. In vain.

The president of the university pulled on the lapels of his coat as he turned to face them from the dead end of the lab, a single rain-streaked window at his back. The fluorescent light bars overhead did nothing to soften the impatience and resentment in his features, only adding a sickly color to his skin. "This lab is responsible for recent progress in cancer treatments and major depressive disorder, Marshal Ford. The researchers here have created implantable devices to deliver much-needed medications that won't be rejected by the human body. Every project produced by this lab has massive potential benefits in the health field."

"Who has access to this room?" She'd noted the security measures on the way in. No cameras. Each door in the building required a six-digit PIN, most likely unique to individual users, but they'd been forced to use one of two manual keys carried by the university president and security. There were any number of places their unsub could procure arsenic and cyanide, but she couldn't discount the very lab their primary suspect had worked in all those years ago. Leigh couldn't help but study the closest computer station to the window, searching for something familiar. Dean Groves had spent entire semesters cataloging and coding data for one of the researching professors to garner his lab experience at that station. She couldn't remember exactly what the study had entailed. He'd explained it to her the one time she'd visited, but she'd gone mushy after he'd cleared his desk and lifted her onto it.

"Our assistant professor of chemical engineering, of course, along with four junior researchers, myself, and the security team." The president scanned the room, as though he alone could determine if anything was out of place or missing, but Leigh had the feeling his academic career had ended years ago. "The doors are secured by key codes. Individualized by user. I don't see how whoever murdered Ms. Dietz could've gotten inside without raising red flags."

"Unless her killer was already familiar with the building." Ford had gone still. More imposing than a moment ago. His expression gave nothing away, but it was easy enough to read him now. "What about old codes? Do you deactivate codes when students leave the university?"

"I can't say that we do." The university president realized the implications of that admission, smoothing his expression. The primary suspect in Teshia Elborne's murder could've come back to kill another student after eighteen years without so much as raising questions. "I suppose if a researcher still remembered their code, they could access the building and this lab."

"Or convince another researcher to give them a key code." Leigh forced her attention away from the section of the lab. "What about surveillance? Any cameras in the building?"

The president shook his head, aging in the blink of an eye as reality sank in. "The work we do in this building is highly proprietary. We couldn't risk outside researchers learning about our ongoing projects, but there are several security guards stationed in the building."

"We'll want to talk with them and get a log of key codes used within the past seventy-two hours." She studied the shelves, each container lined with neon-labeled identifiers. Some she recognized from her brief visit the night Dean had snuck her in for a tour. Leigh grabbed for a container of amylase and turned it over in her hand. Handwritten scratches claimed her attention before she replaced it and searched the rest of the shelf. Turning each container backward on the shelves with the same results. "There are logs on the back of all these containers. Measurements, dates, and initials from the last researcher who used it. Where are the more dangerous compounds stored?"

"In that closet near the door." The university president struggled past Ford, ensuring not to jumble equipment or stations. A feat in and of itself. "All of these must be kept in secure containers, out of direct sunlight, and in a cool, dry space."

"What about arsenic and cyanide?" Ford asked.

"Yes. They should be in here." The president pulled the door open, revealing floor-to-ceiling shelves inside with an array of containers similar to the ones she'd inspected.

"I doubt our killer is courteous enough to sign his initials and write how much he used if this is where the poison came from. We probably won't get his fingerprints if he was careful either, but let's get the containers to the forensic techs when we're finished here." Leigh moved into the closet and spotted the cyanide first. After pulling a pair of latex gloves from her still-damp blazer, she gripped her fingertips around the container lid, lifted it free of its position, and set it on the nearest counter. Then did the same with the arsenic. "We can measure any discrepancies between the last researcher's use and the current weight."

"Brilliant." Ford grabbed a postage scale on the other end of the room and brought it to the end computer station, the only section of the overcrowded desk with any space left. He powered the scale on and selected the measurement. Either Ford had seen this model of scale before, or the US marshal had a secret homemade bread hobby. He set the arsenic on first. "According to the last measurement, this container is under-weight. By... a lot."

Leigh handed off the cyanide as the scale reset. "Try the arsenic."

Ford crouched slightly at the knees. "It's underweight, too."

But they couldn't take the scale's results at face value. There were several factors that could contribute to the measurements coming in underweight. Maybe the researchers weren't as careful to mark their last uses as the logs suggested. Maybe the scale was slightly off or another scale in the lab had been used instead. Human error had the potential to destroy investigations and studies alike. They couldn't discount any of it.

Leigh grabbed for another container from the closet without reading the label. She could've been handling an explosive compound or a highly corrosive acid for all she knew, but her need for confirmation exceeded self-preservation at the moment. "Measure this one."

Ford did as she asked without hesitation, keeping both the arsenic and the cyanide close by. They would be registered as evidence, handed over to the forensic techs to pull prints and test against the poison in the victim's bloodstream. "The log and weight match."

"This one next." She pulled another container free. Then another. And another. The next four measurement logs matched the weight on the scale down to the ounce. The limited free space on the desk had vanished in her attempt to find another explanation.

"You want to try another one?" Ford straightened. Waiting. No judgment. No hint of frustration or anger. He was willing to go through every container in this damn lab if it helped find Alice Dietz's killer, but there was no point. They had their answer, didn't they?

"No. I think we've addressed any potential errors in measurement." That was all she'd been trying to do. To prove the poison had been sourced from this lab. And they'd accomplished their goal. A trickle of sweat collected at the back of her neck. Giving her a glimpse of that dark thread of hope she'd tucked away all those years ago, the one that wanted to convince her Dean Groves hadn't turned into a murderer. She hadn't realized until then how desperately she'd been trying to unbury it. To sever it for good or keep the old fight going, she wasn't sure. "We were right. The killer broke into this lab and stole what he needed to kill Alice Dietz. He's replicating the Elborne case as much as possible. Grab some of those Ziploc bags over there on the desk and tag the containers. Forensics might be able to pull prints off the lids."

Leigh let the university president take a back seat to replace all the other containers on their respective shelves. The walls closed in around them as Ford utilized a box of bags to collect the containers. A bitter burn drove up her nose as she helped set the last of the containers back on the closet shelf. Each of the white, labeled canisters were supposed to be sealed to preserve the compounds inside and protect users from accidentally exposing themselves to something potentially hazardous. She shouldn't have been sensing anything in this closet. "Do you smell that?"

Ford finished sealing the bags with the arsenic and cyanide and closed the distance between them. "What is it?"

"I don't know. It smells like... battery acid?" Biting and sour. An olfactory warning to keep your distance. Her father had taught her how to change the battery in their family car when she'd been seven years old. How to jump one, too. Joel Brody was the kind of man who'd never wanted his children to rely on anyone but themselves. He'd spent hours out on the driveway with his head in the middle of an engine between DIY house projects, and she and her brother had been forced to absorb those lessons against their will. She knew that smell better than her brother's body odor on those hot weekends in the driveway. "And plastic."

Ford angled her out of the closet, scanning the shelves. "I don't see anything leaking. Could be coming through the vents."

No. The odor wasn't as strong in the open. All she could

smell was the slight hint of antiseptic she'd noted when they'd come in. "Do researchers work with acids in this lab?"

"Of course," the university president said. "Several. But I can't imagine any of our researchers being careless enough to ignore safety protocols."

That was what she was afraid of. Leigh shoved her way back in the closet, under Ford's arm as he pulled another row of canisters. And found what she was looking for in the back corner. "That one."

Hesitation gripped hard as she considered the thin layer of latex between the skin of her fingertips and what could potentially burn a hole through a human body. "Get me some gloves."

Ford's body heat vanished, leaving her cold along one side. She hadn't realized how close she'd let him get. How she'd gotten used to his proximity. He returned with a thicker pair of gloves. "Be careful. We have no idea who might've tampered with the container."

She was careful. Moving slower than she wanted to go. The container itself wasn't nearly as heavy as she expected, but the burn in her nostrils intensified to the point she had to open her mouth for some relief. It didn't help. The fumes coming off the acid drove down her throat. "The lid is loose."

That was why she could smell it. Whoever had used it last had been careless. Not one of the researchers. Everything else in the lab was pristine. No. This was something else. Leigh pried the lid free and took a step back. Bubbles foamed toward the lip then out and over onto the desk. The reaction was immediate. "There's something in there."

Something to cause the reaction.

She tried to get a better view without letting the fumes touch her face.

"What is that?" Ford asked.

She went for a pair of tongs stored upside down in one of the pencil holders at the computer station and grabbed for the foreign object. The remnants of a golden bear stalked across the near-melted rectangle of plastic.

"A driver's license?" The marshal adjusted his glasses to get a better look while the university president kept his distance. As though merely being in the same room could smother him with guilt.

"Multiple driver's licenses." Leigh didn't have anywhere to set the license down, replacing it back inside the container, and grabbed for another. This one was different. She could still make out hints of a wide smile and tanned skin. "All from states the suspect you're chasing has killed in."

ELEVEN

Durham, New Hampshire

Wednesday, October 9
5:05 p.m.

Their killer was growing desperate.

Feeling as trapped as she did on this campus.

Forensic techs had managed to put a stop to the acid's destruction of what they'd found to be six driver's licenses in the container. The plastic was warped, the photos were nothing more than a mixture of color, and the names had been too hard to read. There was no telling how long the licenses had been left in the acidic mixture, but there was a chance details could be recovered from imprints in the plastic.

Time would tell.

Another wave of restlessness flooded through the groups of staff and students huddled throughout Thompson Hall. She hadn't gotten the chance to check in on other dorms and buildings, but nerves and frustration were universal during shelter in place orders. The last rations of food had been used up.

Running water hadn't been affected, but things were about to get worse without power and an entire night ahead of them. Still, the storm hadn't let up. They had no way of getting news.

"Does maintenance have any kind of update on the generator?" Leigh stripped free of her blazer and tossed it on the bench beside Ava. Despite October temperatures outside, the fabric had started sticking to her in places better left to the imagination. The fifteen-year-old had managed to peel herself away from the group of students to check in with only a slight groan and very little complaint, but the day wasn't over. Given the pattern of the past few weeks together, they were due for an argument Leigh didn't have the energy to fight. "The heat is getting worse with this many bodies packed in together."

Thompson Hall was mostly made of offices and classrooms. There was plenty of room to spread out, but protocols made it safer for them all to stay together. Especially at night.

Ford swiped the back of his hand across his forehead, jarring his glasses. "They managed to strip some wiring from an older unit they hadn't gotten rid of yet, but they're not sure the parts are interchangeable. It'll take at least a couple more hours to get an idea."

"Did you recognize any of the driver's licenses we recovered?" she asked.

"None, but from what you said at least one was from California. Maybe belonging to one of the victims the killer I'm chasing left behind." Ford couldn't even seem to be bothered to look uncomfortable with the humidity clogging her throat. Traitor. "You?"

"Too much damage, but I think it's safe to say the suspect you've been tracking has come to the University of New Hampshire." Driver's licenses were made and stamped by machine. They'd be lucky if forensics could get an imprint with most of the ink burned off the plastic. "You gave me a list of four victims before Alice, but we pulled six driver's licenses from the container. Serial offenders sometimes collect trophies from their victims to later relive the experience when the desired effect wears off. It's a cycle with a cooling-off period between kills, but this killer is mobile. He's carrying his trophies with him, which makes me believe—up until recently—he was convinced he was invincible. Convinced himself he could outwit and outmaneuver police and get away with murder."

The marshal looked over the lobby in thought. Considering the height difference between them, it wasn't difficult. "But ditching the driver's licenses means our unsub might be getting desperate. And desperation leads to mistakes."

"Exactly," she said.

"Six driver's licenses. I only know of four male victims. You think there are two more we don't know about?" Ford asked.

"I think... I think that the killer is currently impersonating someone on this campus, but he's trapped and without resources. Same as us. Durham PD has the entire town shut down. We've also searched this campus to within an inch of its life. There's no getting out until the storm passes. Could be why our unsub ditched his trophy collection. He's taking care of loose ends."

Her attention landed on Professor Morrow, his back turned to Leigh. She couldn't bury the feeling he'd lied to her about knowing Alice Dietz earlier. There wasn't any big reason for her not to believe his statement. Just one little one: He was a sucker for details. Remembered the tiniest bits of information in any given case study, journal article, and paper. It was what made him one of the most sought-after criminology professors in the country. His criminology courses required at minimum two papers submitted by students each semester, which meant he'd read and graded submissions from Alice Dietz. Hard to believe the name hadn't meant anything to him.

"Security can't access video footage of the lab building until the power comes back on," she continued. "Until then, we're

going to have to wait for the president to provide the key codes
used to access the biomedical lab around Alice Dietz's death."

Ford slipped his hands into the pockets of his slacks. A habit
she'd noted since arriving on the crime scene this morning. His
way of exerting control in a situation neither of them had been
in before. "Why do you think he's killing all these people?"

That was the question. The most critical aspect of any serial
case. Motive said a lot about a killer, and one of the primary
approaches was to look at the victimology. The first victims told
the best stories: why they'd been targeted, maybe if they'd even
known their killer. She hadn't gotten the chance to look at the
previous victim files Ford had brought with him. At the same
time, they couldn't sit around waiting for another body to drop.

"To fulfill a need. There's something his victims have to
provide for him, a reason he's drawn to them. You said he takes
over their identities, becomes his victims for days and weeks.
He interacts with friends, family, coworkers without raising
suspicion. Lives in their homes, takes care of their pets, does
their jobs. Like he's living out a fantasy. It's one of the reasons
people love this time of year so much." Leigh eyed the
Halloween decorations strung up. Witches' hats, paper
streamers in orange and black, depictions of Frankenstein's
monster, and stacked pumpkins on the information desk. "But,
by becoming his victims, he gets to mold his own little world
with no one to tell him what to be."

"His life is so pathetic he needs to become someone else?"
Ford's laugh didn't sit well. Judgmental. Condescending.
Stereotypical. But she couldn't hold it against him. That was the
difference between the work she did compared to his. Most law
enforcement officers saw the world as black and white. A file
crossed their desk, and they attacked it with a dozen preconcep-
tions already in place for how the investigation would end. It
took diving into the mind of a killer, tearing apart behavior,
compulsions, and past experiences to understand each crime

was unique. Each serial offender believed what they were doing was the greatest option for survival.

"As I said, each of his victims would've needed to fulfill a need he has. It could be anything, and it may have been different for every victim. Earlier, you said all of the male victims worked remote, a couple even ran their own businesses. Perhaps our killer was envious of that lifestyle. Of being able to structure his day how he saw fit without a boss looking over his shoulder and no one to answer to, so he became them. He gifted himself a sense of freedom." This was all theoretical. In truth, she wouldn't be able to get a better understanding of their killer until she was able to look through each of the investigative files, but without power, limited flashlights, and thirty percent battery life on her signal-free phone, she'd have to wait.

"He's envious of them?" Ford asked.

"In every case I've worked, killing is primarily about control. Control of oneself, control of another—a way to exert a sliver of control in our lives." Everyone needed some semblance of control, but most of the population could keep themselves from killing to find it. "Our unsub is neat, clean, disciplined, and has a great attention to detail in the way he ensures there is no physical evidence to link him to his victims. But it's not enough. He's not happy. So he moves on to the next victim, and when they don't satisfy his craving, he kills another. He's becoming his highest self by testing out personalities and lives. He wants something they have, but the problem is he's never going to be satisfied. He's never going to stop, because manufactured happiness doesn't exist."

Ford had taken on a stillness again. "I'm starting to see why the FBI has kept you their best-kept secret for so long. I wouldn't want to share you either."

"It's all a theory at this point. I'll be able to get a better read on the victimology once I can dive into the files you brought. Until then, none of it tells us why he targeted and killed Alice

Dietz. She's the outlier and where we need to put our focus now." Leigh couldn't help but flush under Ford's unrelenting attention. It wasn't like the other times she'd walked onto a scene and immediately been challenged by spiteful men uncomfortable answering to a woman with more experience, who didn't believe she deserved to be there, or held a grudge against her ability to unearth corruption in their ranks. Ford's attention was... warm. Better than warm. Almost drugging. "Which meant he might not have planned to kill her. She could've gotten in the way of what he really wanted."

"All right." The marshal shifted his weight between both feet. Eager to get back into the hunt. Leigh imagined it was harder than it looked for him to stay in one place for long given the parameters of his job. "What does our killer want here on campus?"

"Another identity." It was that simple. "Durham is a university town with few full-time residents. It's primarily made up of students. No one comes here unless it has something to do with this campus."

"Someone at the university was the killer's target?" Ford scanned the lobby—the same as she did—to find an abnormality. A break in the pattern or a sign that said, "It's me!" stapled to someone's forehead.

Unfortunately, reality didn't work that way. They would have to pull apart every angle, re-interview every witness, and determine who in Alice Dietz's life had motive to kill her. Before the storm let up and their killer slipped away.

Exhaustion settled in. The egg salad sandwich lodged in her stomach wasn't doing great either. "But something stopped him from assuming the new identity."

"Alice Dietz." Ford had a knack for this work. Brilliant enough to connect leads, charismatic enough to charm his way through interviews and get what he needed, intuitive, even. Or maybe they just made a great team.

"Which means the killer's intended target knew her, might even have a connection to her." Leigh set her gaze on Tamra Hopkins, Alice's second roommate. The other had to be sheltered in the dorms, and from the look of it, Tamra was letting her nerves run the gamut. "Both of Alice Dietz's roommates believed she had a secret boyfriend. Someone she didn't want them to know about. She was quick to anger at the possibility of anyone reading her messages and snuck out of the dorm in the middle of the night on several occasions. My bet is it was someone that could've caused a lot of backlash for our victim."

"Because why hide the fact you're seeing someone unless there's a chance you could get in trouble." Ford hiked his hands to his hips. Ready to chase down the next lead. "Considering all our previous victims are male, I'm going to assume Alice Dietz was heterosexual. Boyfriend could've been in a relationship. Married, even. Didn't want the news getting out, so he's laying low. Refusing to come forward to save his own ass."

There was also a chance the killer had succeeded in assuming his next identity. But then where was the body?

"Maybe." Leigh locked on to Professor Morrow. The weight of her attention caught his. Her former mentor tried for a quick smile. "Or maybe he's hiding in plain sight."

TWELVE

Durham, New Hampshire

Wednesday, October 9
5:14 p.m.

"This was everything of Alice Dietz's I was able to find in my file cabinet. I'm not sure how it will help, but I'm certainly happy to assist however I can." Taking his seat across the table, Professor Morrow handed off a stack of stapled papers.

She and Ford had managed to isolate him in one of the psychology classrooms under the pretense of asking for his help analyzing the investigation. Feeding into that magnificent ego. He wanted a piece of the pie, credit for vaulting her into stardom all those years ago, but it'd been her own experience with police investigations and murder that had given her the edge to keep going. He'd just supplied the textbooks.

"Thank you." Leigh flipped through the papers. Crime prevention. Community policing. Economics of crime and patterns in crime. All topics typical of a criminology major, even some she'd studied herself on this very campus under his tutelage. "These will give us a better idea of who Alice Dietz was, her interests, experience, state of mind. All helpful."

Not really, but Morrow was enamored to be here.

Morrow leaned back in his well-loved tweed jacket that looked the same as it had eighteen years ago. Some things didn't change. "How is the investigation going, Leigh? Nobody will tell me anything."

"Unfortunately, there's not much to tell, and we can't give you any specifics of an ongoing investigation." Ford was to play the bad guy in this little conversation. The one who didn't think a professor could add any insight into a murder case. Get their potential witness riled up enough to forget the story he'd told himself. "I'm not even sure why we're talking to this guy. He's a teacher."

"Professor, actually, Marshal Ford, and one of the leading experts in the country on criminology." Morrow was already taking the bait, the muscle in his jaw ticcing with the insult to his ego. They had to play this carefully. Too many attempts to get the professor to talk and he'd see through them. "In fact, I taught Leigh here everything she knows."

She wasn't going to argue. They had more important things to focus on.

"Now that you've had a chance to review Alice Dietz's papers, is there anything that stands out to you, Pierce?" Leigh returned her focus to the paper in front of her. "She sat in two of your classes. Was she attentive? Did anything seem off in the days leading up to her death?"

"No. No. Nothing like that." Morrow folded his arms across his chest, accentuating the leather patches at his elbows. Not one hair out of place. "In fact, things were going well for her, particularly in my classes. She clearly understood the material and went out of her way to exceed my expectations."

Ford's turn. "Did you ever speak to her outside of class? Did she attend office hours, or did she seek any kind of mentorship or research opportunities?"

"No." Morrow dropped his gaze to the papers on the desk. He was shutting down.

"Alice Dietz was killed with a combination of arsenic and cyanide, same as Teshia Elborne was murdered eighteen years ago. From what we can see, there is no connection between the victims." She had to give him a reason to stay engaged. To show off even. "Why do you believe Alice Dietz was targeted?"

"Well, she fits the profile, doesn't she?" Morrow leaned forward in his chair. She had him. "Young, beautiful, successful by university standards. If I recall, Teshia Elborne was also blonde, fit, even had those big brown eyes." The professor raised his gaze to Leigh's. "Seems your killer has a type."

His point was clear. And it was a type that looked identical to her appearance. Of course, he didn't have all the information. He couldn't possibly know there'd been four male victims before Alice Dietz had been displayed on that sidewalk, and she and Ford would keep it that way. Well, unless he was the killer Ford had been hunting. They had one goal here: to establish a personal connection between Morrow and the victim.

Leigh would have to push a little harder. "Do you believe both women were killed by the same unsub? Now, I can't call him a serial offender with two bodies—" That the professor knew of. "But eighteen years is an extremely long cooling-off period, don't you think?"

"May I assume Alice Dietz's body was washed and bleached in the same manner as Teshia Elborne?" Morrow asked.

"From the hints of bleach the medical examiner noted at the scene, the killer most likely used the same chemicals to destroy any trace of DNA on the body. Like Teshia Elborne." Leigh was willing to let that detail slide. "Scrubbed clean with bleach and dish soap."

"Well, then this isn't a copycat you're looking for, seeing as how there weren't that many details released to the public eighteen years ago, which makes me think Teshia Elborne and Alice Dietz were killed by the same unsub. I would conclude your killer is extremely disciplined." Morrow's eyes glazed over, the professor lost to whatever profile he was building in his head. "He most likely discovered the power to manipulate others as a young child, which gave him a sense of control he seeks. He's intelligent, most likely well read. But he wouldn't allow his compulsions to get the better of him. He makes the choice to kill, potentially explaining why he was able to go so long between kills. I would imagine his chosen hunting ground is tied to his past. Perhaps he was a student here or even a long-time resident of Durham. There is some resentment in his ties to this university, but at the same time, he can't escape it. He has a preference for women, that's obvious, but he likes the idea of a student. Believing he himself can teach her something."

Despite the ruse she and Ford had created during this interrogation, Morrow had made a fair point. Manipulation. The killer they were hunting had to be able to read his victims and the people in his victims' lives, and to adapt to any given situation. Become anyone based off face-to-face interactions. Serial offenders weren't always sociopaths as popular media portrayed. They didn't have to play pretend with emotion and try to mirror it back. There were some who simply enjoyed playing with those emotions. Looked at them like a game to be won.

The temperature in the room rose impossibly higher as Leigh worked her way through the stiff-necked, proud layers of the professor's armor. "That would also mean he had a connection with both victims then and now through the university."

"According to administration records, Professor, you've been here for twenty-three years," Ford said.

Morrow flinched back as if he'd been physically struck. His

attention sharpened on Ford, trying to recall everything he'd added to the profile. "I don't see how that has any bearing on your current investigation."

"Unless you're the connection." Ford's voice held a hint of amusement. A cat toying with the mouse he'd cornered. "Teshia Elborne was a psychology major, wasn't she? Didn't you teach a couple psych classes back in the day?"

"Psychology and criminology both deal with human behavior, so yes, I've taught my fair share. Though my expertise lies in preventing crime. Not trying to get it into therapy." Helplessness filtered across the professor's face. He looked to Leigh for help, but she was happy to enjoy the show. "You can't be serious, Leigh. You can't seriously believe I had anything to do with these girls' murders. You know me."

That was true. She did know him. And he wasn't a killer, but she'd thought the same of Ava's mother. "According to her roommates, Alice Dietz has been acting suspiciously. Leaving the dorm in the middle of the night, becoming paranoid about anyone reading her phone. Simply put, Pierce, we believe she was having an affair with someone who could be ruined if the relationship went public. Maybe even get her expelled. Someone like a professor."

Morrow tried to keep himself from shifting in his seat, but it was the little ways his shoulder tensed and the grind of his back teeth that told her he knew exactly where this was going. All those hours he'd spent drilling her on policing procedures, environmental crime, and research methods were being used against him. Was that the definition of ironic?

Leigh slid Alice Dietz's work back across the table, flipped open to one page from the third paper. "You were a good mentor. Probably better than most. The problem is I remember what it's like to be one of your students. In a way, you're right. I wouldn't be here if it hadn't been for you, but I know exactly what you expect of your mentees."

She pointed out a section of the paper, and the color washed from Morrow's face.

Ford leaned forward, hands interlaced on the surface of the table in front of him. Confident, letting her take the lead with this one.

"This section in Alice's paper is almost word-for-word from one of your previous projects. One of the projects I helped you research as your assistant my junior year. I know for a fact your paper was rejected from three journals before you stuffed it in the back of your filing cabinets." She had him. There was no way he could deny it. "There isn't a single person alive you would let read one of your rejected papers unless they were helping you revise and research a new project. Which means, you lied to me, Pierce. Yours and Alice's relationship was more than student and professor."

"You were having an affair with our victim, and you lied about it," Ford said. "What do they call that, Agent Brody? Oh, right. Obstruction of justice. You're familiar with the term, aren't you, Professor? It's enough for an arrest."

"Now, wait a minute. You have it all wrong." This was the part when Morrow would panic, try to come up with any plausible reason Alice Dietz would've gotten her hands on his work. Plagiarism, theft, academic dishonesty. He'd built a career in criminology and criminal justice, but he'd still revert to his survival instincts when pressed. "Please. Just give me a chance to explain."

Bingo.

"When was the last time you saw Alice Dietz alive?" She and Ford had yet to build a solid timeline of the victim's movements leading up to her death, but the picture was getting a little clearer.

"Saturday night, early Sunday morning. We argued. I regret not telling you sooner, but I didn't want to look... guilty." The air leeched out of him, leaving nothing but a husk of the man she'd once looked up to. "Alice was my assistant this semester. She was helping me with a paper on crime mapping and predicting criminal patterns in certain areas to better utilize policing efforts and focus. She was bright and driven and, of course, I took notice of her."

He motioned to the stack of papers on the desk between them. "We'd meet after classes. I'd help her with her assignments. Nothing big, just extra resources she could look into. Then we started meeting outside the office. Within a few weeks, she was coming to my home, and things ... happened. It wasn't planned, and I certainly never expected her to be murdered." Morrow's voice broke at that last word. "We knew if anyone discovered what we were doing, she would be expelled, and I would lose my job. All my work would've been for nothing. I've invested decades into my career as Marshal Ford has kindly pointed out, and I couldn't risk our relationship going public. That's what we argued about that night. She was tired of sneaking around. I told her..." He swallowed, before continuing in a miserable voice, "I would ruin her if she said a single word."

They'd gotten what they'd wanted, and Leigh let it sit between them. The disgrace, the embarrassment, the grief. Morrow and his ego deserved it all. Though he'd probably take this experience and turn it into some kind of benefit. She collected the papers from the desk and pushed to stand. "I don't believe you killed Alice Dietz, Pierce."

"Why wouldn't you consider me a suspect after I confessed I argued with the victim?" It was a good question, but they didn't have the time to try to fit him into all the boxes. There was an actual killer on the loose.

"Because," Leigh said, "I think you were the killer's intended target."

THIRTEEN

Durham, New Hampshire

September 8, 2006
7:23 a.m.

Pounding from the door jarred her nerves.

Leigh peeled her face off the pillow, hand automatically stretching to the other side of the bed.

Cold. Empty.

Dean had managed to sneak out without waking her again. Probably a couple hours ago. Another early morning at the biomedical lab. She didn't mind. She had her own schedule to keep, and she kind of loved this new routine of theirs. Living their own lives during the day but unable to keep their hands off each other at night. Dean didn't want to own her or dictate her schedule. He never asked for her to change her plans for him or choose him over her friends. He didn't want a girlfriend. He wanted an equal. More than happy to take any free time he could get with her but aware he couldn't be her whole world.

Choice. Every day he gave her the gift of making her own choice. It was one of the things she loved about him the most.

Leigh grabbed for her phone on the nightstand. Damn it. Her brother would be waking up soon, and she preferred not to have to explain to a thirteen-year-old where she'd been and what she'd been doing all night when she got back to their dorm.

Another round of knocks thudded through the room.

"Yeah, yeah." Leigh flipped off the covers smelling of spice and soap and headed for the door. All Dean. She'd catch it on her own skin, in her hair, on her clothes as she navigated from one class to the next or when she got to one of her part-time jobs. Always with her. Part of her. She could smell him on her now, and a rush of heat flooded into her face at the memories of last night. And of the past two weeks. He'd done exactly as he'd promised that first time they'd slept together. He'd taken care of her, helped her grow more confident in bed, let her use him as she needed and explore her curiosity without judgment or hesitation.

He'd become her safe place in such a short amount of time. Something she hadn't had in a long time, and she trusted him. In more ways than one. "I'm coming."

She dragged a blanket around her shoulders to counter the fact she was dressed in a pair of Dean's boxer shorts and her thin tank top. No need to frighten the rest of the dorm this early in the morning. And while it wasn't entirely against the rules for students to spend the night in each other's rooms, she wasn't going to advertise it.

Leigh wrenched the door open.

Facing off with two uniformed police officers.

"Dean Groves." The nearest tried to peek around her through the slim crack in the door, both hands gripped on his utility belt. He was over a head taller than her, making it easier, but Leigh didn't want those eyes scouring through Dean's dorm. This was their space. The one place she could be herself instead of the teen

who'd failed to get her daddy out of murder charges. Nobody else had a right to it. "He here?"

"No." Defenses she'd sworn she'd left back home tightened the muscles down her spine. Automatic and suffocating. Both officers set their gaze on her. Waiting for her to elaborate on Dean's location. It was a tactic law enforcement and lawyers liked to use, knowing social expectations usually got the better of most people due to the need to avoid uncomfortable and awkward silences. But she'd made that mistake once. She wouldn't make it again. "Anything else?"

"You are?" the second officer asked.

"None of your business." Leigh moved to close the door in their faces. She didn't know what the hell was going on—why police were looking for Dean—and she had no intention of getting in the middle of it. She'd already lost her war against the police department in her hometown. She couldn't go through that again. Didn't want to put her brother through it again.

A foot jammed against the door, keeping her from closing it fully. The officer held up a photo, nearly shoving it into her face. "You know this girl?"

Leigh glanced at the perfect smiling face then did a double take. The similarities were a bit eerie. Blonde hair with darker roots—obviously dyed and well maintained—brown eyes the color of burnt coffee, straight white teeth that'd seen years of orthodontia and whitening. The photo had come from a Granite State student ID with a section of dark green border taking up one side of the photo. "No."

"Her name is Teshia Elborne. She's a student here on campus." The second officer took in Leigh's presence inside a dorm that obviously wasn't hers this early in the morning, her lack of clothing, and her most likely frizzed hair. "Has Dean ever mentioned her to you?"

Ah. There it was. The judgment of answering the door half dressed in a blanket that didn't belong to her. Leigh narrowed her *gaze on the photo, to give them the impression she was thinking, but she already had her answer. And she knew what kind of games police liked to play. They were trying to use her to establish a connection between this woman and Dean. In her experience, it usually meant someone was dead.* "Why would he?"

"Ms. Elborne was found dead in front of Thompson Hall this morning," the first officer said. "And we have a signed witness statement that says Dean Groves was the last person to see her alive."

Durham, New Hampshire

Wednesday, October 9
5:53 p.m.

"You're very impressive, you know. The way you used Morrow's own work against him to get him to admit a personal relationship with the victim was genius." Ford kept pace with her all too easily as they navigated back to the building's lobby. The sun had gone down completely now, his phone lighting the way through the maze. "Did you really recognize his work in those papers from all those years ago as his research assistant?"

They couldn't arrest Morrow for having an affair with a student, but Leigh hadn't made any promises to keep it from the university administration either. He would lose his job. Lose any chance of publishing in a peer-reviewed journal. Lose everything he'd worked so hard for. It was a little ironic. Morrow had threatened Alice Dietz to keep her mouth shut for fear of staining his already struggling academic career. In the end, it'd been her death that cost him everything. "No. I took a chance."

It'd been a risk, but ego was Pierce Morrow's number one downfall. Always had been. And she'd gotten good at using it against him.

The marshal pulled her up short, staring down at her. The light from his phone carved sharp shadows into his features, making him impossibly more handsome. "You took a chance? Wait. The section you pointed out to him in Alice Dietz's paper didn't come from one of his projects?"

"Oh. I have no idea. I picked it at random." A laugh—genuine and light—escaped up her throat at the shock contorting Ford's expression. She couldn't remember the last time she'd had reason to laugh. Hard to do when getting screamed at or ignored by a fifteen-year-old throughout the day. "Pierce Morrow doesn't grade his own papers. That's what he has assistants for. His work as a professor is secondary to his own research. He's never read one of Alice Dietz's papers. He has no idea what was in there. He's also written on nearly every criminology topic. I was fairly confident I could pick one at random and use it against him."

"That's..." Ford said. "Quite brilliant."

Warmth stretched up her neck and into her face, and she couldn't keep eye contact. She realized exactly how close they'd gotten to each other. Mere inches between them. When had it happened? How hadn't she noticed before now? Leigh fought the urge to add to those inches. Ford wasn't a threat. He was... handsome. Maybe even a bit reckless taking on an investigation so out of his element. But she liked that about him. "Thank you."

"You're good at reading people, aren't you?" He was looking at her with something she couldn't identify. Admiration? Couldn't be right. Despite national headlines, she was nobody. She'd consulted for police departments all over the country before joining the BAU, but the credit had always gone to the detectives. Until recently. She wasn't admiration material. She was just an investigator determined to get to the truth. "It's not about the evidence or witness statements for you. You see the things most people try to hide."

"I'm drawn to patterns." Had she ever told someone that before? Her parents had known, her brother too. She could find a pattern in anything. A piece of wood her father had brought home from the hardware store. The rise and dip of plot beats in her favorite TV shows. In the hundreds of Lego sets she'd put together. Come to think of it, she hadn't touched any since being gifted a set by the man who'd abducted her brother. "Sometimes to my own detriment. I'm good at finding them. Creating them. I can rely on them. Routines and habits tell a lot more about a person and their priorities than their words."

Maybe that'd been one of the reasons Dean Groves had been able to get away with murder for all these years. He'd changed his patterns.

"What kind of patterns do you see when you look at me?" Ford's shoulders expanded, giving her more to take in. Not in intimidation. But hope she could see the whole picture. Deeper than the US Marshal shield pinned to his belt. Deeper than the exhaustion clouding his eyes.

This was a bad idea. While she couldn't avoid cataloging blatant patterns in the tick of a clock or the way Ava chewed on the ends of her hair when she was upset, Leigh had built a filter to keep herself from obsessing. From getting caught up in waiting for the pattern to break. But turning her obsession on someone she'd partnered with to solve this case? She doubted either of them would like what they found. Still, she couldn't help but pick up on the ones the marshal practically wore on his sleeves.

"You chew on the inside your mouth when you're confused by something. Which, during this investigation, has been a lot. I'm sure your dentist doesn't appreciate that. Your hair is also slightly thinner above your left ear, which means you run your fingers through it, especially in the presence of an attractive woman. It's a self-conscious check. You did it when you met me at the crime scene this morning."

Had it really been this morning? Time wanted to convince her she'd been in these halls for days. Thunder rumbled and shook through the building. The storm was getting closer. Cutting them off even more.

"Think so highly or yourself, do you?" Ford closed the last couple of inches between them. Into her personal space.

She caught hints of his aftershave, mixed with the scent of rain and something cleaner. Soap? How had he managed to keep himself from sweating to death in his suit as she had? She was probably dehydrated. That was what this was. She wasn't thinking clearly, letting him get too close. "I'm just telling you what I see."

"Well, you're not wrong," he said. "About any of it."

Her breath hitched as he leaned in. "I know—"

His mouth was on hers. Sliding over her bottom lip in an even rhythm. He was doing it on purpose. Giving her the pattern she needed to predict his next move. The consideration intensified the heat burning through her, and a falling sensation tore through her. Weightless and heavy all at the same time. His lips were softer than they'd looked, and now the tension was bleeding out of his shoulders. Melting. Ford penetrated the seam of her mouth with his tongue, holding her up through sheer strength. He tasted of dark chocolate and something brighter. Oranges. No breakfast of champions, but she would take it. Any of it. It'd been too damn long since she'd allowed herself this small feeling.

Since she'd had a single glimpse at hope. Connection.

Leigh kissed him back, pressed him against the wall at his back, memorizing with her hands. Ford's fingers speared into her hair, holding her as a willing hostage. She wanted this. She needed this. And after everything she'd survived in the past year—everything she'd lost—she deserved something for herself. Didn't she?

But it wasn't just her anymore. Ava. She couldn't start a

new relationship while struggling to get a grip on raising a fifteen-year-old. Leigh pulled away, setting herself back onto the four corners of her feet. Ford's hold strengthened on her hips, and she forced herself out of his reach, swiping at her mouth. "That shouldn't have happened."

"Don't say it was a mistake, Leigh," Ford said. "It wasn't."

No. It wasn't. It was... perfect. "I have a lot going on in my life at the moment. Ava is... making my life hell, and I need to consider—"

Movement caught her attention.

Ava stepped into the pool of light put off by Ford's phone. Tears in her eyes. Then ran.

FOURTEEN

Durham, New Hampshire

Wednesday, October 9
6:05 p.m.

Making her life hell.

"Ava, wait!" Leigh shoved away from the marshal and ran after her adopted daughter. But she wasn't fast enough. "I didn't mean that!"

Ava's wiry frame merged with the shadows closing in from the narrow corridor, and then she was gone.

Dragging her phone from her blazer—still damp in spots—Leigh hit the flashlight feature. There were over a dozen classrooms Ava could've disappeared into in the past few seconds. Her heart rate drowned out any chance of hearing shuffling footsteps or sobs. She had to calm down. Had to think about this rationally.

"Leigh." Ford was on her heels, adding his phone's flashlight to hers. "I'll start searching the classrooms. You see if she made it back to the lobby."

Okay. She could do that. "Message me if you find her. Please."

She didn't want to screw this up, but she couldn't see a way back either. She'd had a hope things would get better between them. Maybe they had the past few hours, but now... Ava had clawed her way into Leigh's life and seemed just as determined to claw her way out. Their union wasn't a typical adoption case. Ava had come to her through violence and trauma and secrets and murder. Leigh had always known it wouldn't be a smooth transition—for either of them—but now she didn't know what to do. Why couldn't she be like her own mother? Where was the unlimited patience, the emotional intelligence, and ability to smile through the hard times?

Leigh jogged back toward Thompson Hall's lobby. Students were beginning to settle in for the night against the walls and on benches with their coats. The stab of rain pelted against the lobby door glass and windows, turning the two-story chamber into a prison. She targeted the first student she saw. "Have you seen a girl run through here? Brown hair, about five-foot-five?"

The woman shook her head. "No, sorry."

She caught sight of the group of five Ava had spent the past few hours with. Panic welled in her chest. This. This was what being a mother felt like. Every time her adopted daughter had taken off in the middle of the night or refused to come home from school, this feeling threatened to crush her. Until all Leigh could do was live in it. Become it. She grabbed on to one of the group's members. "Have you seen Ava? She must've run through here."

Tension thickened under her touch, the poor guy's eyes widening. "Last we saw her, she was looking for someone."

For Leigh. Nausea churned in her gut, harsh and acidic.

"I've searched all of the classrooms." Ford appeared at her side in the blink of an eye. Impossible for someone his size. Or maybe Leigh really was that blinded by worry. "There isn't any sign of her."

The pounding of her heart pulsed behind her ears. Growing louder. More uneven. She was moving again without conscious thought, running to the opposite end of the building. They'd sequestered students to the lobby and main floor, but Thompson Hall was structured with two more floors above them. "She wouldn't leave. She has to be here."

Ford's hands were on her then, tucking her against his chest. She didn't know how much she'd needed that until right then. The support. The reassurance she wasn't in this alone. That she didn't have to do this alone. "We're going to find her. She can't get far in this storm."

"You obviously don't know how far Ava is willing to go to get away from me." Breathe. She'd fought serial killers for the people she loved, she'd been drowned, stabbed, and had her entire future ripped out from underneath her. She could do this. She just had to think. "She'll want to get as far from me as possible."

Leigh pulled free of Ford's arms for a second time. Each time was getting harder and harder, but she couldn't focus on that right now. "I'm going to search the third floor. You take the second."

"Got it." Ford headed for the stairs ahead of her.

She'd faced each of those life-ending events without a single thread of hesitation. But Leigh found herself pausing at the base of the stairs. She'd wanted nothing more than to have a family, to replace what had been taken from her when her brother had gone missing. She craved the visits from the tooth fairy, registering kids for school, the late nights with newborns, and weekly date nights with the man she loved. She wanted the hard things as much as she wanted the professional Christmas photos in front of the tree and the gap-tooth smiles, all the while knowing she'd earned every second.

But adopting Ava hadn't come close to the picture in her mind, and she certainly hadn't earned the right to call Ava hers. She belonged to another mother. And Leigh was... a place-holder. It was all Ava would let her be. And Leigh couldn't blame her.

She forced her feet to move, to take the stairs two at a time. The surgical sites across her low belly twinged with a hint of pain, but they wouldn't slow her down. Sweat slicked at her temples as she passed the second floor and moved on to the third. She had to trust Ford to keep his word instead of taking full control of the search. Something she didn't enjoy imparting considering her past two cases, but she had to keep her focus on Ava.

Leigh hauled the stairwell door open and crossed the threshold onto the third floor. The president's office stood out at the end of the long hallway with more offices on either side of her. Grant and contract administrators, IT director, career counselors. Too many offices to count. "Ava?"

Her lungs burned with exertion. Out of control. The help-lessness added to the panic ripping through her. All too real, all too consuming, as though she were at the wrong end of a hand-gun. Lightning lit up the sky through the wall of windows. "Ava, please. I didn't mean what I said. You haven't made my life hell. I was... overwhelmed in the moment. I didn't mean it."

Time ticked by effortlessly, out of her hands. There was a killer on the loose. A body in the morgue. A professor keeping secrets. She didn't have time for the dramatics of a fifteen-year-old teenager, but this moment felt important. Her chance at a family was slipping away, and Leigh couldn't stomach the thought of losing something so precious.

"Go away!" Ava's voice warbled on the last word. Cut through with a sob. Thunder boomed directly overhead and threatened to knock the remaining strength out of Leigh's legs. A shadow raced across the corridor ahead.

Leigh picked up the pace. Trying to predict where Ava planned on running. One answer took shape: as far from her as possible. A door slammed. The crushing sound of rain grew louder. The roof access. "Ava, no!"

She charged the length of the third floor and shoved through the heavy metal door with a growing puddle of water squishing beneath her feet. A rubber foot stop demanded attention from the floor, and she shoved it underneath the frame to keep them from getting locked outside.

Wind pelted a wall of rain into her face, and Leigh raised the lapel of her blazer to block the onslaught. In vain. She was soaked in seconds, hostage to the hurricane-force winds on a roof offering little protection. Air conditioning units groaned under the assault, their fan blades spinning wildly. Another round of lightning flashed. Too close. She was exposed out here. In danger. But she wasn't going back inside until Ava was safe. "Ava!"

She searched the roofline. And caught sight of her adopted daughter at the south edge. Directly over the crime scene where Alice Dietz had been left by her killer. "Ava!"

"Don't!" Ava threw one hand out, half turning toward Leigh. One wrong gust of wind and she'd tip over the edge. Her clothing whipped around her, tearing in opposite directions as the storm battered Durham. "Don't!"

Her heart stuttered in her chest. No. No, this wasn't happening. She wasn't going to watch her adopted daughter go over the edge of a three-story building. Tendrils of hair slashed across Leigh's face and blocked her vision. But she still took that step forward. Raising her voice over the thunder of the storm, she reached out a hand. "Ava, please. You don't want to do this."

"You don't know what I want!" Pure venom contorted Ava's beautiful face, a face nearly identical to her mother's. "Nobody asked me what I wanted when she went to prison."

"I know." Leigh attempted another step closer. "It wasn't

fair, Ava. I know, but there's no going back. We're all we have left now."

"I said, don't come near me!" The fifteen-year-old's balance shifted precariously, her toes pressed to the roofline's edge, and Leigh pulled up more than ten feet short. Could she even reach Ava in time? "I don't know you, and you said it yourself, I make your life hell. You don't even want me, so why don't you just leave me alone?"

"I want you!" Her voice broke as the tears pushed into her eyes. "More than you know."

The metal door swung back on weak hinges and slammed against the brick wall behind it. The impact claimed Ava's attention, and her balance failed. She wobbled with both hands stretched out.

Leigh moved to lunge, to grab her no matter the cost of being the most hated woman on the planet. She could deal with that. But she couldn't deal with losing Ava altogether.

"You're lying! You only took me because my mother forced me on you before she went to prison. Like I was some kind of pet that needed looking after." Devastation had replaced rage and stripped Ava's expression down to nothing. She got better control of her balance then, standing straight. Facing off with the one obstacle in her path. She looked like some kind of goddess. Strong. Beautiful. Knowing her power over others. Leigh would be proud if it weren't for the fact the obstacle keeping Ava from what she wanted was her.

"Ava, please." The helplessness she'd avoided her entire life reared its ugly little head. "I don't want you to fall. Please, come back inside, and we can talk about all of this."

"Do you know why I keep running away? Why Officer Caine has to drag me back night after night?" Ava's voice projected over the chaos around them. Even and clear. "You never ask what I want or what I need. You think you know what's good for me, and you make decisions for me, but you're always going to be chasing after the next case. Your job is every-thing to you, and I'm nothing but a case you can't close! That's what he made me. A case!"

Leigh's reach faltered. It was the first time Ava had talked about the man who'd abducted and assaulted her. Up until this point, she'd waited for Ava to broach the subject of what'd happened. To take that first step. Now... she wasn't so sure she'd made the right choice. "That's... That's not true."

It couldn't be true.

"Leigh!" Ford's voice was lost to the howling wind from behind. He'd followed her but, thankfully, kept his distance as he surveyed the situation.

Ava's mother had sacrificed the rest of her free life to keep her daughter safe. To prove the force of a mother's love. And yet, Leigh hadn't really been willing to do the same, had she? Ava was right. Adopting a daughter had been terrifying and confusing, and she hadn't known what she was doing from the beginning. Becoming a mother didn't automatically make you one, as she'd assumed. Her own mom had made it look so easy. Natural. And when it hadn't proven to be the case for her, she'd immersed herself in her work, in the next case to give herself something tangible to rely on. Distracted herself from what was happening in front of her. All this time, she'd convinced herself she deserved the experience of having a family of her own. That she'd more than earned it. But what had she ever really sacri-ficed in return?

"I'm not a case you get to solve. I'm not anything anymore. He made sure of that when he took me." Ava faced the front of Thompson Hall. And lifted one foot in the air.

"No!" Ford's scream lanced through her. His suit jacket penetrated her peripheral vision a split second before Leigh was moving.

She closed the last bit of distance between them, hand outstretched. The wind pounded rain into her skin, into her clothing. Stinging pain prickled along the back of her hand, but she didn't care. About any of it. The storm. Ford. This case. All that mattered was Ava. Getting to Ava.

She fisted her hands in Ava's T-shirt and threw everything she had into wrenching her back. They hit the graveled rooftop as one, but neither of them acknowledged the impact. Leigh wrapped both arms around the fifteen-year-old's shaking frame, trying to absorb Ava into her very skin to keep her safe.

Ford positioned himself to keep the rain from pelting them.

"You're mine," she said into the crown of Ava's head. "You're mine."

FIFTEEN

Durham, New Hampshire

Wednesday, October 9
7:23 p.m.

Her body didn't feel solid anymore.

Pulled in a thousand different directions she couldn't keep up with.

Leigh drowned the urge to fidget as she stroked Ava's hair. It was early evening, but the atmosphere in Thompson Hall's lobby had reached a level of surrender and stillness. There was nowhere they could go, nothing they could do, no one who could help them as long as the storm kept mounting. Students and administration alike had tired of the unspoken social rules between groups. No one wanted to be alone. Instead, staff rotated in turns checking on students, handing over jackets and emergency supplies to get through the night. What they'd assumed would be a short shelter in place order would now certainly stretch into tomorrow. Maybe longer. Acceptance and exhaustion settled over the group of thirty-six and took their last remaining threads of energy. Everyone was tired from worry and questions and fear. Sleep was the only escape.

And Alice Dietz's killer was possibly stuck along with them.

The few flashlights they'd collected from around the building had been distributed with instructions for use only in dire circumstances. There was no telling when they would all get out of here. Food from the vending machines down the hall was all gone, and Leigh couldn't imagine the state of the dorms or any other building campus goers had been sequestered to. She didn't have any way of finding out.

Leigh shifted onto her hip against the cold, hard floor, her elbow tucked underneath her head. The position wasn't remotely comfortable and would be impossible to sustain through the long hours ahead of them, but she'd managed to convince Ava to get some sleep, pressed up against her chest. Next to Leigh's heart. Where she belonged.

What'd happened on the roof... The panic that'd seized her had yet to dissipate. It vibrated through her. There was no way she'd be able to sleep tonight. She'd come so close to losing the one good thing to come out of all the violence of the past. Too blind to see the gift she'd been given. But she'd never make that mistake again. She didn't know where she and Ava would go from here. Probably therapy, maybe an extended leave of absence from the BAU—whatever it took to earn Ava's trust. They needed it. Ava had lost her father to suicide. Lost her mother to a lifelong prison sentence. Had her innocence and freedom stripped away by a man who haunted her nightmares, and her choice of where to live overlooked. And while Leigh had been in a similar situation at her age—desperate for someone to care—Ava deserved the one thing Leigh had never been granted. To feel safe.

No. That wasn't true. Leigh had felt safe once. Protected. Loved. Right up until two Durham PD officers had shown her a photo of Teshia Elborne.

Leigh tried to get comfortable again without waking Ava. The emotional war waging between them was enough to knock Leigh out for a week if given the opportunity. But she wouldn't let it. Not with a killer hiding in these walls. Ava moaned in her sleep, and Leigh ran her hands across the girl's temple again. Ava was alive. That was what mattered. Alice Dietz couldn't say the same. What were the victim's parents going through right now? Unable to reach their daughter, not knowing the details of what'd happened to her. "Shhh. You're safe. I won't let anything happen to you."

Ford moved from his position at the front glass doors, keeping watch. He'd already made his rounds from the front of the building to each exit. Three times. But nothing could take the tension out of his shoulders, and the same restlessness drilled through Leigh. Rest wasn't a word in her vocabulary. At least, it hadn't been up until a month ago when she'd been forced to give up her uterus to cancer. Some habits died hard. She and Ford were similar in that respect. Always looking for answers. Never satisfied with where they were. Constantly looking for the next challenge, the next case, the next answer. It was probably why he'd chosen to become a US marshal. He loved the hunt. Careful not to wake those who'd finally settled in for the night, he headed for the corridor where Dean Groves had vanished.

If he'd been there at all.

Had seeing him been real? Or had coming back on campus triggered her brain to conjure the man she'd been searching for these past eighteen years? Leigh wasn't sure she could trust her own senses, let alone her own memory at this point. She felt like she'd reached levels of exhaustion not yet discovered by sleep scientists.

An outline peeled from the wall near the stairs. Nearly as large as Ford, but there were no other men in the lobby who came close to his size. Instinct froze her to the core underneath the weight of the shadow's attention. As if he was staring directly at her through the dark. Which was impossible. She knew that but couldn't shake the rattling feeling of exposure.

The outline shifted. There one moment. Gone the next.

Darkness absorbed the movement at the base of the stairs. Or maybe her mind had finally broken. All the trauma, the loss, the grief, and desperation to change reality—it was just a matter of time before she lost out to a mental breakdown, right? She didn't need to get up to prove she wasn't crazy. She didn't need to leave Ava to ensure the rest of the people in this room weren't in danger. And she certainly didn't need to be chasing any more ghosts.

Except she couldn't stop staring at the spot where he'd stood.

Leigh pressed a kiss to Ava's temple and smoothed her hair away from her adopted daughter's face one last time before slipping free. Maneuvering through the piles of bodies strewn across the lobby floor, she tried to keep her movements to herself and avoid stepping on any heads or hands in her path to the stairs.

She glanced down the corridor where Ford had disappeared. He was still making his rounds. If he followed the same pattern as the last three times, he'd move on to searching each classroom, ensuring all windows were secure from the inside. Leigh pulled up short of climbing the stairs to the second level, turning instead to the ones leading downstairs.

Hadn't Ford secured the basement door earlier?

Maintenance workers had given up on trying to bring the sabotaged generator back to life. The wiring stripped from another unit wasn't interchangeable. They just had to ride out the storm, same as everyone else. It didn't make for the best conditions, but they were safe as long as they remained quarantined to this building and didn't turn on each other. Leigh found herself descending into the basement, grabbing for her phone's flashlight.

She tapped the button on the screen, and white light seared her vision as she crossed the threshold. Quietly closing the door behind her so as not to wake anyone in the lobby, she faced off with a long corridor smelling sweetly of rot. Pools of water puddled in the cracks along the cinderblock walls and cement flooring. Overhead bare bulbs added to the creepy factor as she took the first few steps. "Ford?"

Had the marshal slipped down here for his security rounds, and she hadn't noticed? No. That didn't fit his pattern.

Drip. Drip. Drip. Water pelted her shoulder from above. Several tons of rain had soaked the surrounding property and was trying to work its way inside a non-waterproofed foundation. Then again, who could've predicted a hurricane in the Atlantic reaching this far inland? Leigh's flashlight failed to illuminate anything more than a few feet ahead of her and reflected back at her from puddles spreading across the floor. Some several inches deep. She raised the phone's flashlight ahead of her.

And landed on a human shape.

Back turned to her, she couldn't make out any details other than mountainous male musculature, short dark hair, and black clothing and boots. Not Ford. Energy charged into her free hand as she reached for her holstered sidearm and raised her weapon. "Hey!"

The figure sidestepped into a corridor to his left.

Out of view.

Leigh pressed herself against the wall and heel-toed toward the corner as silently as puddles and her shoes allowed. She couldn't ignore the instincts screaming at her not to follow, but she couldn't ignore a potential lead on Alice Dietz's murderer either. The killer was trapped on this campus with them. What better hiding place than a series of underground tunnels administration only ever used for maintenance purposes?

Back pressed against solid cinderblock, she forced her breathing to slow. Charged nerves lost a bit of their influence as she craned her neck around the corner and raised her flashlight beam.

Empty.

Leigh stepped into the corridor, her focus honed on any potential threat. Water soaked through her shoes, much deeper here, as if the foundation itself sloped steeper into this section of the building and collected the storm's tears. Each step had her wading until her slacks were plastered against her legs from her knees to her ankles.

A trap. This was a trap. Whoever had killed Alice Dietz was intelligent enough to realize they weren't getting out of Durham until police cleared the roads, but escape would still be his number one priority. The first step to getting away with murder? Make sure you're not being chased. But the lure had already hooked into her. Pulling her deeper into the building and eviscerating her survival instincts.

Leigh built a mental map back to the door leading up to the lobby. It would be easy to get lost down here without anyone knowing where she'd gone and just five percent left on her phone battery. She glanced at the screen. Make that three percent.

She should turn back now. Wait until morning when Ford could accompany her in another search of the basement. But by then, the killer could be gone. She couldn't wait for backup.

She caught sight of movement ahead. Her lungs suctioned to her ribcage as she raced against the deepening flood to catch up. "FBI! Stop!"

The water thickened here somehow, and she really didn't want to think about what she was wading through as she approached the end of the corridor. Ice worked through her feet and cut off feeling in her toes the deeper she trod. Leigh pulled up short of a dead end. That didn't make sense. He'd been right here. Spinning in place, she lost her grip on her phone. The device hit the two feet of water increasing by the second and blacked out.

Throwing her into darkness.

"Shit." If the killer had wanted her out of the picture, he was certain to get his wish in the next few minutes. Leigh stretched her free hand out to test for a wall—something—to lead her out of this fresh hell. She'd never had a problem with small spaces, but the corridor closed in too tight. Too dark. Unknown. Crouching, she allowed the rest of her outfit to soak through as she searched for her phone. She couldn't leave it, but saving it might be a waste of time if she died down here. Her fingers grazed the powerless brick, and she attempted to turn it back on. In vain.

Water sloshed against her legs.

But she hadn't moved.

And the feeling she was being watched again hardened the muscles along her spine. Leigh raised her weapon. Completely at the mercy of the darkness—and the killer—closing in.

His voice cut through the thudding pound of her heartbeat behind her ears. "I've been looking forward to this moment for a very long time, Agent Brody."

SIXTEEN

Durham, New Hampshire

Wednesday, October 9
8:01 p.m.

A flashlight beam seared across her face.

Leigh blinked to force her vision to adjust, throwing up the hand still clutching her phone to block the onslaught. It didn't do a damn bit of good, but she wasn't dead yet. She at least had that going for her. But why was she still alive? "If you're trying to escape, you're doing a really shitty job. Starting with giving away the advantage with a flashlight."

A low laugh rumbled over the *tick tick tick* of water leaking through the foundation. Deep and warm and nothing like a killer should sound.

No answer.

A tremor wracked through her legs, and she clutched her weapon tighter. Was hypothermia possible at this temperature? She didn't know. Didn't want to know. But at this rate, this entire basement level would be under water within a couple hours. She had to get out of here. Preferably in one piece.

Still, he hadn't moved. Hadn't done a damn thing but stared at her. She couldn't make out his features—hidden behind the flashlight's beam—but she could feel him watching her. Waiting. But she wouldn't be the one to make the first move.

"You are one of the dumbest killers I've hunted." She redirected her weapon's aim. For the outline centered behind the flashlight. She might not be able to identify him, but his size provided an easy target. It was hard to gauge from their current surroundings, but Leigh had the distinct feeling she wouldn't be a match for his sheer strength in a physical altercation.

He extended the flashlight toward her in response. She could barely make out the hand holding it out.

He wanted her to... take it from him? This was a trick. At attempt to force her to give up her balance, to shove her off guard. Distract her. If she reached for that flashlight—and every cell in her body wanted it—he would take the opportunity to surprise her. She would be putting herself at a disadvantage.

Leigh sucked in a shivering breath. "Why don't you keep it? Give me a look at that pretty face."

Withdrawing his offer, he tossed the flashlight. Into a room she hadn't noticed until then. The beam twisted down into a watery grave.

Leigh couldn't let her curiosity take control. She had to keep her gaze on him. She wouldn't give him the upper hand. She'd made Ava a promise to be there. To make an effort. She couldn't break her promise mere hours later. "I'm not a dog who likes to play fetch."

He backed up a step in the muted light put out by the drowning flashlight. Then another. Why wasn't he saying anything?

Leigh squared her stance, ready to shoot, but he hadn't attacked her. Hadn't done anything to warrant a bullet to the chest. Still, her heart climbed her throat with his retreat. Instinct said this was the killer they were looking for—who'd killed Alice Dietz, who'd set his sights on Pierce Morrow's identity—and yet he'd left Leigh alive when given the chance.

No. This was something else. Like he was... giving her a choice. Follow him or follow her curiosity into that room to her left. Her mind raced to come up with the correct answer. He was almost out of reach now, barely more than a thin outline at this distance. Then gone.

"Leigh!" Her name echoed down the corridor a split second before two flashlights punctured through the darkness. They bounced in erratic rhythms as water parted from the ambush. Ford.

Leigh raised her hand to block the sear of light on her eyes, weapon still raised. "I'm here. I'm fine."

"What the hell are you doing down here?" The marshal stripped his windbreaker from his shoulders, transferring the flashlight from one hand to the other, then wrapped the thin fabric around her shoulders. He gripped her upper arms and stroked up and down as if trying to start a fire. "Shit. Your lips are blue. We need to get you upstairs."

It wasn't until then she realized she was shaking. Cold. Her joints had stiffened in her ankles and knees, and she lowered her weapon to her side, phone still clutched in her other hand. It would take someone else prying it from her fingers to get the waterlogged device free. Her teeth chattered. That was good. That meant her body was fighting back instead of giving up. "He was here."

She could barely make out the words, but Ford understood her. He did that uncanny thing where he went absolutely still despite his size. As though he could sink back into the shadows as easily as the killer had. "Who was here? Dean Groves? You saw him?"

Had it been Dean? It'd been hard to tell in the dark. Leigh

rolled her lips between her teeth and bit down to give her body something more worthwhile than survival to focus on. The windbreaker holding Ford's body heat was helping. She shook her head. At least, she thought she shook her head, but it could've been the tremors threatening to unravel her from the inside. "My phone died. I couldn't see anything, but he had a flashlight. He tossed it. In there."

The flashlight at Ford's back swung into the room, and Leigh was just able to make out what looked to be one of the campus police officers. She couldn't remember his name.

"We need to get you out of here." Ford closed the distance between them, locking his arms around her upper body. The movement was entirely too intimate, and yet exactly what her body needed. His heat, the sensory input, that unique flare of citrus and something darker and velvety—it all worked to keep her in the moment.

"He didn't want to hurt me. He wanted me to follow him." Leigh moved to secure her weapon but missed her holster. She tried again, until Ford clamped his oversized hand around hers. Taking her weapon. It disappeared behind his back. Most likely in the waistband of his slacks for safe keeping. Probably the right thing to do considering she could barely coordinate her brain's commands with her hands' actions. Shooting him by accident was sure to test the relationship between USMS and the FBI. Not to mention their partnership. "I think he wanted me to go in there. We don't have much time. The water is getting deeper."

Leigh could practically feel the nerves coming off Ford and the campus police officer as she put everything she had into taking that first step. The flashlight the killer had tossed into the room acted as a beacon, something for her to focus on while her body fought to give up. How long did it take hypothermia to set in anyway? She'd have to look that up when she got a chance.

The marshal slid his hand around her waist. Holding her up

or trying to stop her from going into that room? Both were valid reasons in her current condition. "Leigh, your body temperature is dropping by the minute. You need medical attention."

One of the flashlights hit the nearest wall. To the points where water leaked through the stone itself.

"Then, by all means, go back, but I'm staying." The last word came out more muddled than she'd meant. Stupid failing body. There had to be a reason the killer had focused on this room. Why he'd led her through the maze of the university's basement. It wasn't just to confuse or isolate her. There were easier ways to accomplish either or flat out kill her. Leigh grabbed for the killer's flashlight. The water was deeper here. Flooding this room faster. It must be the lowest point of the basement, collecting every drop breaking through from the surface.

"Get upstairs. Ask Durham PD if they have pumps to control the flooding. I'll stay with her." Ford's flashlight cut ahead of her and hit a row of shelves made of two-by-fours. The racks were empty apart from what looked to be an old pressure canner and... mason jars? "What the hell is this place?"

"Emergency storage." Leigh clutched on to Ford's borrowed windbreaker as a different kind of chill emanated from her very bones. Frigid water reached thigh deep here and siphoned her strength little by little as she surveyed the shelves. Cloudy green liquid inside those jars told her whatever was inside had gone bad a long time ago. "The school must've had some kind of emergency preparedness class. Used this room to store pressure-canned goods. See? There are lids and rings for the jars in this box. And a dozen canned peaches in the corner."

"Doesn't look like anyone's been down here for years." Ford branched away from her position, studying the rest of the room.

"Seems whoever used this space for emergencies literally forgot it existed in an emergency." She searched the rest of the shelves. More of the same. Broken mason jars, mold, and canned goods that had long expired past their due dates. She was hungry, but she wasn't that hungry.

"It's you," Ford said.

Leigh tried to shake her head, but the headache punching at the back of her skull made it all the more difficult. "I'm pretty sure I've never taken an emergency preparedness class."

"No, I mean. Look. It's you." Ford raised his flashlight farther up the opposite wall of the shelves, highlighting a cork board full of posted notices and notes.

She waded through the water nearing her hips. She'd been wrong before. The water was rising faster than she'd originally estimated. Time was working against them here and in her body. But none of that compared to the chill freezing her to the core as she stared at a photo... of her. Except it wasn't just one. At least a dozen. Cut out from printed newspaper articles, headlines highlighted and pinned to the board. Meticulously collected and displayed on a board at least three feet in width and three feet in height. Every inch dedicated to her.

"Some of these are from when my father was arrested for murder."

Over twenty years ago. The edges had yellowed over the years, but there was no mistaking their age. Newspapers hadn't accepted the digital age then. Everything concerning her father's case had been in print and delivered to her family's door each morning. To ensure she understood her family was no longer wanted.

"He's obviously kept these preserved." Ford scanned the rest of the makeshift shrine to her career. Her life. If he'd ever wanted a look inside her head, it was displayed right in front of him. "Why leave them here to be destroyed?"

"No one expected a hurricane to reach this far inland." Leigh focused on one newspaper clipping. She thought she'd seen every piece of coverage concerning her career. It was, after all, hard to miss, but she hadn't seen this one. It'd been printed from what looked to be a low-level news site. She tore it from its pin. "He must've been forced to abandon it. Give me your phone."

"What for?" Ford asked.

"Mine is dead, and I want a picture of these clippings in case the room floods and we lose more evidence." Leigh took his offering and got shots of the photos, including the one she'd torn from its post, and pocketed the clipping itself.

"Good point." The marshal moved into the rest of the room, taking his flashlight with him, but Leigh could only catalog the clippings in glimpses. "It feels like he's trying to get your attention. Coming to your alma mater, killing Alice Dietz with an old MO, targeting your mentor. Like he has something against you."

"I have that effect on people." This couldn't be it. A bunch of old newspapers weren't enough to understand the killer's motive or final endgame. There had to be more here. A reason he'd led her to this room. Leigh turned her focus to the rest of the space. The flashlight shook uncontrollably in her hand. To the point she nearly dropped it. But she held on long enough for the beam to land on the largest piece of furniture in this room, and her stomach knotted tight.

A tub. Complete with a bottle of bleach and a smaller bottle of blue dish soap. The same combination of chemicals used to wash the victim's body clean. A darker lump took shape at the other end, hidden near the drain. Drawn, Leigh fought the rising flood and crossed the room. A backpack? She hauled it out of the tub by the top handle, setting it on the edge, and ripped the top open. Brushed metal reflected the flashlight beam back at her. A laptop. The weight of the bag shifted as a textbook fell forward. She went for one of the smaller pockets and drove her hand inside. Pulling a phone with a clear plastic case from the depths. Alice's phone.

Leigh's breath caught as she scanned the room a second time. "I think Alice Dietz was killed in this room."

SEVENTEEN

Durham, New Hampshire

Thursday, October 10
6:34 a.m.

The water had gotten too deep.

She and Ford had attempted to grab everything they could carry out, but the scene was gone. The containers of bleach and dish soap, a compressed syringe, the newspaper clippings, Alice Dietz's backpack—it was all that was left. Whatever secrets had been preserved in that room were now lost. Everything else had gone straight to the forensic team for eventual processing with nothing more than their mobile kits used on the crime scene.

Another shiver wracked through her arms. Pain ricocheted down into her hands. The cold wouldn't relent. Two students had been nice enough to come together to supply her with a dry hooded sweatshirt and a pair of sweats once she'd emerged from the basement, but cuddling Ava hadn't done a damn bit of good to bring her core temperature up. She'd only gotten a couple hours of broken sleep on the floor, and it was taking a toll on her brainpower. "Who says I never let you have junk food for breakfast?"

Ava licked the remnants of melted chocolate from her fingers. "I'm pretty sure you're supposed to advocate for protein, greens, and fruit to promote my growing body."

Rain fell in sheets outside the double doors, though the winds had died down considerably. There was a chance Mother Nature had gotten tired of beating this small university town black and blue, but it would be hours before Durham PD reopened the roads. Hours which their killer would surely use to his advantage.

Leigh tried to hug her knees closer to contain what little body heat she had left. Really, she just didn't want to think about what could happen if they didn't catch this killer. "Please don't say those words to me again."

"What? Growing bodies?" A spark of amusement lit up Ava's coffee-brown eyes. She had the uncanny ability to find almost anyone's weakness and use it against them. Like a super-power. "What about intercourse—"

"Finish that sentence, and I'll handcuff you to me for the rest of the day." A chill that had nothing to do with the beginning symptoms of hypothermia and everything to do with not wanting to have this discussion in the middle of a lobby surrounded by students swept through her. "I'm sure your new friends would appreciate the entertainment."

Ava narrowed her eyes on Leigh in challenge. "You wouldn't dare."

"I have them right here." She pulled a set of cuffs from the back of her waistband. "What's the point of making threats if I can't back them up?"

Pure, unfiltered shock contorted the fifteen-year-old's expression before she shoved to stand and rejoin the friends she'd made. One of them being Tamra Hopkins, Alice Dietz's roommate. The redhead gave Leigh a half-smile as Ava slid into their ranks.

"Coward." She'd have to file that threat away for later. For now, she'd try to salvage any melted chocolate from Ava's candy bar wrapper. A pair of dress shoes and slacks penetrated her peripheral vision. Leigh froze. With her tongue slicked against the inside of the wrapper as if it'd been superglued.

"Please tell me you didn't get that out of the trashcan like a raccoon." Ford crouched beside her, somehow looking as handsome and clean as ever. He'd been in that water too. Maybe not for as long, but he didn't seem to be suffering a single symptom. That just wasn't fair.

Leigh forced herself to retract her tongue back in her mouth, even though she'd found a particularly good glob of caramel left at the bottom of the wrapper. "Would it change your opinion of me if I did?"

"Not in the slightest." A smile deepened the creases around his eyes, and she wasn't sure she'd ever seen something so... genuine. Ford dug into his windbreaker pocket. "Here. I got this for you."

Her heart hiccupped at the sight of a full-sized candy bar. She grabbed for it. "Where did you get this?"

"Would you believe me if I said I found a stash in one of the professor's desk drawers upstairs and did not fight a freshman for it?" he asked.

"No, but I appreciate it all the same." She tore into the wrapper and nearly devoured the entire offering in one bite, his gaze on her. "You weren't expecting me to share, were you?"

"Not anymore." Ford held up his hands in surrender.

She talked around chocolate and caramel and peanuts. "Sorry. Hypothermia made me hungry."

"Why do I have a feeling you'll be using that excuse for a while?" Ford's smile slipped. "How's Ava doing today?"

Leigh trained her eyes on her adopted daughter perfectly fitting into the group of the friends she'd made. Practical strangers. Ava had a way of doing that. Luring people in, getting them to care about her and look past her hardened veneer. Had it really only been last night they'd found themselves on the roof, desperate to bring Ava back inside? "Better, I think. There's a lot we still need to talk about, but I'm happy she's willing to try. The real problem is, I have no idea what I'm doing."

"I'm pretty sure every parent of a teenager has your same problem." There was that charisma, the way he could take any conversation and situation and extract her nerves from the formula.

"Yeah. But I didn't really get a chance to prepare." The candy bar lost its taste then. Too thick in her mouth. "Ava kind of fell into my lap, and now I feel like we're both sinking, but she's pushing my head under water to keep me from getting to shore."

Ford unpocketed another candy bar from the breast pocket of his suit jacket. Where was he producing them from? How many more could he possibly have? "That's... graphic. I've heard of babies being brought by a stork, but I didn't think there was any truth to that particular fairy tale."

"No." A lightness wrapped around her mind. Instant sugar high after being depleted of any real calories over the past twenty-four hours. "I adopted Ava two weeks ago. Her parents... They weren't able to take care of her anymore."

"Isn't that around the time you arrested your best friend for murder?" Ford settled his attention on Ava, the candy bar in his hand forgotten. His eyes widened slightly, and Leigh couldn't stop the surge of acid forcing its way up her throat. "She looks exactly like her mother."

"Nobody knows." A desperation she hadn't experienced in a long time entered her voice. He was a better investigator than he gave himself credit for, able to connect two random facts into one cohesive whole. She should've seen it before now. "I mean, nobody but her mother and the state and my family. She's too young to consent to media interviews or be followed by photographers."

Ford shifted his attention to Leigh. "You're worried she'll be subjected to the same treatment you were at her age."

"I was a couple years older, but yes," she said. "I don't want her to have to go through all that. She deserves to have the chance to make her own choices and mistakes."

"She wouldn't be alone. She'd have you." Ford remembered the candy bar in his hand and peeled the wrapper. There was no way he allowed himself to indulge in sweets as often as they had in the past twenty-four hours with that physique. But desperate times called for desperate measures. "Either way, her secret is safe with me. Honestly, I'm not even sure who I would tell. Even before I joined the marshals, I've never liked talking to people. I'd rather shoot them."

"We have that in common." Leigh found herself smiling again. It was easy to do with him around. "Thank you. For... everything."

"Can't let the FBI's number one serial offender investigator go hungry in the middle of a case, now, can I?" He took a bite of his candy bar. "I guess we're really not going to talk about earlier. I don't know about you, but I don't usually go around kissing attractive women while I'm on assignment. Let alone other investigators. I tend to have a lot more control."

Which meant he'd lost his prized control. Because of her. Heat charged into her neck and face, chasing back the permanent chill she'd taken up. That shouldn't make her as happy as it did. Investigators had to keep their heads in the game, but it'd been a long time since she'd allowed her wants to take the lead. And she definitely wanted Ford. "I don't go around kissing attractive men while I'm on a case, either, but here we are."

"Am I barking up the wrong tree, Agent Brody?" Ford asked.

Indecision seized her. Her initial instinct was to let him down easy. To move on as if nothing had happened between them, but the past few months had blown up in her face so cataclysmically none of her future plans remained intact. Leigh watched Ava throw her head back in laughter. Some joke Leigh was sure she wouldn't understand, and her heart double-timed. She'd dedicated her entire life to fighting for those who couldn't fight for themselves. Now felt like a good time to fight for herself. To become more than her job. "No. You're not barking up the wrong tree, Marshal Ford."

"Good." There was that smile again. A little shy and a whole lot crooked. Like Ford was uncomfortable with his own emotions. "Then maybe once we've got our unsub in custody, I could take you out sometime."

"We'd have to find him first." She returned his smile.

"Right. I was hoping Alice Dietz's devices we recovered from the basement could help us in that regard, but they're both dead, and we have no way of charging them as long as the power is out." Ford grabbed for his phone from another suit jacket pocket. The man was practically a Swiss Army knife in a much prettier package. "I've been thinking about what you said about the previous victims. That the killer targeted them for a specific need. I went back through the case files with your perspective in mind."

The sugar rush from eating nothing but a candy bar in the past twelve hours simmered enough to let her focus on Ford's screen. "The first victim was from Santa Ana. He worked remote, and if the killer was looking for a sense of freedom in his life as you suggested, this guy would've provided it. No spouse or children. According to his laptop's history, this guy worked from all over. From the beach, one hit led us to a cabin in the woods, another to a small internet cafe downtown. He was a scientific journalist. Read complicated science journals I can't even begin to summarize and rewrote them for easy public consumption for an array of outlets."

"Able to work and write from anywhere." Freedom, indeed. "All right. What about our next victim?"

"Here's where it gets complicated. Wanting to take over someone's identity for a sense of freedom, I understand." Ford swiped his finger across the screen, pulling up the next file. "But what the hell would he want with a competitive bungee jumper from Glendale, Arizona?"

Leigh took the phone, reading through the second victim's background. Good question. "Most jumpers are adrenaline junkies. Humans abhor boredom and create bucket lists a mile long to give their lives excitement. Our unsub may have been craving some spontaneity after living life as a science journalist."

"Okay. Victim number three, Garland, Texas." Ford moved on to the next victim, a professional headshot taking over the screen. "Guy was a police officer for over ten years."

Now that one was surprising. "Did he have a partner?"

"Yeah. Going on two years together," Ford said. "Saw each other nearly every day. Knew each other's families. Even had been in a couple shootouts together. They'd been tight, right up until the partner started noticing some changes in our vic. Things like a sudden change in rooting for Dallas Cowboys when the vic had been a lifelong Houston Texans fan and wearing contacts. After the vic's body was recovered, partner said he'd never needed corrective lenses in his life. That was one of the first things that tipped him off."

"Relatedness." It was what she experienced with her team, working with the BAU. For years, she'd always been on the outside looking in. Brought in to consult but never actually part of the team. What better way to connect with someone than by sharing that danger together? Living it. Relying on someone else to help you through the hard times. It was what was happening between her and Ford now. "A common goal."

"Last victim was from Boston. He was some kind of professional runner-slash-influencer. Ran a bunch of marathons for a living. I'm not sure how crazy you have to be to put yourself through that. Got sponsored by one of the big running brands a few years ago." Ford brought up a snapshot of the victim's social media. Lots of gear unboxing, photos of shoes, and coastal runs in progress with times. "Our unsub made the transition seem almost flawless on the guy's social media. Only problem is he doesn't show his face in any of the photos."

"The unsub wanted attention. Probably didn't get a whole lot in his life. So he targeted someone who did." Leigh caught sight of Professor Morrow, a little more worn around the edges than he had been last night during their interview. Wrinkles in his clothing, his jacket looking heavy on his dropping shoulders. "But none of these victims' deaths explain why our killer would want to assume the identity of a criminology professor with a failing career."

Ford handed off his phone with the photo of the newspaper clippings they'd recovered from the basement. "Unless it has something to do with you."

EIGHTEEN

Durham, New Hampshire

Sunday, September 10, 2006
9:24 a.m.

Teshia Elborne's killer was an artist.

Leigh couldn't describe these photos any other way. It was twisted—she was well aware—but there was something beautiful in the way the woman's killer had cleaned and taken care of the body then almost laid her out on the ground. An offering to some forgotten god.

No wonder Professor Morrow had approached her with the opportunity to contribute to his research. She was seriously messed up.

She flipped through the next set of crime photos, a cold chill coming down from the air-conditioning vent overhead in his book-packed office. The breeze ruffled the incident report and witness statements Durham PD had already collected and filed. Not a lot of detectives would've handed over confidential case files, but Professor Morrow had his contacts. And now she did too.

"What do you make of the case?" He'd been watching her from behind his desk, those beady eyes never wavering. "Anything jump out at you?"

It didn't make sense. Why he wanted her opinion. He was the expert. A god among men in the criminology world. She'd read all his published works. He'd recruited her from the psych program to study under him. She was nobody. A freshman with too much emotional baggage, trauma, and a thirteen-year-old brother secretly living in her dorm. Leigh moved on to the next photo, a close-up of the victim's face.

It was hard to deny Teshia Elborne had been beautiful, even at the center of a crime scene. Blonde hair, almost the same shade as Leigh's, spread around her in a halo highlighting chocolate eyes and full pink—well, now pale white—lips. Seductive and manipulative. With a wide smile that promised a ringing laugh and that Teshia knew her effect on people. Used it against them to get what she wanted. Leigh couldn't help but be drawn in. Heaven help those who'd come face to face with the victim before her death. Had Dean been one of them?

"I think the killer has done this before." While she had extensive knowledge of death investigations, this one felt... out of reach. Disconnected. She hadn't known the victim, but she couldn't pass up the opportunity to study the case either. Not if she wanted to apply to Concord's police academy next year. "Teshia wasn't his first."

"Oh?" Professor Morrow leaned forward in his seat. "What gives you that impression?"

Her mouth dried under his attention. One wrong word and he could take his offer back. Leigh slipped her index finger between the first two pages of the report. One name stood out among all the others in the witness list. Dean Groves. The last *person to see Teshia Elborne alive. She put that small detail aside for now.*

"According to the medical examiner, the killer washed and bleached the body before depositing her at the scene. He knew to clean under her fingernails and ensured not to leave any prints or fibers on her clothing. That kind of discipline is honed over a long period of time and with practice."

"Very good." Professor Morrow made a note on the legal pad. Was he really taking her suggestion or was this some kind of blind test? "Durham PD hasn't made that assessment. So we'll want to look into past histories of violence when suspects are inevitably identified. What else do you see? What of the victim? Why was she targeted?"

It took everything inside of her not to straighten under his praise. It would be easy to chase the high, but Leigh took another look at the case file in her lap. Upwards of seventy percent of murdered women were killed by someone they knew, half of them by a partner. Chances were Teshia Elborne's death hadn't been random. And with police looking to question Dean, she had to assume they'd been close. Possibly a couple.

"Witness statements tell us she was well-liked. Academic transcripts and records show she was involved in a number of social organizations over the years and did well in her classes. I think that got the killer's attention, but it wasn't the most important detail for him. She was... popular, held a lot of power. But not over her killer."

"Perhaps her killer was jealous of all that power. Wanted it for himself." Professor Morrow made another note, his pen nearly cutting through the thin yellow lined paper. "Or she tried to use her power on him and failed."

"No. I don't think this was a crime of passion. The mode of operation tells me the killer is calculated. He doesn't make a single move without considering all the options available. Based on his high level of intelligence and preparation, I would say he

viewed Teshia Elborne more as a tool than a person. He was more than likely using her for something specific." Leigh couldn't take her eyes off the witness statement that'd slid free from the stack. One provided by Dean Groves. The text blurred the harder she tried to make sense of his words. Relationship. Two years. Cheated. Confrontation. Her lungs shoved every molecule of air free from her chest. The man she'd started falling in love with wasn't just the last person to see the victim alive. He'd been betrayed by her. "And then he wasn't."

Durham, New Hampshire

Thursday, October 10
7:03 a.m.

A power line sparked and collapsed.

Students grouped tighter at the windows facing a distant Main Street, flinching as one at the impact. Low murmurs expressed disbelief and sorrow at the destruction tearing through town. The storm wasn't passing. If anything, conditions had somehow gotten worse over the last hour. Hail had reached golf-ball-sized proportions, and Leigh thanked foresight for getting the insurance on her rental car. There was no way she was driving out of here with a car that didn't resemble Swiss cheese.

Ford took up one side of the bench she'd occupied last night, her on the other, as they crowded into Professor Morrow's space. Cutting him off from escape. How the hell did he manage to look put together after swamping through the basement with her twelve hours ago when it took everything she had not to smell her own breath?

"All right, Professor. Let's talk. Setting aside your personal connection to Alice Dietz, we believe you are the killer's target. Have you noticed anything out of the usual recently?"

Morrow interlaced his hands between his knees. Exhaustion had puffed the bags under his eyes to monumental proportions. Leigh wasn't sure she'd ever seen him like this. So very... ordinary. He would hate that. To admit he was human like the rest of his puny subjects. "You mean other than the fact you hold information which could cost me my job at this university?"

"Marshal Ford is asking if there's been anyone new in your life? Maybe someone who's been asking personal questions or become interested in your work?" She hadn't meant that last one to sound so biting, but she didn't feel bad about it either. Pierce Morrow had gone out of his way to obstruct the investigation into Alice Dietz's murder. He'd broken a cardinal rule as a criminologist, one he'd instilled in her from the very beginning of their mentorship, and had cost himself her respect in a record amount of hours. "Or have you noticed anything missing or moved from your apartment or office?"

"No. Nothing like that." Weariness coated the professor's voice. He shook his head, but it didn't have the same effect as it used to with his eyes cast between his feet. The case was getting to him—all of them. Or was this sudden surrender something else? "I mean, except my driver's license."

Leigh snapped her gaze to Ford. "What about your driver's license?"

"It's missing. Has been since the night Alice and I... fought." Morrow rubbed at his face, aging in front of her eyes. Where he'd been a perfect picture of calm and collected yesterday morning in the president's office, the mask vanished. Leaving nothing but a shell of the man she'd known. "I thought I must've dropped it leaving campus. I didn't think anything of it until now. You think someone is trying to impersonate my identity?"

"While we can't share details of our investigation, we believe the killer has a personal connection to Agent Brody." She didn't miss the twitch of Ford's mouth. Concern? The marshal's eyes lifted to hers. No. Not concern. Defeat. As if the mere thought of her working this case cut him on a physical level. "And may be trying to use you to get to her."

Well, that certainly didn't sound insane.

Except they had an entire wall of newspaper clippings, dates, photos, and details about her career and life from the time she'd been seventeen years old. Forensics was still running an inventory, but the killer had done a thorough job. Even down to a mere mention of her name as a consultant for a past police department. Leigh stopped herself from shoving her hand into her blazer for the article she'd taken from the board. One neither Ford nor the techs would ever see. But the killer had. He'd left it where she would find it. Like he'd known she'd step into that room. Calling her out.

"Leigh and I haven't been in touch in years," Morrow said.

"But you said you followed my career. That you've read about every case, that you used your law enforcement and federal contacts to get copies of my case files." The hairs on the back of her neck stood on end as those nights in his office took shape. Memories and feelings she'd shoved to the back of her mind. She'd worshiped the ground her mentor had walked on for so long. Wanted nothing more than his approval. At least up until she'd learned his nasty little secret.

"I did." Morrow nodded, his eyebrows arching to deepen the age lines streaking across his forehead in uneven patterns. "You were one of my favorite students. I was proud of the work you'd done as a consultant and then for the FBI. Of course I followed your career."

Right. Because in his mind he'd made her. Thought that he deserved the credit for her success. It wasn't her merits and personal study of more than two hundred serial cases that shaped her into the investigator she was today. It was him. "Or were you looking to gain my insights again by showing interest in my work?"

Blood drained from the professor's face as he shoved to stand. Escape. That was what the guilty did. They tried to escape. "I don't know what you're talking—"

"That's why you reached out so many times over the years, right?" Law enforcement had stopped requesting his contributions. Just as journals had stopped publishing his research. The problem was, it'd all been done before. It'd all been said. Pierce Morrow was stuck in the past and refused to adapt to or embrace changing policies and technologies. He preferred to live in an outdated and underserving landscape that had no use for him. And it was only now hitting him how useless he'd become to the field. "Why you'd send me case files you'd been asked to consult on. Just like the Elborne case." Leigh kept her seat and her voice rose. It was enough to draw him back in. To try to contain her accusations. "Don't you remember? Asking me to come to your office and get my take on the case. Why the victim had been targeted. Helping you to understand the killer's motive. Of course, at the time, I wanted to impress you. I trusted you. I'd known Durham PD asked you to look at the case. What I didn't know was that you'd take credit for my insights. I also didn't know you'd had a personal relationship with Teshia Elborne, just as you did with Alice Dietz."

Ford craned his head up toward Morrow, all emotion void from his expression. It looked as though the marshal was doing everything in his power to remain seated, hands tense in fists. And that absolute stillness. She saw it for what it was now. An attempt at control. "Is that so?"

"The insights you made, while noteworthy, Agent Brody, were child's play compared to those I've made over my career. I have been integral in helping police solve upwards of fifty homicides over the course of my career. Not to mention been published in a dozen criminology and abnormal psychology journals." Morrow was practically shaking now. Exposed for the fraud he'd become and not even a little bit comfortable with it.

He must've seen the end in sight. And now... Now he was trying to save himself by any means possible. "I never needed a college freshman's insights. I saw something in you. Something great, and I fed it. I turned you into the agent you are today. You needed me."

"No. You used me. And you used Teshia Elborne and Alice Dietz." Leigh straightened, a full head shorter than the professor but more than capable of putting him on his ass if necessary. What would've happened had she agreed to stay to assist with his research instead of joining the Concord police academy? Would she be dead now, too?

"What do you think, Ford?" She couldn't deny the connection to both victims, then and now.

"I think the killer we're hunting becomes his victims." Ford rose from the bench, closing in on the professor. "Who better to steal someone else's identity than a professor who's lost his own?"

NINETEEN

Durham, New Hampshire

Thursday, October 10
8:41 a.m.

Pierce Morrow was under arrest.

Well, confined to one of the classrooms on the main floor by force. Turned out, those handcuffs did come in handy. Leigh could still hear her former mentor yelling as she and Ford made their way back toward the lobby. Students and staff alike tried to keep their stares brief, but there was no hiding the shock. Or the confusion plastered on Ava's face. One of this university's professors may have been involved in the deaths of two students. Officially, they couldn't charge Morrow with anything until the storm retreated and they got him to the station, but cuffing the man who'd used her profiling insights without giving her credit to solve those fifty-plus cases he'd bragged about sure put an extra pep in her step.

"Anything from the forensic techs?" She'd been so focused on not dying from hypothermia, she'd almost forgotten the evidence they'd pulled from the basement. Priority number one: avoid any and all reflective surfaces. She didn't want to think about what she looked like right then in mismatched sweats, frizzed-out hair, black semicircles under eyes, and with a permanent blue tint to her skin. Probably less FBI agent, more carnival psycho. It was a promising career change.

"Not yet." Ford angled around the nearest grouping of students. In vain. They parted as effectively as the Red Sea as he approached. "Seems the killer made sure not to leave his prints behind on the bleach and dish soap containers. Without a way to access Alice Dietz's devices, we have no way of knowing if he tried to erase evidence of contacting her, but they're still trying to pull DNA off her belongings. My guess, he was wearing gloves when he killed her, but we didn't recover any from the room, which means he most likely took them with him to dispose at a separate location."

It would've been the smart move. Couldn't have all the evidence in one location. That would make it too easy.

Ford motioned her ahead of him as they crossed the main floor back toward what was now their favorite spot by the lobby doors. The perfect perspective to keep an eye on civilians and the storm alike. "There's a chance he wasn't so careful with the newspaper clippings. If we can get even a single print, we'll have what we need to bring charges."

Except the man who'd led her to the kill room hadn't been Morrow. She would've recognized him, right? Though the more she tried to recall details of those tense minutes face to face with a potential killer, the hazier her memory became. Her brain took the opportunity to let her know Pierce Morrow wouldn't have been caught dead in a flooded basement, and his clothing hadn't shown any signs of distress. Unlike hers, which had practically fallen apart by the time she'd changed. But who else would've known the location of where Alice Dietz had been killed if not the man who'd killed her? A partner? Morrow didn't like those either. "Have the techs been able to get anything else from the room?"

The marshal took position at her side, keeping an eye on the rest of the main level. "Water's too deep, but there were no signs of blood."

"There wouldn't be." A different kind of energy shifted within the huddled masses. Leigh could feel it as she watched them, the glances in her direction, the questions on their faces. Up until now, it would've been easy to pretend this investigation hadn't hit close to home. But the students and staff couldn't ignore it now. At least not with Morrow still shouting his innocence from down the hall. Did the man have to be so dramatic? "Teshia Elborne's killer was careful, almost gentlemanly about the way she was handled. The body had been washed and cleaned before he'd left her in the court-yard, but the medical examiner never found lacerations or bruising. Not even tape residue around her mouth, wrists, or ankles. The ME believed the killer used padded handcuffs, but there weren't any recovered with the remains or on campus."

"You accused the professor of taking credit for your insights on the Elborne case. I assume that means he was consulting and gave you a peek at the investigation file." Ford turned that dark gaze on her. More intense than she expected. That same energy coursing through the crowd had finally reached him. Restless-ness. Confusion. Anger. This case was getting to him. More so now than before, and something inside her wanted to soothe that itch he suffered from. "We could use those insights now. What's standing out to you?"

Apart from the fact that she'd been sleeping with a murderer? "Teshia Elborne's killer cared about her. Maybe even loved her. I would go as far as to say she knew him. Trusted him enough to let him get close. But the way he left her exposed to the elements also testified to his anger. He cared about her, but he wanted to see her punished. As much as I hate to say it, Morrow isn't in it for love. He uses people. And Dean..."

"Teshia cheated on him." It wasn't a question. Ford had already written Groves as their villain. And Leigh couldn't deny the similarities between this case and the Elborne investigation. Couldn't deny she'd seen Dean Groves in this very lobby twenty-four hours ago either.

His involvement was the most likely explanation. But there were still too many missing pieces to the puzzle. She couldn't pick out the pattern. Why come back after all these years? Why risk exposing himself now for a murder he'd already gotten away with?

"It was a good theory at the time." But was it the right theory? Their only connection between the past and the present was Pierce Morrow, and he'd made his feelings more than clear about helping her since she put him in cuffs.

A male student broke away from the pack. "Hey, agent lady, when are we getting out of here? You can't keep us here forever."

More students joined in agreement, and, in an instant, she and Ford were facing a wall of unrest. Shouts hiked her blood pressure higher as she scanned the crowd for that one familiar face. Ava. Where was Ava? Leigh caught sight of her adopted daughter's gaze toward the back, her chest squeezing with the anxiety written there. "The shelter in place order hasn't been lifted. We need to stay indoors until the police tell us otherwise. Besides, it's hailing golf balls out there. Where are you going to go?"

"We have a right to leave!"

"What are we supposed to eat?"

"Yeah. Let us go home!"

Administration and staff tried to raise their voices over the throng of panicking students, but they were greatly outnumbered. There was no getting through. No logic involved. The lobby doors shuddered as though the storm had picked up on the collective emotions of its prisoners.

"Stay alert. I'm not sure this is going to end well," she said to Ford. Leigh could feel the electricity coming off the students in waves. "For them, I mean. We'll be fine. We've got tasers."

Ford looked her up and down. "You have a taser in that getup?"

"Don't you?" She suddenly didn't feel so self-conscious in the sweats she'd borrowed with him looking at her like he wanted to search her for weapons himself.

He patted the back of his suit jacket. "Must've lost it chasing you down into the basement."

"That's unfortunate, because I really don't want to use my tactical baton. We have one taser between the two of us." Leigh eyed the two campus police officers shifting their weight between their feet at the outer edges of the crowd. One wrong move and this could turn deadly if they weren't careful. "And nearly forty students who want out of this building."

"Please, everyone needs to remain calm. We will get through this together." The president's voice of reason failed, his power stripped from him when he needed it the most. Hurricanes didn't care about authority, and neither did these kids right now.

The first student raced straight past Leigh. She caught him by his coat collar before he hit the doors. The shelter in place order was for everyone's safety. There was no way she would let him put the rest of these people at risk. "Come on. You don't want to do this. It's not safe."

She shoved him back a few feet.

Her warning had little effect. She braced her legs as much as possible as his head collided with her belly in an attempted tackle. If she still had a uterus, he might've taken her down. Training and instinct had her thrusting her hips forward. Leigh used his own momentum to shove his face into the floor, landing on his back. Knee positioned into his spine, she grabbed for both of the student's wrists and pinned them to his frame.

It was over within seconds.

Blowing her hair out of her face, she wished Morrow wasn't currently occupying her only set of cuffs. A pair penetrated the edges of her vision, and she looked up to find Ford staring down at her in approval. She grabbed for his cuffs and ratcheted them around the student's wrists. The two campus police officers moved forward to take custody. They'd put him in the same room as Morrow. Maybe then the professor would stop trying to get attention. "Thank you."

Leigh shoved to stand and faced the now silent crowd staring wide-eyed and a little nervously at her. "Right. Anyone else want to put the lives of all your fellow students and teachers in danger by opening those doors?" She waited a beat. The doors weren't shuddering anymore, but she could still feel every thrust of wind like a pulse at her back. "No? Great. Nobody else do that. I'm running out of handcuffs."

Pinpricks in her hands told her the adrenaline would take a while to drain from her system, and she forced herself to breathe through the encroaching nausea. She turned toward Ford. "You wouldn't happen to have saltines or some other kind of cracker in that magic suit jacket, would you? Oh, how about more candy?"

"I'm not sure I'd consider it magic." The marshal drove his hands into another pocket and pulled free a stick of silver-wrapped gum. "But it does its job, and I think if you eat any more candy, you're going to end up in a hyperglycemic coma."

She took the stick, instantly drawn by the heavy scent of mint as she unwrapped it and folded it into her mouth. The effect was instant. Calming. Just like him. Her heart rate would take a couple more minutes to settle, but her stomach seemed happy for the time being. "Lifesaver."

"Funny, I was about to say the same thing about you." That

crooked smile was back, like he was trying to keep it to himself and failing. It fit his personality with a little bit of bad boy flair. Every schoolgirl's fantasy and every father's nightmare. She could imagine a younger version of him. All charm and no rules to hold him back. The kind of guy who wouldn't lift a finger if told what to do. Interesting that he'd chosen the US Marshals Service. Then again, Ford mostly worked alone from what she'd observed. No partner. Free to chase fugitives across the country. His own boss, in a way. "That was impressive."

"You can't blame them for being scared." Leigh buried the urge to swipe invisible dust off her sweats. What was the point? "But I don't think we'll have any more trouble. Now that they've seen what will happen if they turn on us, I doubt they'll want to end up in the same room as Morrow. He's not the best company right now."

"You didn't answer me before," Ford said. "Go out with me."

"You're persistent, I'll give you that. Probably makes you perfect for this job." A flush that had nothing to do with adrenaline heated her skin. She was stalling, and they both knew it.

"I know you're committed to your career, and we both travel for work. I know you're trying to figure out how to be a mom, and this is a terrible idea." Ford cocked his head slightly. As though she was something worth studying. "But I've got to be honest, I've never met anyone like you. And I want to know more. Just one date."

"Weren't you paying attention? My entire life story is in the hands of the forensic techs down the hall right now. All you have to do is read it." Nerves coated her hands in a thin layer of sweat. She had no reason to decline. She was single. He was single. They had the same interests... in that they enjoyed chasing killers. She could do this. She could move on. Start a new chapter. When else would she get the shot? "All right. One date. After the case is finished."

"It's a deal." Ford nodded.

Ava shoved through the horde of students.

Nerves contorted into full-blown concern as Leigh closed the distance between them, Ford pressing in at her back. Her senses scanned the room for the next threat. "What's wrong?"

"It's Tamra. I can't find her anywhere." Out of breath, Ava dug her nails into Leigh's arm. "She's gone."

TWENTY

Thursday, October 10
9:02 a.m.

Tamra Hopkins wasn't missing.

She was dead.

Leigh jerked Ava away as the body came into sight. Left right there in the middle of the second-floor corridor of lower administration offices. A scream-like gasp escaped the fifteen-year-old's throat as reality crashed down around them. She twisted around to push Ava toward the stairs, but the damage had already been done. "Don't look. Don't look."

They couldn't disturb the crime scene.

But Ava wasn't in her right mind. None of them were. A sick color of green infiltrated Ava's face a split second before she slapped her hand over her mouth. "I'm going to be sick."

Leigh grabbed for the nearest garbage can and passed it to her, holding Ava's hair back as she emptied all those coveted calories into the bin. "It's okay. I've got you."

Ford's frame maneuvered past them. He closed in on the body and gently tested the victim's neck for a pulse. Raising his gaze to Leigh, he shook his head. Dead. He shoved to stand, his gaze searching around the scene intently.

The two campus police officers she'd noted downstairs rushed up the stairs. Then slowed in horror.

She could read their thoughts as clearly as if they'd spoken aloud. How had this happened right under their noses? How long had it been since they'd seen Tamra downstairs? An hour? Less? Leigh couldn't help but run through every interaction, every change in the young woman's expression, every word out of her mouth over the past twenty-four hours.

"I don't understand. I just saw her." Ava tried to breathe through the next round of heaving, but it would take a few minutes to work through the shock. "Who would want to hurt Tamra?"

"I'm sorry. You shouldn't have seen her like this." Leigh tried to rub small circles into Ava's back, wishing it would do a damn bit of good for her own furious rush of loss. She hadn't known Tamra Hopkins more than a day, but the young woman on the floor hadn't deserved this. Any of this. She couldn't stop that internal pull to check out the body. This didn't feel like the meticulous premeditation the unsub had utilized in disposing of Alice Dietz's remains. This was impulsive. A survival tactic. A mistake. "I'm going to take you back downstairs. Okay? We'll get you some water, and you can rest until I'm done here."

Man, she was really failing at this whole work–mom balance. Who the hell brought their child to a crime scene? Ava continued to clutch the garbage can—better to be safe than sorry—and Leigh set her hand at her daughter's low back.

"No!" Ava twisted out of Leigh's reach. "You can't just put me somewhere out of sight and forget about me again. You said you would try harder. So try harder, Leigh."

The girl certainly knew how to twist the knife poisoned

with guilt for the kill. Leigh shifted her hands to Ava's arms, squeezing all the love she could into that hold. It wasn't enough. She had the feeling it would never be enough, but neither of them was exactly in a position for more at the moment. She couldn't do this right now. They had to act fast while the evidence was still preserved.

"Ava, a girl is dead, and I'm responsible for finding out what happened to her and making sure no one else gets hurt. This is what I do, and I can't do that job if I'm splitting my attention between you and trying to stop the man who hurt her."

"You're not even going to try, are you? Everything you said before, it was all a lie. You're always going to put your job ahead of me." The vitriol—unlike anything Leigh had witnessed—leaving Ava's mouth invaded and pooled at the base of her spine. "I'm never going to be enough for you."

Ava didn't wait for an answer, ripping free of Leigh's hold and heading for the stairs. In seconds, the fifteen-year-old was gone. Taking what little of Leigh's heart was left with her.

"You all right?" Ford had managed to sneak up on her.

She didn't understand how that was possible considering his size and intensity, but that wasn't important right now. Her nose burned as she stared after Ava. Where had she gone wrong? Why couldn't she figure this out? She wouldn't cry at the utter failure tearing through her. Not here, and sure as hell not now. "I don't have a choice. We have a body."

Leigh closed in on the remains.

"I think it's safe to say Pierce Morrow isn't our killer," he said. "He's been cuffed downstairs for the past hour, but Tamra Hopkins doesn't exactly fit our victimology."

"She knew of Alice Dietz's and Morrow's affair. Told me she'd accidentally read Alice's messages when she'd mistaken her roommate's phone for hers." Crouching a few inches away from the body, she took in everything. The arrangement of Tamra's limbs. Not handled with care but as though she'd been dropped. No blood or blunt force trauma from what she could see without turning the body over. Lack of bruising around the wrists and neck. There weren't any signs of a struggle, but healthy sophomores didn't just drop dead. "We need to talk to her friends. Find out how long she's been gone and what she might've been doing up here."

"Can you two handle that?" Ford asked the campus police officers obviously at a loss—in shock—a few feet away. University campus police handled the same types of crimes as every other law enforcement agency. Assaults, rape, theft, robbery, car accidents. But here in pristine Durham, New Hampshire, death had made its violent entrance twice in the past two days.

Neither seemed overly committed to the task, but Leigh had to trust they'd follow through. Every detail mattered. She searched her borrowed sweats for a set of latex gloves. Right, those were in her other pants.

Ford offered a bright blue pair from above. Knowing exactly what she needed. How did he do that? First with the cuffs he'd let her borrow downstairs, then now with the gloves. Just as he'd known not to push her for a date after that kiss and to give her space where Ava was concerned. If she didn't know any better, she would think he could read her mind. Or maybe she really was that transparent.

She snapped the gloves into place. Protocol dictated no one was to touch or search a body until the medical examiner or coroner had a chance to assess it, but the ME wouldn't be able to get here until the storm was done tearing Durham apart piece by piece. And Leigh needed answers. She pried Tamra's right eye open with her index finger and thumb, careful not to jar the body.

Ford's body heat pressed her right shoulder. "What are you looking for?"

"Teshia Elborne was poisoned with arsenic and cyanide eighteen years ago, but no matter how many times the ME searched for a puncture wound, she couldn't find it." Nothing in this eye. Leigh moved on to the left. "It wasn't until I was reviewing the investigation files with Morrow a few days later and Durham PD had determined Dean Groves had killed her that I noticed something off about one of the victim's eyes. It was irritated more than the other."

There. Up under the left eyelid. Out of sight unless you knew right where to look. She leaned back to give Ford room. "See? Same irritation in her left eye."

"Well, I'll be damned." He was right above her. Close enough her breath skimmed his jawline. "The son of a bitch injected the poison into his victims' eyes?"

"The ME will most likely find the same irritation in Alice Dietz's eye once he's able to complete the autopsy." Leigh withdrew her hand, looking over the body. She'd seen too many in her life. Starting when she'd been seventeen years old. Only a couple years older than Ava was now. She hadn't stomached it well then either. The guilt was back, trying to get her to choose between her old life and the new. But was there a right answer? She wasn't sure.

Tamra Hopkins looked as though she'd simply been picked up and dropped in the middle of this floor. No blood or skin beneath her polished fingernails. Almost... ambushed.

"There are no signs of a struggle on her arms. No bruising or blood that says she fought back. The killer would've had to have separated her from the herd downstairs. Which meant she trusted whoever wanted to get her alone. She came up here willingly." Leigh wasn't sure who she was talking to. Herself or Ford.

"One of the other professors?" Ford asked. "Or a student?"

"They're not the only ones in the building." She looked up at him.

Surprise arced into the marshal's face, and he drew back. Going still all over again. It was one of his patterns. A coping mechanism to handle the overwhelming emotions he either wasn't comfortable with or didn't want her to see. "You think one of the campus police officers had something to do with this?"

She tried to superimpose the two officers' frames over the one she'd faced in the basement. One fit more than the other. A little leaner, more muscular. Someone who took his job seriously and stayed in shape, but the height didn't match. Neither of the campus police officers was as tall as the man from the basement maze.

She'd made the mistake before of overlooking the fact law enforcement officers were themselves in the perfect position to commit murder, and she'd nearly paid for her oversight with her life. Detailed knowledge of crime scenes and forensics, automatic authority, familiarity with the campus. Maybe even the tunnels below it. It all gave their unsub the advantage in this sick game. Campus police would certainly have access to a key-coded biomedical lab where they'd sourced the arsenic and cyanide used to kill all three victims. Not to mention control of the security surveillance systems.

Leigh tried to memorize every line, every curve of the victim in front of her. They wouldn't be able to move the body until the medical examiner got here. And who knew when the storm would clear? For now, they could only preserve the scene.

But something was wrong with this picture.

She shoved to stand, unstable. It was a wonder she was still upright after only a few hours of sleep, suffering hypothermia symptoms, running off two candy bars, and riding the emotional upheaval of raising a teenaged terrorist. But she didn't really have a choice. "If someone was coming at you with a syringe—no matter what you believed was in it—would you hold still to let them stick it in your eye?"

"I think I would do whatever it took to make sure I didn't get stabbed." Ford slipped his hands into his slacks pocket, focused on the body. "But I'm one of those graced with a phobia of needles."

"So why didn't she fight back?" And why hadn't she put it together until now? Teshia Elborne. Alice Dietz. It'd been right in front of her for eighteen years. Leigh pointed to the body. "Why didn't Alice Dietz fight back? Even Teshia Elborne's body didn't show any signs of a struggle. Their clothes were intact. There was no indication of pulled hair, DNA in their mouths from a defensive bite, or vaginal trauma. It's like they—"

"Were unconscious when he poisoned them." A brightness she hadn't witnessed before lit up Ford's dark eyes. It was the same feeling she experienced when a case took a turn and the pattern became more clear. Addictive and satisfying. As though her whole life had led to that exact moment. Ford turned his attention back to the victim at their feet. "He never even gave them a chance."

"There are two ways to knock someone unconscious. Either you hit them, which leaves contusions, bruising, and blood. Or you knock them out with a quick-acting compound that can't be detected during an autopsy."

"There's only one chemical I can think of that knocks out its victims without leaving a trace," he said. "Chloroform."

"The medical examiner agreed. Except the use of chloroform was never indicated in Teshia Elborne's autopsy report, which confirms whoever killed her eighteen years ago," Leigh said, "is killing these women now."

TWENTY-ONE

Durham, New Hampshire

Thursday, October 10
10:11 a.m.

"You don't want to believe it's him, do you?" Ford was giving her that look again, the one that convinced her he could see directly into her thoughts. Or maybe she was seeing what she wanted to. Wanting someone else to feel this burden of help-lessness. Share it. Take some of it from her. "You don't want to believe Dean Groves had anything to do with this. Alice Dietz. Tamra Hopkins. The four men who died in the past year. You still think he's innocent."

"We don't have enough evidence to make a determination." Part of her wanted it to be Dean. The other wasn't so sure. Either way, no amount of time could hide her hesitation as she fidgeted with a highlighter she'd found in one of the open desks on this floor. They'd managed to find a blanket tucked into one of the desk drawers, using it to cover Tamra Hopkins's body. Now it was a matter of waiting. Making sure no other unsus-

pecting students stumbled onto the scene. Securing this floor
until the medical examiner and forensics teams could do their
jobs.

She hated waiting. What she really wanted to do was find
Ava, and she knew that the longer she let her hesitation rule, the
larger the chasm between them grew. But she didn't know how
to go back. To fix... whatever this was between them. There was
something Ava wasn't telling her. A reason that no matter how
hard Leigh pushed or how often she made an effort, Ava
wouldn't accept, and that something was festering between
them a little more each day. Ava couldn't seem to let Leigh in.
She didn't want to let anyone in, and whatever she was hiding
had started eating her alive.

"I've made assumptions during an investigation before.
People like us get it into our heads that the crime worked out
one way, and then all we're looking for is evidence to support
it." She leaned back in her chair, more than willing to go back to
pretending the past hadn't come full circle. Interlacing her
fingers over her stomach, she kept herself in the moment. Away
from that part of her life where the entire world had turned
against her and her family. She didn't want to go back there.
Because there was nothing she could do to change it. But she
could do something now. She could keep fighting for the truth.
No matter how hard it was to hear. "It's led to more than one
innocent person behind bars."

"Confirmation bias." Ford folded his arms across his chest.
He didn't have to be here. It didn't take more than one of them
to secure the scene, but he'd chosen to stay with her. It was...
nice to have someone to talk to. Made her feel as though she
wasn't entirely alone in this mess. "Is that why you alibied him
for the night of Teshia Elborne's murder despite the evidence
showing otherwise? You didn't want to believe Dean was
capable of something like that?"

"There was no physical evidence showing Dean Groves

killed Teshia Elborne." That was the problem. They didn't have anything. It'd been washed away with bleach and dish soap. "Everything Durham PD had was circumstantial. The source of the poison, Dean's connection to the victim, the statement about the argument they'd had. There was no blood or DNA on the body. They couldn't even find the murder weapon."

It'd had the potential to make a very compelling story.

His sardonic laugh cut her deeper than she expected. "And if the president comes back with a list of key codes used to access the biomedical lab and Groves's old code shows up, would you believe he killed these women then?"

The mere thought of it dried her mouth. She didn't know the answer to that question, but her beliefs didn't matter in the end. She had a job to do, and she was very good at compartmentalizing to get it done. No matter the consequences.

"Then I'll re-evaluate." That was all she could do unless the unsub decided to expose himself. A signed confession, a "Hey, it's me. I'm the problem." Even leaving something—anything— for them to identify him would be great right about now. But experience said most serial offenders would rather die than give up an ounce of self-preservation. "If Dean's old code doesn't show up on that list, are you willing to look for evidence that someone else is responsible for these deaths?"

"I'd be willing to... re-evaluate." Ford threw her a gut-wrenching smile, and the uneasiness of the past few minutes released the vise around her chest. "That's all we can do, right?"

"Right." But he had a point. It was getting harder and harder for her to separate her past from this current investigation. There were too many similarities, dead ends, and obstacles. At this point, the BAU was solely being utilized to solve all the secrets she'd buried in her life. First, her brother's murder then Elyse's disappearance. Now police were forced to focus on her romantic entanglements. There wasn't a single area of her life that hadn't been touched by murder, lies, and loss. No wonder Ava didn't want any part of it.

Leigh stretched her legs out in front of her, crossing at the ankles. No matter where she turned, death followed. It was already closing in too fast on her and Ava. And yet she'd agreed to a date with a US marshal she'd met yesterday morning. Sooner or later, Ford would become a victim. Whether by her job or her inability to let anyone get inside her head, he would suffer. Because of her. Maybe it would be better if she was honest up front, if she let a couple skeletons slip free from the closet to put his fascination in perspective. And if those skeletons got under his skin—pun intended—he could get a running head start from the disaster that was her life.

"You weren't far off base, though. About Dean Groves."

Ford looked at her as though she was suffocating, and he didn't know what to do about it. Setting those dark eyes on her, he studied her as if to memorize every detail, every hair, every change in her body language and expression. Looking for a crack in her armor. "What do you mean?"

"Dean and I met my freshman year at college. The first day I moved into my dorms, actually. He was the RA, and he offered to help me move my stuff in." Leigh couldn't look at him. Couldn't face the disappointment sure to hit her upside the head with judgment and disgust. "After that, he asked me out. I said yes, and we started dating. He was..."

Was she really going to talk about losing her virginity to a suspected killer? No. No, she was not. "In a matter of weeks, I fell head over heels in love with him. I thought he was, you know, the *one*."

Ford didn't answer. Didn't even seem to breathe.

She could slice through the tension between them with her father's old pocketknife. Four seconds. Five. Leigh tapped her fingernails on the chair's arm, her heart rate climbing the longer he refused to react. "I'm going to need you to say something now."

The marshal cleared his throat as he leaned forward, eyes on the floor. "So when you alibied him for the night of Teshia Elborne's murder..."

"I wasn't actually with him." She whispered her confession. She'd lied in the statement she'd given to police eighteen years ago. It hadn't been the first time, but it was certainly the lie she regretted the most. Would Alice Dietz and Tamra Hopkins still be alive if she'd been honest? That was the thought haunting her now, only a few feet from Tamra's body. Could this all have been avoided if she'd accepted that she'd been dumb and in love? That she'd been wrong? "Dean was spending a lot more hours than normal in the lab that week. He'd been working on an early Capstone project, and he was close to wrapping up his experimental study, but I don't know where he was that night. I just knew I couldn't lose him, too."

Not like she'd lost her father. Never again would she let someone be taken from her due to the whims of power-hungry predators. Even those with official titles.

"Leigh." Ford scrubbed at his face. "You lied on an official police report. If the FBI discovers you obstructed a murder investigation—"

"I know. And if you feel the need to be the one to tell them the truth, I wouldn't blame you." She would lose her job. She would face criminal charges. Every case she'd ever worked would be torn apart and assessed. Air lodged at the top of her chest. She hoped he didn't run straight to Director Livingstone with her admission, but she wouldn't ask him to keep her secret. Secrets killed, and he deserved better than that. "I wouldn't blame you for canceling our date either. Not that those are comparable. But it's not every day a woman you've asked out admits to committing perjury."

"Is it technically perjury if it happened outside of the courtroom?" He'd shut down his expression. Locked her out with that stillness that said he was feeling too much and didn't know what to do with it.

"That's a good question." The words left her mouth as nothing more than a whisper. Because she knew he didn't really care about the technicalities of perjury. He cared that she'd lied. What self-respecting law enforcement officer wouldn't? "What happens now?"

Ford cut his gaze to the body mere feet away, him on one side of the divide, her on the other. It'd been a body that'd brought them together. Another one might thrust them apart. And then who would she have?

"You said whoever is killing these victims is disciplined and focused. He does everything for a reason. He stalked his victims, learned everything he could about them. Right up until he killed Alice Dietz. She's the outlier, but now she doesn't seem to be the only one. What purpose did Tamra Hopkins's murder serve?"

So they were going to gloss over the fact she'd had a personal relationship with one of their suspects? All right. The tendril of defensiveness unwound from around her ribcage. "She must've seen something she shouldn't have."

"What makes you say that?" Ford asked.

Leigh wasn't entirely sure. "As much as Tamra theorized about Alice Dietz having a secret relationship, I don't think that's why she was poisoned. She'd read a couple messages from Alice's phone, but she couldn't recall the number they'd come from and didn't know who Alice had been involved with. I think our killer has made his first mistake."

Ford's eyebrows nearly hit his hairline. "How so?"

"It won't be possible to confirm until the medical examiner can get us a narrower time of death, but based on the amount of heat still in the body, I'm fairly certain Tamra Hopkins was killed after we had Morrow cuffed to the desk downstairs. But he did have the means, the motive, and the opportunity to murder Alice Dietz if she'd planned on taking their relationship public."

The marshal's gaze floated off to Leigh's left. Not really focused on anything in particular. "What could she have seen to gain the killer's attention?"

"I don't know yet, but the way she was left—without wiping down her body with bleach or arranging her as Teshia Elborne and Alice Dietz had been found—tells me killing her wasn't planned," she said. "It was a reaction."

"Well, that... doesn't make me feel good." Ford practically melted into his chair, legs splayed wide and away from his body. The posture didn't look natural. A forced calmness and ease that didn't match his personality. "So now what?"

He was trusting her to do the right thing. To get this investigation back on course. Willing to move past her admission and forge ahead toward the truth.

"If our unsub has a law enforcement background, everything we've recovered in evidence has been compromised. The bottles of cleaner, the containers of arsenic and cyanide, the driver's licenses we recovered—we can't rely on them to build our case. The primary crime scene is gone. Any evidence he left behind has been destroyed by the storm, and the medical examiner can't get to Alice Dietz's autopsy until the electricity comes back on." Leigh pulled in a deep breath, waiting for the marshal to come to their next step on his own. "But there's still one key piece of evidence the killer didn't expect us to find."

Ford narrowed his gaze on her. He lost the casual posture, pushing back in his chair. "You have to be joking."

"It's the only way." A shiver tremored through her, and Leigh's body temperature dropped in preparation. "We have to go back to that basement."

TWENTY-TWO

Durham, New Hampshire

Thursday, October 10
11:36 a.m.

She couldn't force herself to take the next step forward.

Leigh stared at the foot-deep pond pooled at the bottom of the steps leading into the basement. There was no telling how deep the water had swelled in the past twelve hours. Certainly enough to make her hesitate.

She'd changed back into her slacks and blouse. No point in ruining the perfectly dry sweatpants and hoodie she'd borrowed.

"You don't have to do this." Ford took position over her shoulder. The lobby was silent as students and staff lapsed into a seemingly temporary acceptance of their circumstances, intensifying his voice to the point she felt it in her bones. "According to the officers the chief sent over, Durham PD is clearing the flooding from City Hall. They can be here in the next couple of days with pumps. Whatever evidence is down there isn't going anywhere."

"Who else might die in that time?" She didn't have to look at him to feel his attention burning between her shoulder blades. It was cute the way he worried, but she could do this. She had to do this. "Besides, it's not like the killer would risk drowning just to wait for me to go back into that room."

"Screw the plan. There's no way in hell I'm letting you go down there alone." The marshal stripped off his suit jacket and tossed it into the lobby.

"We talked about this." They'd already agreed. "You need to stay here. Make sure no one disturbs Tamra Hopkins's body before the medical examiner can get here."

Ford unlaced his shiny shoes next. Then discarded his black socks and tie. In a matter of seconds, the marshal was stripped of his armor. "I sent one of the forensic techs to guard the remains, and campus police are more than capable of controlling the crowd. You're not going back in there by yourself. End of story."

"Fine." She wanted to argue, but Leigh couldn't deny the acid charging up her throat at the idea of going into that black underwater hole alone. She descended the final step, flinching as freezing water soaked through her shoes. The door fought against her push, and she powered the flashlight in her hand. Hopefully she wouldn't drop it this time. "Stay close."

She stepped into the blackness.

Water churned against her calves and continued to seep through the cinderblock walls as though they were sobbing. *Drip, drip, drip.* Every cell in her body focused on that consistent rhythm. A combination of comfort and terror rippled through her veins at the sound. They wouldn't know how deep the flood went until they worked their way back to the room. Her toes were already aching at the cold assault. The muscles in her legs ached with every push forward. Damn, she needed to get back into the gym if she was already losing her breath.

Ford shone his light ahead, scanning the walls and the ceilings. She imagined he hadn't gotten a great view of the tunnels in his rush to get to her last time. Then again, they didn't really have all the time in the world. "I guess I should've asked if you knew where we were going before I agreed to come back here."

His voice echoed off the long stretch of corridor and exposed pipes overhead and settled into her body.

"I remember." Leigh tried to tamp down the shivers tensing the rest of her body. Expending too much energy. Burning calories she didn't have in the first place. She cut her flashlight beam to the first corner. "Here."

Taking the first left, they confronted another corridor. The water slid around her waist here. Taking her breath in an instant. She bit the fleshy inside of her bottom lip to distract herself. Her heart rate ticked up every inch they gained.

"You okay?" Ford's beam crested over her shoulder as though he could read the tension along her spine through her blouse.

"If you define 'okay' as still having a pulse." The pattern of dripping water she'd relied on to keep her focused changed. Becoming more of a steady stream this far into the maze. "Yeah. I'm doing great."

"Oh, good. Because for a minute there I thought you could hear my brain screaming at me to get the hell out of here," he said.

A near-hysterical laugh escaped her chest. He was trying to distract her. Doing a good job of it, too. Leigh angled her flashlight to the next corner. "So that's what that was. I was worried an animal had gotten trapped down here with us."

They approached the final turn, putting the ultimate dead end in their beams.

"Shit." Ford grabbed for a pipe over her shoulder to keep his balance. His flashlight beam confirmed the sickening feeling in her gut. "We're too late."

He was right. Water climbed to her chest at the start of the hallway but one more step would sweep her off her feet if she wasn't careful. The hallway itself sloped as a pool would leading unsuspecting victims into the deep end. Collecting at least eight feet of water between her and the kill room. Leigh sucked in a breath to counter the cold jerk of air leaving her chest, but it was no use. She kicked off her shoes and pulled her socks free. It was a risk exposing even a single inch of skin in water so black they couldn't pick out debris, but they'd already come this far. There was no turning back. Not for her. "We're going to have to swim it."

"No, Leigh." Ford reached out, faster than she thought possible, and pulled her back into his chest. "That entire room could be underwater."

"There's a reason he led me here, and I don't think it's for cleansers and a syringe we couldn't pull prints from or Alice Dietz's dead devices." Whoever had lured her here—killer or not—may have been willing to sacrifice evidence he knew would lead nowhere in exchange for protecting the answers they needed. "Don't follow me. You're the lead on the investigation. You know this killer better than anyone, and they're going to need your help to catch him."

He didn't answer.

"I can do this," she said. "In and out."

"This is a bad idea, and you know it." Ford released his hold, but let his touch linger at her shoulder. "You're risking your life for this case."

Ignoring him, Leigh tightened her hold on the flashlight in her hand and grabbed for an exposed pipe above with the other. She could use the network to pull herself closer to the door without expending too much energy. "If I'm not back in five minutes—"

"Just get your ass back here as fast as you can." His hand threaded through the hair at the back of her neck. Ford crushed his mouth to hers. The kiss wasn't anything like their first, full of punishment and unbridled anger. He was the one to pull away. "We have a date, remember?"

Leigh nodded, more out of breath than ever. Her initial weight strained the joint in her shoulder, but she used the water —now to her shoulders—to her advantage. "This is nothing like *Tarzan*."

Within a few feet, the water lapped at her chin, then crested her mouth. She pinched her lips together to avoid swallowing it down. She was going to need a hepatitis shot after this. Leigh blew a strong breath as cold invaded her nostrils. This was as far as she could go keeping her head above water, yet she still had at least five feet to the door to the kill room. There were no guarantees she'd find air pockets in that room. Plan for the worst. Hope for the best. As good a motto as any.

The flashlight beam warped under the watery surface in her grip. With one last glance back to Ford, Leigh took a deep breath.

And slipped beneath the surface.

It took too long for her vision to adjust. Clouded water assaulted her eyes as she waved a hand forward. Not like a chlorine burn. More like a stabbing ice pick sensation. She could make out the doorframe. She kicked with everything she had, propelling her as far as possible before kicking again. Every thrust burned through her oxygen a little faster. She had to stay calm. Use her head. That was what would get her out alive.

Sliding her hand along the doorframe, she pulled herself over the threshold. The water changed. Murkier. Disturbed. As though the walls were closing in and squeezing her insides. Leigh mentally mapped the shelves immediately to her right and kicked past them.

What had they missed?

The corkboard once holding her entire life's story was gone, swaying directly above her. Sweeping the flashlight overhead, she tried to identify pockets of air, but the entire room had been consumed. The realization pressurized the oxygen in her lungs. She'd ever been able to hold her breath for long. She had two minutes—maximum—before her lungs spasmed for relief, and she had to turn back.

Leigh kicked into the farthest section of room from the door. A dark bump-out housed another hand-built shelf measured precisely behind the tub where they assumed Alice Dietz had been bleached and washed before her remains turned up in front of Thompson Hall. Except the wall was darker here than in the rest of the room.

A door. She didn't remember that from her and Ford's initial search. The shelf stood as sentinel, blocking off access. A maintenance closet? Bubbles escaped her nose and mouth as she kicked closer. Her heart rate climbed every second she forced herself to stay in this room.

One minute. She had to make a choice. Go back to Ford, tell her what she'd found. Or risk running out of air. But who knew when they would have this opportunity again? By the time the pumps did their jobs, their unsub could be long gone. She couldn't risk it.

Leigh released the flashlight. The beam hit the floor and carved off to one side but still managed to provide enough light for her to make out the shelf. She closed the distance between her and the shelf, hauling it up. Her lungs screamed to exhale, and she lost another few precious seconds of air. The shelf lifted away, and she guided it over the porcelain tub a few feet away. But her luck was running out.

She wrenched the doorknob. The door refused to budge. Setting her feet against the edge of the tub, Leigh pressed her shoulder into the swollen wood door and shoved.

The wood splintered and swung inward.

A water-logged, bloated face lunged at her.

Her scream was absorbed by the surrounding depths. Water infiltrated her mouth and throat and pushed out the last remnants of air from her chest. The body escaped the confines of the closet and floated toward the ceiling. Dark clothing, pale skin, and purple bruising would haunt her nightmares until the end of her days.

She grabbed for the body's collar and dragged it behind her. Desperation threw logic out the window. She kicked with everything she had to get back into the hallway. To Ford. To air. The drag increased the ache in her muscles with every kick and sweep. Ten feet. Five. She was almost there. Leigh could just make out the shape of the doorframe ahead. She was going to make it.

Gloved hands wrapped around her neck.

Twisting, she released her hold on the body. Clawing at the pressure around her throat.

But she'd already used up the last of her oxygen. Leigh reached for the ceiling.

As the attacker dragged her down.

TWENTY-THREE

Durham, New Hampshire

Sunday, September 10, 2006
9:06 p.m.

She couldn't move.

Leigh pressed herself closer to the man next to her, her back to his front. Her muscles ached in the best way possible. Her lungs had caught fire. She could feel Dean's heartbeat pounding into her spine. Rhythmic and soothing. This. This is what she'd been craving for so long. The warmth of another person. The... acceptance he offered. In this moment, in this bed, trauma and anger and loss and suspicion couldn't reach them. She wanted to stay forever. Right here. With him. This was where she belonged. "That was—"

Dean grasped her chin, turning her mouth into his. His lips slanted over hers in a claiming and punishing tide. As though he could somehow climb inside her and never leave. She could live with that. Dark eyes met hers as he secured one hand around her waist, drawing her closer. "Yeah."

They had a lot of moments like this. Where they didn't have to use their words. There was an understanding, bone deep and soul baring. Like they'd been together for years rather than a few weeks. How had they gone from strangers to... this in the blink of an eye? Dean had consumed her thoughts since the moment she'd met him in the stairwell. Then more so since he'd asked her out. Since she'd offered him her virginity. Since she'd exposed her family's history. All of it had led to this moment. To... what was this? Lust? Infatuation?

Love?

Leigh set her head back into the hollow of his shoulder. Her chest tightened. She registered the moment he noticed the change.

"What's wrong?" Dean pressed a kiss into her temple, securing both arms around her. As though she was something precious. Worth holding on to. Protecting.

"Professor Morrow asked me to look into the case of that murdered student. Teshia Elborne." Now it was his turn to tense. Leigh dug her fingertips into the backs of his hands. Trying to keep him here as long as possible, but it was only a matter of time, wasn't it? Everyone she cared about was taken sooner or later. Why did she think Dean would be any different? But she had to know. She had to know the truth. "The police showed up here a few days ago. Looking to question you about her murder. You knew her, didn't you?"

His exhale fluttered across her bare shoulder. And the bubble they'd created to block out everything but these four walls popped. Dean extracted his hold from around her ribcage. He rolled from the too-small twin bed, taking the top sheet with him. Leaving her cold. Empty. Confused. "If you read the file, then you know I gave a statement. And that I ended everything between me and Teshia before I met you."

Leigh's insides soured as she dragged the comforter smelling of him to cover herself. "You claimed she cheated on you with her high school boyfriend. Another student said she heard you argue with Teshia a few weeks before her death. The police... They think you had something to do with what happened."

Stillness unlike anything she'd seen before flooded through him limb by limb. In that moment, she wasn't sure she knew him as well as she thought she did. If she'd been wrong all this time. "Are you asking me if I killed my ex-girlfriend, Leigh?"

"Did you?" she asked.

Dean melted then. He threaded both legs into a pair of sweatpants and arched a T-shirt over his head. Inch by inch, he closed the distance between them. He framed one side of her face with a calloused palm. The warmth was back in his eyes. Focused solely on her, and she couldn't help but want to stay in it. To be the center of his entire world again. "You're going to make an excellent criminologist one day, little rabbit."

His dorm room door shuddered under three hard pounds. The assault from the outside world electrified her nerves. "Dean Groves, we have a warrant for your arrest in connection to the murder of Teshia Elborne. Open up!"

No. They were supposed to have more time. Leigh latched on to his wrist with both hands. Wanting him to stay. Memories of watching her father cuffed in the middle of the living room while her mother shouted and cried charged into the present.

"They can't do this. They don't have any physical evidence." She wanted those words to be more than a panicked wish, but experience had taught her well these past couple of years. Leigh shot off the bed and grabbed for her clothes as Dean faced the door. Her heart threatened to beat straight out of her chest. "Don't say anything. I know a defense lawyer. I can fix this."

He waited until she'd dressed. Then locked those depthless eyes on her. "This isn't for you to fix, Leigh."

She froze. Taken aback by the crush of emotion stuck in her throat.

Dean opened the door, turning to face her as two Durham PD officers wrenched his hands into handcuffs.

Durham, New Hampshire

Thursday, October 10
11:51 a.m.

She was going to die.

Black webs spidered at the edges of her vision. The pressure around her throat increased. She couldn't breathe. Couldn't think. The body overhead swayed with every kick she attempted to get free. But it was no use.

Leigh threaded her fingers underneath the vise circled around her throat. Soft fabric prevented her fingertips from getting a grip. She shook her head as though that would rewind time. As though it would help her disassociate from suffocating in the next few seconds.

Throwing her head back, she failed to connect with her attacker's nose. There was nothing she could do. Her movements were already slowing. Getting harder to control. The darkness was closing in, and there was nothing she could do to stop it.

Her elbow knocked against the nearest shelf hanging on to preservation supplies. One of the mason jars—full of green slime that would kill anyone who dared get close—knocked over onto its side and rolled closer.

She didn't have time to think. Leigh shot one hand out while clawing for release with the other. Her fingertips slipped off the curved glass and forced it farther away. It rolled back in the next second. She tried again and secured her hand around the heavy jar.

Her attacker's grip threatened to crush her airway.

The black edges across her vision transformed into a thick wave that overwhelmed her senses. But she hung on. She wasn't going to die today. Not like this. And sure as hell not in this room like Alice Dietz. Leigh brought the slime jar into her ribcage, then slammed it against the edge of the shelf.

The thud barely registered in her ears. Or was that one of the last thuds of her heart in her ears? She couldn't tell the difference. Her pulse weakened in her throat, barely bulging against the hands crushing her. She dragged the increasingly heavy jar back to her chest. Then hit it against the shelf.

Pain spliced across her palm. Keeping her alive. She focused on that pain, on the feel of shattered glass in her hand. Leigh clutched it tighter. Cutting herself deeper as a heavy weight dragged her into a watery grave.

She brought the shard to her neck. And sliced down.

A filtered groan reached her ears. The grip around her throat disappeared. A rush of pressure expanded in her chest, but she couldn't let herself inhale. Bits of light bled into her vision. This was her chance. Leigh didn't bother aiming for the flashlight rolling back and forth across the floor and kicked for the door.

Her arms protested every swipe, as though she were swimming through mud.

Out. She needed out.

A dark shape blocked her escape through the door. Two... of them? No. She wasn't going to stop. Couldn't stop. Leigh braced for impact as the second attacker extended a hand. For her.

Strong hands latched on to her arms and dragged her close. Finishing what the first had started. Except Leigh was still moving. Being shoved through the door into the hallway. The second shape released its hold, his features blurred in her vision. Propelling her out of the kill room.

Waves mocked her from overhead. Promising an air pocket. She clawed for the water's surface with all the grace of a T-rex. One hand broke the surface. Then her head.

Her gasp echoed off the walls. Leigh gulped a burning lungful of air as she clung to an exposed pipe in the dark. Ford.

Where was Ford? A sob pressurized in her chest, but she wouldn't let it out. Not here. Not yet.

A flashlight beam cut through the water around her feet. Her throat barely managed to produce a sound. "Ford!"

The marshal's head broke free of the inky depths. He stretched to grab on to a pipe next to hers with bare hands, worse for wear around his mouth and eyes. Blood mixed with water at his temple. "Shit. Are you okay?"

Fury burned through her veins. Leigh shoved at his chest. "You were supposed to wait for me." She hit him again. "You were supposed to go back if I didn't make it."

"I just saved your life! Not sure if you know this, but someone tried to kill you." Ford swiped a mixture of water and blood from his face. "I think that deserves a thank you."

"Where is he?" She struggled to catch her breath, shaken straight to her core. She'd come close to dying multiple times over her career, but this... This had felt personal. Or maybe she just had more to lose now. "Where did he go? What happened?"

"The son of a bitch clocked me with one of those mason jars." Ford tested the contusion beside his left eye, coming away with watery blood. "Must've gotten away while I was trying to figure out which way was up. You didn't see him escape?"

"No." Leigh couldn't help but search the depths underneath them. Tried to pick out the shape of her attacker beneath the surface but was met with only darkness.

He was right before. Of course he was right. But the idea of losing yet another person she cared about had taken hold. Her brother, her father, her mother, Dean, Elyse. They'd all left her to fight alone. And now she'd almost lost Ford. Leigh tried to control the tremors coursing through her body. From adrenaline, nearly dying, or another round of hypothermia, she didn't know. Her teeth chattered. "Thank you."

"You're bleeding." He pointed the flashlight at her exposed

forearm, rivulets of blood snaking along her skin. The cut across her palm could get infected if she wasn't treated soon. The marshal grabbed for her elbow, guiding her back the way they'd come. "Come on. We gotta get you out of here."

"We can't leave." Leigh tightened her hold on the exposed pipe overhead, shaking her head as if that would make a convincing argument. "Not without the body. It's... it's floating around the ceiling. We can't leave without it."

Her strength was waning. She couldn't stop shaking. The past few minutes blurred into fragments. Why couldn't she feel her palm? Shock. This was shock.

"Some asshole just tried to kill you, and you want to go back in there for a dead guy who might not have anything to do with this case?" Ford tightened his grip on her. Almost painful. "We'll send someone else. You're not going to make it."

"I'm fine." Now if she could stop shaking to make that a little more convincing. Leigh tried to take a full breath, but she suddenly forgot how to breathe. She had to snap out of... whatever this was. They needed that body. Shifting her grip, she moved to descend back into the depths. "I can do it."

"Damn it. No, you can't." Ford pulled her against the hard muscle of his chest, keeping her head above water. "Can't believe I'm saying this, but I'll do it. To be clear, is this really what homicide investigators have to go through to solve a case?"

"Remind me... to tell you about the time I had to walk through a wall of spiderwebs to get to a crime scene," she said.

Ford pointed a strong index finger at her. "Stay here. If you move, you'll be the next body I drag out of here. Got it?"

Leigh nodded. Because that was all she could do.

In seconds, the marshal was gone. His flashlight beam wavered before extinguishing completely as he entered the room. One minute. Two.

Was the water churning faster or was that her brain trying to stay awake? Her grip slipped from the pipe above, and her head dipped beneath the surface. Weightless and a little tired. Okay, a lot tired. Her heartbeat sounded... off. Far away and slow. Like it couldn't keep up with the rest of her.

But then Ford was there. Pulling her up. Leading her down the corridor. She used him to get her balance, and right then, he felt so much... bigger than she remembered. Strong hands kept her upright. She only had a second to wonder how he was dragging a body behind them and simultaneously keeping her on her feet. Her head rolled back on her shoulders.

"Stay with me," he said.

A rectangular white light assaulted her vision, blurring his features. Growing bigger. Leigh stumbled against the stairs leading into Thompson Hall's lobby, her face pressed against the cement.

"Leigh?" A flurry of sound and motion added extra strain on her brain, but Ava's voice reached over it all. "Leigh!"

The black spiderwebs were back. Pulling her under.

TWENTY-FOUR

Durham, New Hampshire

Thursday, October 10
1:39 p.m.

"Why isn't she waking up?"

Ava. She'd know that voice anywhere. Though the worry was new. Leigh wasn't sure she'd ever heard it before now.

"Give her a few minutes." Another voice she was supposed to recognize. Ford? "She's been through a lot, but she'll come around. Your mom is strong."

"She's not my mom." There was the fifteen-year-old Leigh knew and loved.

Intense aches closed in around her throat as she swallowed. Something moldy and acidic lodged at the base of her esophagus. Oh, hell. Had she swallowed some of the green slime in those mason jars? Gross. The thought was enough to turn Leigh onto her side and force her stomach into a heave. Pinpricks pinched her palm. She could only imagine the kind of damage thirty-year-old botulism could cause.

"There you go." Pressure circled into her back. "Just breathe."

She summoned the energy to crack her eyes.

And stared directly into the face of a corpse.

Shoving to all fours, Leigh lost the minimal contents of her stomach into a garbage can thrust into her chest. It took a few minutes for her to get her bearings. Recognize the amphitheater seating, the narrow windows punctured across the room, and the industrial carpeting currently darkened by the shape of her soaked outline. She set her gaze on Ava—enjoying that small tinge of relief—then the marshal crouched a few feet away. "Not cool."

"Sorry. Didn't really have any other place to put him." Ford stood. "We're running out of places to store bodies. Besides, you're the one who insisted he come back with us."

Was he… angry with her? Leigh wasn't sure her head was in the right place to argue the significance of finding a body in the very room their killer had murdered Alice Dietz. What the hell had happened down there? Her grip tightened around the garbage can as she studied the swollen features of the remains. Tall, most likely male. His clothing seemed intact. Though there weren't any distinguishing features due to purple marbling and swelling. But, if she had to guess from the way he'd been hidden in a closet in the basement, he'd been murdered. Maybe even before Alice Dietz. Only the medical examiner could tell.

"Ford, can you please find a blanket or something to cover the body?" The urge to strip the remains down to a series of details and patterns surged, but her head was still pounding. She couldn't feel much of her feet and hands. And she was sure she'd scared the shit out of her adopted daughter. Leigh reached for Ava, grasping on to the fifteen-year-old's forearm. "I'm not sure my stomach can take another close encounter."

"Yeah, sure." He was looking at her as though he wanted to

argue but thought better of it. In seconds, he was pushing through the door at the top of the amphitheater seating and letting it close behind him.

Leigh set the garbage can to one side, the carpet beneath her growing damp. "Ava, are you okay?"

"Me? You're the one who nearly died." A similar anger contorted Ava's graceful expression. Then vanished. "Why did you go down there? Why did it have to be you?"

The concern was back in Ava's voice, clenching something deep inside Leigh wasn't sure she could identify. It'd been a long time since someone had been worried about her. Least of all the one person she was sure hated her more than anyone else in the world. "This is my job, Ava. This is what I do. I hunt for answers so people like Alice Dietz's and Tamra Hopkins's families can move on. So people who hurt others don't get away with it."

People like Ava's mother. Though she didn't have the heart to voice that thought. Didn't Ava understand? This was who she was, who she'd become to cope with reality. Finding answers, solving puzzles, healing herself by getting the justice she couldn't, case by case—she couldn't do anything else.

"You could've died." Ava tore her forearm from Leigh's grip and added a few feet of distance between them. "And then what? Who would look after me? Did you even think of that?"

Understanding hit, and the fight drained from Leigh's veins. No. She hadn't thought of Ava before going down into that basement. She'd followed her instincts. And put herself in danger. Because Ava had a point. What would've happened if Ford hadn't been there to fight off the killer? What would've happened to Ava if Leigh hadn't come back? Leigh scooted across the floor, threading her arms around the fifteen-year-old. Ava tried to push away, but even in Leigh's shocked and exhausted state, she wasn't letting go. "I'm sorry. I'm so sorry."

"You promised to take care of me. You said you would put

me before your job." Ava swiped at her face. "You're all I have left."

"I know." They'd started rocking together, using their grip on one another to soothe the mutual hurt they'd inflicted on each other. It wouldn't last forever, but Leigh forced herself to memorize every detail. Sans the corpse staring in their direction. "You're right. And I'm going to keep my promise. Okay? I'm not going to leave you. Ever. You're mine. And I'm yours. I'm not going anywhere. Understand?"

Leigh forced herself to lighten her hold on Ava, smoothing hair back away from the girl's features to get a better view of her face. "I'm sorry about Tamra. I know you didn't know her long, but sometimes time is irrelevant. I'm going to find out what happened to her."

"I know." Ava swiped at her face, but her expression said there was more. "Leigh, there's something I need to tell you. About what happened in Gulf Shores—"

The door at the top of the stairs opened, centering Ford in its frame. He clutched a US Marshals windbreaker. The same one he'd let her borrow after her first confrontation with the room in the basement. "Couldn't find another blanket or a tarp. Figured this was better than nothing until the ME is able to get here."

"Thank you." He might still be mad at her, but Ford had somehow managed to get her out of that basement alive. "For saving my life."

His brows dipped toward the bridge of his nose. Almost... hesitant. "You would've done the same for me. That's what partners are for."

"I wouldn't know. I've never had one." Leigh ducked her mouth to Ava's temple and planted a kiss there, wanting to stay right here. Where the dangers of this case couldn't get to them, and they'd somehow come to an even deeper level of understanding one another. Except there was a dead guy in the middle of the floor. "I need you to go back to the lobby so I can examine this body. I'll be there in a few minutes to come check on you. All right?"

Ava nodded, slipping free of her grasp. As effortless as a professional dancer.

Leigh waited until the door at the top of the classroom closed behind her adopted daughter before turning her attention to Ford. Her clothes clung to her like an uncomfortable second skin. Too heavy. Infected and stained with whatever had been in those jars. "I'm guessing since the entire basement is flooded, maintenance has given up on fixing the generator."

"Considering it's under four feet of water, yeah, I'd say attempts to replace the damaged wiring have been aborted." Ford let himself smile, and in an instant, they were right back where they'd started.

"Any reports on when this storm is supposed to pass?" Leigh forced herself to move. Her body had other ideas, but she couldn't let it win.

"Not yet," Ford said. "One of the campus police officers located an old emergency radio. The batteries are dead, but the university president has the staff searching the entire building for the right size. No luck yet."

Good. That was good. Looked like the radios they'd accepted from Durham PD's chief were coming in handy, keeping them in the loop. Any information could change the tide in this case. Or at least allow them to do their jobs. "Any identification on the remains?"

"Not that I could find." Ford kept his distance from the body. "It's hard to tell with all the swelling, but I'm guessing our friend here is a middle-aged male, Caucasian. A few bits of gray around his temples."

"Slacks and button-down suggest professional." There wasn't much more to tell considering the damage done to the remains. Leigh maneuvered to stand, angling for a better view of the man's face. "I don't see any signs of hemorrhagic edema, so he didn't die from drowning."

"Hemorrhagic... what?" Ford asked.

She tried to get closer without touching the body. While it was unlikely the medical examiner would be able to pull much from the remains now that they'd been moved, she didn't want to take any chances of transference. "White foam in and around the mouth and in the airway. Mucus in the lungs mixes with water and creates a foam during drowning. He doesn't have any."

Leigh caught sight of a band of bruising at the victim's throat. Reaching toward Ford, she wiggled her fingers. "I need your flashlight."

"What for?" He grabbed it from the floor nearby and handed it off.

"There's something here on his neck. It's hard to see with his chin tilted down." Leigh hit the power button and managed to eliminate another inch of distance. There. A sliver—maybe half an inch—of discoloration. "That looks like... a strangulation mark."

Ford tried to get a better view. "How can you tell?"

She wasn't a medical examiner, but that didn't stop the memories of previous victims from infiltrating this case. Three bodies. Two young women. One adult male—Ava's abductor and rapist. "I've seen marks like these before."

Leigh forced her attention back to the body in front of her and not on the past. "He wasn't supposed to be there."

"You think the unsub is responsible for this?" Ford had gotten close without her noticing again. Right over her shoulder. Probably to get a better view of the remains, but she hated the feeling she couldn't shake the sogginess in her brain.

She was tired. Running on fumes. Had nearly died—twice. Not to mention the drain of emotionally losing Ava hour by hour. A heaviness she wasn't prepared to fight intensified in her muscles. Shards of memory—of being guided out of the basement—fit back together as she looked up at Ford's face. Almost the same angle he'd been at pulling her down the flooded corridors. Except she couldn't make his features fit. Then again, she'd been disoriented. And it'd been dark. *Stay with me.* The voice filtered into the present, but she couldn't assign it to the man in front of her. Too many differences.

"There's no way the killer set up shop in that room to kill Alice Dietz or Pierce Morrow without noticing a body in the closet. He would've searched and memorized every inch of that basement to get the advantage. I think our new friend here surprised him, and the killer had to adapt in the moment."

"By strangling him instead of poisoning." Ford looked as though he wanted to nudge the body with the toe of his matte black shoe. "So who is he?"

"Let's ask campus police if they're missing one of their officers." She ran her gaze over the body again, trying to pick up something—anything—to tell them what'd happened. But the headache at the base of her skull thudded harder. "I want to check in with the university president on the key codes used at the biomedical lab while we're at it."

"Good idea. Until then you look like you could use a nap or an exorcism." He circled her face with a finger. "You've got something green and a little terrifying on your face."

"How nice of you to notice." She would not throw up again. Shower. She needed a shower. And a nap. "It's not like I almost died."

His laugh filled the oversized classroom. But there was something in it that didn't quite reach his eyes. "Let's go, Brody. I'll check in with campus police and the university president."

They'd made it to the top of the amphitheater stairs—not without a few stops along the way—when the classroom door wrenched open. One of the forensic techs looked between her and Ford. "Agent Brody, we managed to pull some information from one of the driver's licenses you recovered from the biomedical lab."

"Whose is it?" she asked.

He handed over the warped plastic. "It belongs to Pierce Morrow."

TWENTY-FIVE

Durham, New Hampshire

Thursday, October 10
2:07 p.m.

She couldn't get the slime out of her hair.

Leigh shoved her slacks, blazer, and blouse into the garbage can inside the door of the women's shower. No amount of soap, shampoo, and conditioner was going to get rid of whatever had been in those preservation jars. The smell alone churned her stomach. She only hoped whoever had tried to strangle her was having the same issue. Would serve him right, after all. And it'd make him much easier to identify if they came across a drenched man with a cut on his forearm and slime in his hair.

Which begged the question: How had her attacker managed to stay hidden all this time? The network of tunnels beneath campus must have alternate entries and exits. She made a mental note to ask maintenance for blueprints of the flooded maze.

With the slightly green tint to her blonde hair, she was

beginning to fit in with the school's witchy decorations and she had to admit that despite it all, she felt a little more human. A dull thud pulsed behind her eyes. Ish. Turned out, it took more than a shower to recover from nearly drowning, but they'd long run out of food with no supplies able to get onto campus. People were going to start getting sick if they didn't do something.

"Look at that. She lives." Ford shoved away from the wall where he'd stationed himself while she showered.

The smile was automatic. Honestly, she liked his barbs. His sarcastic sense of humor. "Thanks to you. Can't say the same for my clothes, though. I had to call dead on arrival."

"I've gotta say. I like the sweats." The marshal stared down at her, more at ease than he had been after pulling her from the basement. She understood his reaction. The sense of helplessness that came with not being able to do anything for someone you cared about. It told her a lot about the importance of relationships in his life. Ford slid his hands into the front pockets of her borrowed hoodie and skimmed her belly through the rough fabric. "Takes away some of your intimidation."

"You find me intimidating?" She couldn't help but tip her chin up to meet his gaze head on. This was a power struggle, one she didn't intend on losing. His hair was slightly askew, and damp. He'd taken his own shower, and the effect pooled heat low in her belly. Uncomfortable and a little desperate.

"Well, not anymore." He cocked his head to one side, increasing the intensity of his strokes through her sweatshirt. A renewed heat trailed from every touch, and she had to remind herself they were working a case. Getting this close was sure to come back and bite them in the ass if they weren't careful. "Kind of hard to be intimidated by someone once you see them throw up."

"That's not fair. I was covered in goo." Her attention caught on a section of his hair, and Leigh struggled to hold in her laugh. Made sense. He'd gone into that room after her and fought the killer to save her life. There was no escaping the sludge. She wanted to kiss him for that. Wanted to push this as far as they could without crossing the line between professionals. "In fact, I'm not the only one."

"What?" Ford reached for his hair, coming away with preserved mold. "Damn it. I thought I got it all."

"Serves you right for coming after me when I told you to stay in the corridor." Her smile got too heavy. Leigh raised herself onto the toes of borrowed sneakers and pressed herself to him. Her hands splayed across his chest, feeling his heartbeat—strong and sure and even—beneath her touch.

Ford notched his chin down, seemingly unable to ignore the pull between them. "If I hadn't, you wouldn't be here." His voice went gravelly; it told her exactly how much she affected him.

She pressed her mouth to his. Hunger tore through her, the kind that couldn't be sated with one of the candy bars he'd stolen from the vending machine. Leigh slanted her mouth into his, inviting him deeper. Needing him to consume every hurt inch of her and make it better. Her heart shot into her throat as his thumbs shifted over the waistband of her sweats and skimmed her stomach. She arched into him. More.

Ford took the lead. Latching on to her hips, he spun them until her back hit the nearest wall and hauled her mouth level with his. His groan urged her to hike her legs around his waist and lock her ankles as the marshal pressed in closer. Right where she needed him. He kissed her as though he were an entire meal and he'd been starving up to this point. Furiously with no mercy. Her lips—and the rest of her—burned at the contact, but she wanted this. She wanted him. The connection that made her feel a little bit more put together after life had shattered her in every regard.

She hadn't experienced that since... She didn't want to think about that. Didn't want to think about *him*. Not while

Ford's hands were pulling these sensations from her. Her resulting moan echoed through the corridor.

The fluorescent tube above them exploded.

Leigh jerked back as hundreds of pieces of white glass hit the tile around them. She brought her hands to shield her face. Once the shower of glass ceased, Leigh unlocked her hold on Ford and tried to see the damage around his massive frame. A surge of joy flickered within her. "The power must've come back on. Maybe the tube couldn't handle the surge."

Ford held on to her hips until she managed to get her feet under her. He stepped aside, testing the nearest light switch. Nothing happened. The marshal scanned the corridor. Absolutely still. "I don't think so."

There. Amid the shattered pieces of glass. Leigh maneuvered around the marshal, picking up the rock. It wasn't anything special but said so much. Someone else had been here. Watching them. A sick knot tightened in her gut. "We should talk to Professor Morrow again. Seeing as how we recovered his driver's license, he's the only one of the killer's targets that's still alive. He may know who's behind this."

"I'll be right behind you." Ford didn't give her any room for argument. "I'm going to take a look around."

Except she didn't want to leave him to face whatever this was alone. Leigh squared off with him, every sense she owned on high alert. Watched the shadows as if they would come alive. She could still feel the imprint of those gloved hands around her throat. Still feel the life draining from her bubble by bubble. "What happened in that room?"

"I was counting the seconds you were gone, Leigh. And when three full minutes passed, I knew something was wrong. So I dove into that room. That's when I saw him behind you, strangling you. You managed to get away, but he was coming after you, and I had a chance to stop him. We fought. Long enough for you to make it out, but I had a choice to make." Regret singed his voice. "I chose you."

She didn't remember anyone else there. But Ford had somehow managed to save her life and recover a body the killer might not have wanted them to find. And barely escaped. With a nod, Leigh pushed as much gratitude into her expression as she could while ignoring that fired-up part of her that wanted him to press her back against the wall and continue to distract her from this case. She'd never had this problem before. Never wanted to step back into the world of dating and relationships and having to shave above the knee. What was it about Max Ford that called to every primal need she'd buried over the years?

She navigated back to the second classroom branching off the west side of the lobby and shoved inside. Professor Morrow had quieted his protests over the past few hours, but the headache that surged when she set sight on him was enough to make her reconsider coming in alone.

Morrow wrenched his head up from where he sat at the bottom of the amphitheater-like classroom, one wrist lowered at an angle and cuffed to the leg of the table centered between him and his students. The papery skin beneath the cuff had grown angry. He'd obviously tried to pry his way out, but his voice was much softer than she expected. "Leigh."

There were parts of him she still recognized after all these years. His clothing, for one. His ego, too. Others not so much. She hadn't been prepared for the added lines around his eyes and mouth or the prominent gray in his beard and hair. Had he always been this... worn? Or was that another layer of the mask he insisted on wearing? Leigh fisted the handcuff key in her sweats. She didn't like seeing him like this. Because no matter what role he'd played in the deaths of two—now three—students, Pierce Morrow had been one of the few who'd believed she could solve her brother's case. And she had. With things she'd learned right here in this classroom.

"Your driver's license was found with a collection of others the killer tried to destroy in a container of acid here on campus. Trophies."

The words were merely whispered but held so much power. "How many others?"

"Five." She dragged a chair from the other side of the table and took a seat. Her bones hurt, but for the first time since stepping foot back onto this campus, she enjoyed the familiarity of conversations like this with her old mentor. The two of them working a case together. Except he hadn't been in cuffs then, and she'd been nothing more than a naive freshman in love with her first real boyfriend. "Forensic techs were able to identify yours, but they're still working on the others. From what we can tell, four of them most likely belong to the unsub's previous victims whose identities he became. We believe that's what he intended to do with you."

"Why me?" Morrow shook his head. "What makes me so special?"

"That's a good question." She studied the man in front of her. Trying to find something recognizable in his movements. In his way of speech. Then again, she might not be the best person to assess him. Their relationship had been... strained over the years. Limited to video calls and emails with months of no contact passing in the blink of an eye. The killer Ford had described became the people he targeted in every way. Career, lifestyle, routines, social circles. "Have you come across a killer like this before? One who becomes his victims? Lives their lives?"

Another shake of the professor's head. He wasn't as polished as he had been yesterday standing in the corner of the president's office beaming at her. This man had lost everything he'd valued in the span of twenty-four hours, and it showed.

"No. Nothing like this. Whoever killed Teshia Elborne and Alice... He's on a level I've never imagined possible."

There was almost a hint of admiration in that statement.

"How far do you think this chameleon would go to become his victims?" She wasn't sure why she was asking Morrow. Leigh leaned forward in her chair. She considered his earlier question. Why him? Why this identity? What need did Pierce Morrow fulfil for this particular killer? "How far would you go to become someone else?"

"Still think I'm the one killing students, Agent Brody?" The question didn't hold any hint of emotion. As though Morrow had accepted her as the expert in their field. No argument.

No. She didn't think he was a killer. He couldn't have killed Tamra Hopkins while cuffed to this table, and he certainly hadn't been the one to try to drown her in the basement.

"You've been hiding your failures for years without raising any red flags here on campus or in the field. As far as your network knows, you're the one they come to for answers." Stolen answers. But answers nonetheless. The ultimate long con. Leigh let the theory take shape, molding it out loud. "What if the killer we're hunting saw that in you? Even admired it. He's a fraud, too. He could've been drawn to that familiarity."

Morrow's voice went breathy. "What are you saying?"

"This unsub chooses his victims because they offer some kind of value to him," Leigh said. "I think your value was what you do best as a professor. He was looking for a mentor, and he found it. In you."

She kept her gaze locked on Morrow's and saw exactly what she was looking for. Fear. "So tell me, Professor Morrow. Who have you been teaching to get away with murder?"

"I don't know what you're talking about." Color drained from Morrow's face. The pulse at the base of his neck thudded too hard for a man of his age merely sitting in a chair. Enough that Leigh spotted it from her position. He shook his head, maybe trying to convince himself more than her.

"I think you do." Leaning forward in her chair, Leigh refused to break eye contact. It was one of the lessons he'd taught her all those years ago. To never give up the power in an interrogation. "I think you know exactly who's behind these murders. I think you know what he wants, and I think you got more than you bargained for in whatever arrangement you two had. Who is he, Pierce?"

The professor's bottom lip trembled. Just before he pulled himself together. "I want my lawyer."

TWENTY-SIX

Durham, New Hampshire

Thursday, October 10
2:31 p.m.

Leigh shoved through the classroom door into the corridor, nearly taking out Ford with the momentum. "He wants his lawyer."

While the professor wasn't technically under arrest considering they couldn't get him to the Durham PD station for processing, Morrow had shut down completely.

"I take it your conversation didn't go well." Ford's ability to both make light of their ever-darkening situation and drive her up the wall at the same time had reached new heights. He fell into line beside her. A support she hadn't had in a long time.

She stepped back into the lobby, heavier than ever after noting the lost stares cutting straight to her. Students and staff alike questioned her without so much as saying a word. They'd moved from flat-out anger to fear, but Leigh wasn't good at offering words of comfort. She couldn't even do it for her own adopted daughter. "Was forensics able to find prints or identi-fying markers on the chemicals we collected from the basement?"

"Nothing. The killer ensured to wipe everything clean, but even if we still had access to that room, which we don't"—Ford hit her with a hard stare as if to remind her they would not be going back down into the basement until pumps could be utilized—"we most likely couldn't get anything new from it."

She didn't have any intention of going back down there. Ever. The memories she had now of her time in the basement would last a lifetime. Why was it anytime they got their hands on a lead, it was ceremoniously ripped from their grasp? Leigh targeted the university president, cornered between two other professors and who she assumed was his executive assistant. "Have you been able to verify the list of key codes used to access the biomedical lab between two nights ago and yesterday morning when Alice Dietz was found dead?"

Color fled the president's face. "I'm sorry, Agent Brody, but without power, I'm not able to access the system. The access I have is through my desktop computer in my office."

Of course not. Because that would've been too easy. "What about security, campus police, or other researchers? Would they be able to get to it from their tablets or phones?"

"I'm not exactly sure what our security team or campus police have access to, Agent Brody, but the other researchers won't be of any help. Each code is kept private to ensure approved access to the lab and its equipment."

Leigh notched her head to meet the marshal's gaze. "Ford, let's get those two campus officers down here. Ask them if they can get us a list of key codes."

"You want to pull them off babysitting duty?" His eyebrows arched toward his hairline.

Tamra Hopkins's body. The headache pulsing at the back of her skull urged her to close her eyes. Okay, maybe it had something to do with almost dying, too. But for now, she had to scramble for all the little pieces of this case and try to hold them together. The lobby doors shuddered as if to emphasize no one was going anywhere anytime soon. Lines of water branched across the outer door glass, thickening and thinning with the onslaught, and snuck under the barrier.

"Leigh?" Ford lowered his voice. "Agent Brody."

Case. Right. Damn, she was tired. Leigh rubbed at her head. "Ask them if they can get a list of key codes used in the biomedical lab."

"Sure." He reached for her, as though to steady her in case she lost consciousness, but her pride wouldn't sweep her off her feet. "Are you all right?"

Was she all right? Hard to tell between the lack of calories, the lack of oxygen for those terrifying three minutes, and the lack of sleep in the past two days. She refused to cross her arms over her chest as she normally would under someone else's scrutiny. "I'm good."

"I asked one of the officers to keep an eye on our dead guy from the basement down the hall and the other on Tamra's remains. I'll be back in a few minutes." He headed for the stairs leading up to the second level.

Lighting flashed in the corner of her eye. Then the boom of thunder sounded overhead. A few gasps reached her ears. A collective bracing for the worst. Damn it, she didn't know how to do this. To... make it seem as if she had everything under control. When was the last time things were under control? Before someone she'd trusted to help her solve her brother's case had tried to kill her? Before she'd been told the cancer had come back? Before a murderer had asked her to adopt her then fourteen-year-old daughter? Her entire life was a case study in not having control.

These kids were scared. Ava was scared. People were dying, and none of them—not even Leigh—knew why. She faced off with the university president, and a rush of dizziness nearly knocked her off balance. Leigh's hand hit the wall beside her. Apparently, she'd been ignoring her body's needs long enough. There was about to be a mutiny. She buried the urge to shake her head. Not wanting to upset her brain any more than she already had. "Marshal Ford said something about an emergency radio. Were you able to find batteries?"

"The marshal didn't tell you?" Confusion contorted the president's face. "We replaced the batteries. We gave him the radio to contact the local Marshals office for help."

"Oh." Leigh didn't remember that part of her and Ford's conversation. But she wasn't remembering a whole lot at the moment. Like a sudden fog had rolled in and started shutting down her executive functions. She needed to sleep, but one could argue she needed to catch a killer more. "I'll check in with him."

She maneuvered through students until she reached Ava, crouching to meet the fifteen-year-old on her level. "You doing okay?"

Ava eyed her from toe to head, barely turning to meet her gaze. "You look like you're about to pass out."

"You say the nicest things." She'd caught sight of herself in the bathroom mirror before her shower, but Leigh would bet the bruising around her neck had darkened to an ugly black and purple. "Are you doing okay?"

"Everyone is scared. They think they might be... next," Ava said.

Leigh wasn't sure she could ease that worry with Tamra Hopkins's body upstairs. There didn't seem to be any strategy other than survival to Tamra's death. She'd claimed to have seen private messages between Alice Dietz and an unknown man, most likely Professor Morrow, but was that motive enough to kill her? Or had she simply been in the wrong place at the wrong time and paid the price?

Leigh rubbed at her temples. She'd have to find some ibuprofen to get through the next couple of hours. Otherwise, her head might explode from the pressure.

All right. If the killer had seen a potential mentor in Morrow as she'd once done herself, why add his driver's license to the killer's trophies? Pierce Morrow was still alive and every ounce the egotistical, thieving investigative consultant she remembered. Maybe becoming a target meant the professor had already outlived his usefulness...

Tension radiated down her spine. Leigh settled her attention on the group of six students huddled in a circle, Ava included. "Listen, as long as you guys stick together, don't go anywhere alone, and stay in this lobby, you're safe. I know you're confused, and you're scared, and we have no idea when we'll be able to get out of here, but Marshal Ford and I are doing everything in our power to get you through this in one piece. I give you my word."

She had nothing else to offer. No heroic speech that could fix any of this. She just had her instincts, and right now they were telling her Pierce Morrow was still in danger.

Leigh forced her legs to move. Though it took everything she had to put one foot in front of the other. Running on fumes and adrenaline—and, let's be honest, a whole lot of uncertainty —tended to have that effect. She retraced her path to the second classroom west of the lobby.

"Hey." Ford somehow ended up in front of her. Like her brain had stalled with her hand on the classroom door. "I just talked to both campus police officers and got the same answer. They aren't able to access the key code history for the biomedical building without an internet connection."

Leigh rubbed at her head. The headache had spread from behind her eyes up her forehead and clawed down the sides above her ears. More intense than a minute ago. "Is there some kind of monthly report emailed to authorized parties showing who accessed the building?"

She was grabbing at straws at this point.

"Not that anyone has offered," he said.

Great. "So we can't narrow down who had access to that lab and the arsenic and cyanide used to kill Alice Dietz."

"What I'm wondering is how Tamra Hopkins was killed when we'd already submitted both poisons into evidence." Ford had a point. "You might be onto something with your law enforcement theory."

"One of the forensic techs." It wasn't a question. Leigh tried to mentally picture the two techs that'd been forced to shelter in place with them. She didn't know either personally. Homicide investigations fell to local police who supplied their own teams unless specifically asking for the bureau's assistance. Both techs had a pulse on the investigation, the ability to manipulate evidence, and the knowledge to clean up after themselves. "Let's get their names and find out what we can about both. I'd like to talk to Morrow again."

Ford set a hand on her shoulder, holding her in place. His gaze narrowed, and she didn't even have the energy to give in to her usual self-consciousness. "Hey, are you all right? Your pupils are dilated, and you look like you're having trouble staying on your feet. Did you hit your head when you were in the basement?"

"I..." Did she? Dilated pupils didn't come from exhaustion. The world tipped on its axis, and suddenly she was looking up at the marshal from a much lower angle than she had a second ago. "I don't remember. I'm fine. I need to talk to..."

"Whoa. It's okay. I've got you." Ford caught her under the arms, sliding her back against the wall until her butt hit the cold stone floor. "Here, sit down."

She didn't have time to sit. There was something she had to do. Wasn't there? Leigh shook her head. Big mistake. Her vision swam, closing in then bursting back out. "I'm okay. I can do this."

"You shouldn't move until we can get an EMT in here to assess you." Ford set both hands on her shoulders. "At least let one of the campus police officers have a look."

Yeah. Like that was going to happen in the middle of a hurricane. Leigh almost laughed. She just had to remember what it was she had to do. She reached for the door handle above her head, pulling herself to her feet. She closed her eyes as the world started swimming. Focus. She had to focus. Okay. That was better. She didn't feel like throwing up anymore. Maybe she had hit her head. Or was this an extended symptom of hypothermia? She didn't know. "I need to talk to Morrow again."

"Leigh, you can barely stand. Wait here. I'll get you some water." He didn't give her a chance to argue, darting down the hallway back toward the lobby.

Every second they wasted was another opportunity for the killer to escape. This was what she was trained for. This was what she was good at. She swung the door inward. To find Pierce Morrow dead in his seat.

TWENTY-SEVEN

Durham, New Hampshire

Thursday, October 10
3:07 p.m.

Heavy footsteps aggravated each pulse of the pain in her head.

Something hard pressed into the left side of her body. Rough. And smelly. Leigh craned her head back, the rest of her body following. Bright lights punctured through the haze still clinging to her vision. When had she lain down? Where the hell was she?

An outline centered over her, growing larger as the person above her neared, but she couldn't make out many details of a face. Her brain refused to catch up to her senses. Ford?

"You're going to be okay." Calluses caught against her jawline, a trail of sensation from ear to chin. Careful. Controlled. Soft. "The drug will clear your system soon."

"Drug..." The word echoed over and over. Intensified the hard thud between her ears. Her tongue felt too big for her mouth, and her head... The more she tried to focus on his face, the further away he seemed to be. Leigh tried to reach for him, barely grazing a shirt. Her depth perception was off. Her entire body was off. And slow. Helplessness iced her veins. She was at the mercy of... whoever this was.

"Just a little something I came up with to buy us some time together." Dark eyes came into focus then blurred all over again. "It's temporary and fast-acting. There won't be any permanent side effects once the drug leaves your system, but you might have a headache for a couple hours. I didn't know of another way to get you alone."

"Why? Who... you?" Wait. Did she actually say the words or was that in her head? She couldn't be sure. Her thoughts weren't making a whole lot of sense, and she hated it more than not knowing who'd killed Teshia Elborne, Alice Dietz, and Tamra Hopkins. And... someone else. Why couldn't she think of their name?

"We don't have much time, Leigh." Her name leaving his mouth soured her stomach. It was familiar. As though they knew each other. His hand shifted to her forehead, sweeping hair away from her face. Too gentle. Too intimate. "I never planned for you to get involved. Did everything I could to make sure this didn't blow back on you, but I need you to stop chasing this case. If you don't, you'll be the next body in the morgue, and I can't finish this if you keep getting in my way."

She pressed one hand against the industrial carpet in an attempt to sit up, but her body thought better of it. Slumping back to the floor, she tried to latch on to the man above her. To test that he was real. Her hand slipped right through him. Nothing but a ghost. "Morrow."

Where was Professor Morrow? He was in danger... She had to stop the killer from finishing what'd he started. No. That wasn't right. She'd been too late.

"Stop working this case, Leigh." His outline shrank. Getting farther out of reach. "It's the only way you'll get out of this alive."

Wait. Again, she wasn't sure if she'd voiced the words aloud or if they'd gotten stuck in her head. Leigh rolled back onto her side to follow as his bottom half then his distant frame retreated and closed her eyes. It was harder to keep them open this time, and she sank back into unconsciousness.

Durham, New Hampshire

Thursday, October 10
4:16 p.m.

The outline took shape above her. One clarifying breath at a time.

"Shit, Leigh. I was getting worried." Ford's features solidified the longer she stared at him, but her neurons still felt fuzzy. Concern etched at the corners of his eyes. "Take it easy. I couldn't find any evidence of head trauma, but people don't usually pass out at random."

"What... happened." Her mouth dried on the words. She could taste the acid in her throat, feel it clogging her airway. The headache behind her eyes wasn't as intense as before. *You might have a headache for a couple hours.* A mere whisper of voice lodged at the front of her mind.

Setting one hand on the hollow of her back, Ford took her hand and brought Leigh to her feet. His grip clamped down on her arm. "I went to get you some water, but when I got back, I found you unconscious in here. You must've collapsed."

"Morrow." The name was stale on her tongue. Her body didn't feel like her own. More like something that'd been possessed. Too disconnected and otherworldly. Guess that fit in with the Halloween themes plastered all over this classroom. "He's dead."

Leigh reached for a table to get her feet under her. As much as she appreciated Ford's assistance, she couldn't work this case glued to his side. That just wasn't professional. *I need you to stop chasing this case.* There was that voice again. Hell. Why couldn't she get it out of her head? Had to have been a bad dream. Something her unconscious mind created to appease the internal drive to solve this case.

"Same MO as Dietz and Hopkins. Teshia Elborne's, too." Ford ensured she wouldn't fall flat on her ass, retracting his hold on her. Though he kept close. "Whatever the killer had wanted from the professor, he obviously got it."

"Except the unsub didn't become Pierce Morrow." She was sure of it, but the only confirmation they would get was through DNA, dental, or fingerprints. Those were the things that couldn't be replicated by an imposter. "He's deviated from his pattern again."

"First with Alice, now with Morrow." Ford backed up until his thighs hit the desk behind him, and suddenly he looked as beat as she did. The circles under his eyes were more pronounced now, his skin paler than a few hours ago. Then again, living off stolen candy bars from the vending machine wasn't doing either of them any favors. While she'd gotten to take two naps—against her will or not—he'd been awake for more than twenty-four hours at this point. He wasn't going to make it much longer without making mistakes. "Why now?"

"We've been running off the theory the killer chooses his victims and becomes them to fulfill different needs he can't fill himself. I think the unsub sought out Morrow as a mentor." The world wasn't swaying anymore. Little by little she regained control of her limbs. *Temporary. No permanent damage.* Leigh scrubbed at her face. Pieces of the dream twisted into place. Shards as broken as the fluorescent light tube that'd shattered while she'd been wrapped around Ford. None of them fit together as a whole. Except it didn't feel like a dream. More like... a memory. "Morrow has been living a lie for so long, it was bound to catch up to him. And it did. Just not in the way we thought."

Leigh shoved that part of her that would mourn Pierce Morrow's death deep down where she could ignore it for the next decade. "He wouldn't tell me who'd approached him. Honestly, he seemed... scared. It's possible the professor could identify whoever is carrying out these murders and was too ashamed to admit he hadn't caught the red flags before now."

"Another student?" Ford asked.

"No. Our killer has been traveling across the country over the past year. Not attending classes." A student didn't fit into their makeshift profile. They were looking for someone with an interest and knowledge in forensics. Someone practiced, potentially spanning decades. "As much as this unsub targets victims to fulfill certain needs, Morrow liked to collect professionals in his extensive network."

"I talked with both forensic techs after you collapsed. They claim neither of them has been out of the other's sight since the shelter in place order went into effect." Ford pressed away from the table, unsteady. The change in his stance didn't fit the marshal she'd come to know, the one who'd held her against that wall with his strength alone. It didn't feel right to see him this vulnerable. "But if Morrow took on a mentee, there has to be record of our killer in the professor's office or on his phone. Emails, video, and phone calls."

"I can search Morrow's office. As one of his former research assistants, I'll know what to look for." She closed the distance between them, testing her own balance, and stared up at him. Grabbing for the lapels of his suit jacket, Leigh forced his attention to her. "When was the last time you slept?"

"A while." He pinched the bridge of his nose as though to chase back a headache. Reminding her of the one pulsing behind her eyes. His expression shadowed with the overhead lighting positioned at his back, and she tried to fit Ford's features into that dark outline still vying for her attention from the dream. "I didn't want to let my guard down or give this asshole an opening to come after you or any of those people in the lobby."

I didn't know of another way to get you alone.

Her brain worked to match the cadence and tone of the voice in her head to the man in front of her. Ford had her alone now. Why would he have needed to incapacitate her to buy them a few minutes together? The answer was already there. Waiting for her to come around. He wouldn't have. Someone else had.

Someone had drugged her.

She'd been in this room with them. Talked to them. Leigh's grip loosened, and she took a clear step back. Had she come face to face with the killer and not even realized it? Air stalled in her chest.

"Leigh?" For the first time, panic tainted the marshal's use of her name. His hands slid along her arms. "You just went white. Are you about to pass out again?"

"I'm fine." No. No, she was not. He'd been right there. Within reach, and she'd done nothing to stop him. Leigh moved for the door. "I... You should get some rest while you can. I'll interview the forensic techs again and check out Morrow's office."

"You sure you're okay?" Ford asked.

"Yes." Another lie. Seemed they were starting to pile up, but how the hell was she supposed to explain to Ford that she may or may not have been in the same room as the killer and let him get away? The shame she'd hidden behind alibiing Dean Groves eighteen years previously stabbed through her as hot as the bullet she'd taken seven months ago. "Get some rest."

Leigh shoved into the corridor, attempting to get her bearings. She'd been brought to a classroom at the opposite end of where they'd detained Professor Morrow. She wasn't sure, but she could almost see Ford wanting to keep her as far from the bustle of the lobby and the room where Morrow's body would have to wait for the ME. That made three now. And no answers as to who had killed them.

The unsub had managed to get to Morrow with no intention of letting him live. But Ford had a point. How was the killer managing to poison these victims when they'd already submitted the arsenic and cyanide from the biomedical lab into evidence?

Unless they'd never lost access.

Interview the forensic techs. Search Morrow's office. Her goal was simple, but she found herself navigating back into the lobby in search of Ava. She'd made a mistake in bringing her adopted daughter here—she'd put her in danger—but letting Ava face this storm alone in a hotel room hadn't sat right either. This was what they had to work with, and Leigh wasn't sure it would ever be good enough. If she would ever be good enough.

Approaching Ava's circle of friends, she pulled up short. "Where's Ava?"

Five sets of eyes landed on her but only one student answered. "She went to the bathroom about twenty minutes ago. I was about to go check on her."

"Thanks. I'll do it." There was only one set of bathrooms on this floor. Broken glass crunched under her shoes as Leigh cut down the corridor. She'd have to have someone in maintenance come clean up the remnants of the fluorescent light before someone cut themselves. Pushing inside, she picked up the sound of one of the showers running. Steam slid underneath her clothing as she approached. "Ava, everything all right?"

No answer.

A pooling sense of dread puddled at the base of her spine as she approached the shower door. Locked from the inside. Leigh tried to get a look through the too-narrow crack. She knocked. "Ava, open the door."

The dread festered into something feral and panicked. Water crept beneath the foot-high space between the bottom of the thick metal and white tile. It was the only way in. "I'm coming in."

Leigh didn't wait for an answer, getting down on her hands and belly, and pulled herself through the opening. Her clothing soaked up burning hot water, but she didn't care as she took in the sight of her adopted daughter huddled in the corner of the stall. "Ava."

Brown eyes cut to her. Glassy and empty at the same time. "I killed him."

TWENTY-EIGHT

Durham, New Hampshire

Thursday, October 10
5:00 p.m.

She'd never meant for any of this.

Putting Ava in the middle of a homicide investigation. Letting her career take the lead in this new life they were supposed to be building together. Breaking her promise to try harder.

"Are you hurt?" Leigh shoved to stand in the too-small shower stall and turned off the spray. Her sweats were instantly heavy as they soaked up water, pulling at every tired and sore muscle in her body.

The fifteen-year-old shook her head, knees drawn to her chest. She looked so much smaller in this moment. Afraid and alone.

Leigh's heart threatened to break apart right there in her chest. She took another step forward, careful, hesitant, as though Ava might run at the first sign of being spooked. A cornered animal ready to strike out to protect itself. No matter the damage left behind.

"Talk to me, Ava. Tell me what's going on."

Those caramel-colored eyes raised to meet Leigh's gaze. "It was supposed to be me."

"What do you mean?" Sitting in front of Ava, she blocked out the rest of the world. It was just the two of them here, and nothing else mattered. The fight between her career—this case —and showing up as Ava's guardian burned. But Leigh was beginning to see there was no middle ground. There was no choice. Not for her.

"Mom is in prison for killing the man who took me." Ava's voice softened. Trembled with something caged and guilty. "But it's supposed to be me. I'm the one who killed him. I was there. He'd locked her in the storage room under his house. She'd gone there to protect me. To make sure he never touched me again. But he was going to kill her, and I couldn't let him. So I killed him first."

Leigh crossed her legs together. Kept herself from reaching out, from disrupting this sudden open line of communication. Not communication. Admission. Ava had admitted to killing the man who'd abducted and raped her. A murder her mother was serving a life sentence behind bars for. Tears burned in her eyes as the impact of that truth took shape between them.

"This is what you wanted to tell me earlier. Why you've been running away. Why you shut me out? You've been dealing with this alone?"

"I didn't know what else to do." A fresh round of sobs echoed off the cooling tile around them. Ava swiped at her face, but it didn't erase the hollowness that'd deepened over the past few weeks. "You're a cop. I was scared if I said anything, they'd take me away again. You're not my mom, but you're still the only person who gives a shit what happens to me."

Leigh couldn't keep the distance between them anymore.

Not caring about her borrowed sweats, she scooted closer until her knees framed Ava's.

"Look at me." She set both hands on her adopted daughter's face. This was the moment. The one that would make or break them, and Leigh couldn't lose anyone else. She couldn't give up on the family she'd worked so hard to find. Waiting until those brown eyes met hers, she held on to the hope that they would make it through to the other side. Together. "I already knew."

Confusion warped Ava's beautiful face. She pulled out of Leigh's hold, trying to melt into the wall behind her. But there was no escaping this. For either of them. They were bound in a way Leigh hadn't let herself be bound to another person in a long time. Unfiltered trust, and she wasn't letting Ava go so easily. "What? How?"

"Your cell phone GPS. Gulf Shores police narrowed down the signals in the vicinity of the murder. There was your mother's, the burner your abductor used to lure you to his house. And then there was yours."

"You knew? You knew, and you didn't say anything?" How quickly sorrow had been replaced with rage. They couldn't ignore it or soothe it. There was no escape or avoidance from this now. Ava would have to live with what she'd done, but she didn't have to do it alone. The veins in Ava's neck pulsed with her erratic heart rate. She released her hold on her knees. Ready to strike. "My mom is in prison. If you knew she didn't kill him, why didn't you tell the judge? We could be together right now!"

"Because she wouldn't let me, Ava. If I had told that courtroom you'd been there, that you were the one to kill him, you would be the one behind bars right now. He might've abducted and raped you, but the evidence at that scene told a clear story. It wasn't self-defense. It was murder. You would've been arrested, and your mother couldn't handle that. She was willing to sacrifice herself to keep you safe." Leigh fortified her voice. Tried not to feed the hurt she'd carried all these years. There'd been nobody there for her when her father had been sentenced for the murder of her brother. No one to fight for her. She'd had to fight for herself for so long, she wasn't even sure she remembered what it was like to have someone else consider her needs, but she wouldn't put Ava through that. "She wanted to protect you from this. She didn't want you to have to handle the fallout of what happened alone, and she knew I was the best chance of helping you deal with whatever came next. And I agreed. She loved you. That's why. That's what parents do, and I'm so sorry."

The fight left Ava then, but it took a few moments for her to pull herself together. The tears returned in full force, a renewed sense of hopelessness resonating in her voice. "What do you have to be sorry for?"

"Because you didn't feel like you could trust me." The pain leaking from Ava became Leigh's then. Fully, without remorse or regret. She took it and made it hers as she'd wished someone would've done for her all those years ago as a teen. Shared it, soothed it, broken it apart until there were only tiny pieces left to carry. "I'm sorry that you thought you had to deal with this on your own. And I'm sorry I didn't make it clear you could come to me when you needed me and that I used my work to drive a wedge between us."

Ava launched herself forward, securing her arms around Leigh's neck. Wracking sobs tremored through her chest and straight into Leigh's heart. Resentment, rage, drive, grief—she'd held on to it all for so long, used it to get her from one case to the next. But none of it had really served her. Not until now. She wouldn't utilize her experiences and pain as a weapon to keep everyone out any longer. It was worth far more. For Ava.

"I lied on my application to the FBI." Her commitment to this precious soul poured into her admission. Leigh smoothed Ava's hair down her back. "They asked me if I'd been involved in any criminal investigations, and I lied. I was the one who found that body underneath my house when I was seventeen, but my father insisted on leaving me out of the report. He told police it'd been him. And eighteen years ago, when a student was killed on this campus, I gave their only suspect a false alibi. I lied then, too."

Apparently, she'd reached capacity for holding her secrets in. First with Ford. Now Ava. But this was important. Uttered promises meant nothing. So she would show Ava how far she was willing to go. "If the FBI ever found out, I'd lose my job. I'd be charged with obstruction. They could arrest me."

Ava's grip relaxed, but she held on. "Why are you telling me this?"

"So you know I'm here. No matter what." She shifted Ava back to look at her face, swiping tendrils of hair behind her adopted daughter's ears. "We're in this together now. I have your secrets, and you have mine. To be fair, yours is a lot bigger than mine, but you get the point."

A wisp of a laugh escaped Ava's lips. Her eyes had swollen from crying, but there was a strength in their depths, too. "I get the point. Just don't be expecting me to call you Mom or anything. You can turn me in for murder, and I can tell your boss you lied, but we're still mortal enemies."

Leigh took a chance, catching a tear from Ava's face. This was the most honest they'd been with each other. It was uncomfortable and new, but there was also a sense of relief. Of shared hurt neither of them had to shoulder alone anymore. "Wouldn't have it any other way."

Ava's gaze shifted to the stall door. "So now what?"

"Now we raid these lockers and hope we can find some dry clothes. Then we go back out into that lobby." Leigh needed to check in with the forensic techs and take a look at Professor Morrow's office. If he'd taken on a collaborator, there could be evidence that led them straight to their killer. "I need you to stay close to the friends you made. I don't think you will be a target, but it's not safe for anyone to be alone while Marshal Ford and I work this case. Understand?"

"I understand." Ava got to her feet, sopping wet. "I'm sorry. For running away all those times. For distracting you from this case. I know you're trying to keep more people from dying."

"You don't ever need to be sorry for asking for your needs to be met, Ava. Not from me." Leigh fought the added weight of her clothing and unlocked the stall door. Hitting up the first locker, she tossed something that looked like oversized basketball shorts and a T-shirt in Ava's direction. Probably wasn't the cleanest, but it would keep her from catching a cold in this damn storm. "And I hope you'll keep coming to me long after this case is concluded."

Ava dressed quickly, sans socks. "Are you close to solving this case?"

She heard the question her adopted daughter wasn't asking. When could they go home?

"Yes. We're close." The killer was tying up loose ends as the end of the storm approached. Getting ready to flee. But she wasn't going to let that happen. Leigh pulled a second set of sweats from another locker and found a T-shirt perma-caked with deodorant in the armpits. Could be worse. "There are things I can't talk to you about when it comes to my work and my life before you, but I will always be honest with you if you'll try to be honest with me. That means no more running away in the middle of the night. And it means talking to me when you're upset. All right?"

Ava kept her chin high. "All right."

"And we'll be seeing a family therapist together when we get back to Quantico. I know you like yours, but we have to be in this together." Leigh pried off her wet sweats, changing into a set one size too big and a T-shirt one size too small. Tossing the soaked clothes in the nearest trash, she met Ava at the exit.

"One hundred percent, Ava. We need to be a team if this is going to work between us."

Nodding, Ava no longer looked as though she'd rather be in any other room than the one Leigh stood in. "Can I visit my mom?"

"That's up to her," she said. "But, if she approves, yeah. Anytime we can arrange it."

Mere minutes had passed since she'd sought Ava out, but the entire world had shifted in that time. And a little bit more of Leigh's damaged heart had pieced itself back together.

TWENTY-NINE

Durham, New Hampshire

Tuesday, September 12, 2006
9:11 a.m.

She hated police stations.

A nauseating film clung to her every time she had to be here. Durham PD's station wasn't much different from the one she'd spent countless hours in back home. It wasn't the buildings themselves. It was the empty promises. The values every officer was supposed to live by yet failed to uphold when it came to getting justice for the people they claimed to serve. It was the massive hole in her heart she couldn't get rid of no matter how many times she told herself this time was different.

It wasn't different.

It'd been two days since Durham police had arrested Dean. His parents had passed away in his freshman year. He had no siblings or family to rely on or to get him a defense attorney. She was all he had left, and she wasn't going to leave him to fight this alone. But the investigating detective in charge had refused to give her any information over the phone despite her connection to Professor Morrow. He hadn't been any help either. *Be patient, he'd told her. The criminal justice system takes time.*

Well, Dean didn't have time. Because at a certain point, every officer in this station and every citizen in this town would start believing the lies departments like this spewed to reach their arrest quotas. She'd seen it before. Witnessed the corruption and sickness that took hold when authority and assumed power was left unchecked. People like her father had paid the price for that power. Especially with a case of this magnitude. Small town, big murder. The accusations had already started spreading. Dean was on the verge of losing everything. His scholarship to attend UNH, the research opportunities in the biomedical lab, the job offers, his friends and professors.

But she could stop it.

She hadn't been able to save her father. She could save Dean.

Leigh approached the front desk sergeant, a bleached-blonde woman who could only peck at her keyboard with the inch-long neon nails. "Excuse me. I need to speak with the investigating detective in charge of Teshia Elborne's case."

"Those are some big words for a pretty little thing like you. You watch that Dateline show?" A snap of gum scorched along Leigh's nerves as the officer gave her barely more than a quick assessment at her lack of an answer. Passing her a clipboard, the desk sergeant nodded toward the chairs lined up against the wall. "Sign in and take a seat. The detective is in the middle of an interview. He'll be with you when he gets a minute."

Sign in. Leigh clutched the pen. Frozen. Her name hadn't done her any favors back home. In fact, it'd made things much, much worse. She scribbled something unintelligible in the box next to today's date. In the end, her name wouldn't matter. It was what she had to say.

Stepping back, she took the nearest chair. And waited. Ten minutes. Twenty. Thirty. She'd miss her psychology class if she *didn't leave soon. This was more important. This was a man's life. She counted off her heartbeats, just as she had in a lobby almost identical to this one to pass the time waiting for police to realize they had the wrong man.*

After forty minutes, the investigating detective shoved through the door in his wrinkled brown suit with the smell of cigarette smoke clinging to his skin and breath. His button-down stretched too tight across his midsection. Not a man who saw field work often. He was most likely betting this case would be the one to see him through to retirement. "You here about the Elborne case?"

"Yes." *Leigh sucked in a breath, but her confidence had leaked with every minute she'd had to sit in that damn uncomfortable chair. Getting to her feet, she steadied her voice.* "I came here for information on Dean Groves. Officers arrested him two days ago, and no one will tell me when he's being released."

The detective's jaw tightened. That was it. The only reaction he was going to give her. "Now why in the name of all that is holy would we release the man suspected of killing Ms. Elborne?"

"Dean Groves didn't kill anyone." *She kept her head held high. She could do this. For Dean. She'd lied to police once. What difference would another make if it saved the man she loved?* "And I can prove it."

Durham, New Hampshire

Thursday, October 10
5:23 p.m.

Leigh stood over the body.

Pale. Bloated. And very dead.

Almost exactly how she felt. She should drag the remains into the classroom where Ford was sleeping. Would serve him right for putting it in her line of sight when she'd come around after surviving that hellscape in the basement. But she didn't want to cause any more damage she wouldn't be able to explain to the ME or disrespect the victim. "Who are you?"

The swelling in the victim's face hid any recognizable features. Lips four times the size of normal, a too-wide nose that didn't fit in the man's face. Even the ears were out of proportion. The man's hair was dark with signs of silver. Natural, from what she could see. Clean shaven. Took good care of his nails. No wedding ring. None of the staff knew who this man was and what he'd been doing in the tunnels beneath Thompson Hall. There wasn't much for her to decipher any patterns, habits, or clues as to who this man had been. Or even when he'd died.

Leigh was careful prying his eyelids open, looking for that telltale irritation.

The classroom door protested on its hinges as Ford entered.

"I see you finally got your beauty sleep." She sat back on her haunches, hands still connected to the corpse. The medical examiner was going to have a hell of a time determining time of death with the changes in environment and temperature. It wasn't a conversation she was looking forward to.

"You think I'm beautiful?" The marshal's crooked smile triggered a chill up her spine as he crossed the classroom to her position. Not a single wrinkle in his damn suit.

Hell, she couldn't even keep one set of clothing dry, and he looked like he'd stepped out of the office. "Can't say you're hard to look at. This guy, on the other hand, has seen better days."

"We figure out who he is?" Crouching, Ford met her eye line.

"No. Not yet." She settled the victim's eyelids back into place. "But I can tell you he wasn't poisoned, which confirms my theory our unsub wasn't planning on killing him. It was an impulse decision, but he's been stripped of any identifiers, including his ID. It's possible his is one of the six driver's licenses forensics is working on restoring, but I found something much more interesting."

Ford's attention shifted from the body to her, and the entire world closed in around her. Just as it had when he'd hauled her against him in the hallway. "Oh?"

Her breath shuddered out of her at the memory. So much had happened in the past two days—almost dying, for one—but in those short minutes, Ford had brought something in her alive. Leigh pointed to the remains' white button-down shirt. "Yeah. His clothes are too big."

"His clothes?" He scanned their unidentified victim from head to toe, and she was reminded that studying dead bodies wasn't actually part of his line of work. He was a hunter.

"Gas builds up the longer a body is left to decompose. Primarily in the torso. That's why he floated to the ceiling when I let him out of the closet." Leigh pointed to the line of buttons bisecting the remains. "The bacteria in his intestines start releasing gas at time of death and it stretches the skin like air in a balloon. If you push down on his stomach, you can feel the gas is there, but the buttons on his shirt aren't straining against his torso. Same goes for his pants. There are wear marks on the third hole in, but his belt is buckled on the fifth. So either he's recently lost around fifty pounds without updating his wardrobe, or the killer stripped and dressed him."

His mouth parted. "You got all of that just from looking at him?"

"What can I say? I'm perceptive." A bolt of grief shot through her. "Professor Morrow used to have me assess random photos of death scenes and bodies as his research assistant. I'd find them in my backpack, in my email, or sometimes waiting for me in a file slipped under the door of my dorm. One time he built a diorama with handmade dolls and used corn syrup for blood. He wanted to know how the victim died and who was the most likely suspect given as little information as possible. It was probably one of the most effective pieces of my training. Now I can walk onto a scene and tell you everything that's wrong with it."

"I'm sorry." Ford kept his gaze on the body, obviously out of his element in the "offering condolences" department. "He obviously meant a great deal to you."

She hadn't considered how much until now. "Yeah. Well, he wasn't exactly who I thought he was in the end."

"Are any of us?" Ford said.

His statement wedged into her mind as she turned the remains to one side. She let her grip slip. The body rolled back into place. "What if that's true?"

The marshal examined the remains. "What? That none of us are who people think we are?"

Leigh gave herself permission to verbally piece the theory together, even if Ford couldn't see inside her brain. "Serial offenders typically have one goal. They like to exert control over others, but our unsub has two. He has two sets of victims. The five—potentially six if the driver's licenses can tell us more—males whose identities he absorbed or used to fill a need, including Professor Morrow, and the three females all killed on this campus. What if he's trying to become someone else with his male victims, and he's trying to bring our attention back to Teshia Elborne with his female victims?"

"What? Like a split personality?" Ford braced one forearm against his leg.

"No." She reached for the pieces to shape the puzzle in her head. "We were right before. I think whoever is killing these women now murdered Teshia Elborne eighteen years ago. There's no other way he'd know to use chloroform to knock out his victims before poisoning them with the syringe. That detail was left out of the reports, and only the medical examiner and investigating detective learned of it after the autopsy had been completed. But I think he regrets killing her."

A foreign expression contorted Ford's features. "Guy's got a weird way of showing regret by killing two more women on campus."

"That's where the identity theft comes in." The more thought she put into the theory, the more solid it became. Real. "He's doing everything in his power to become someone else. He's running away from who he was. Teshia Elborne's death broke something in him, and he'll do whatever it takes to convince himself he didn't hurt her."

"Then he knew her," Ford said. "He had to be at this school eighteen years ago. You and I both know Durham PD only had one suspect then, Leigh."

"But Dean Groves wasn't the victim's only point of conflict at that time in her life." Her heart jerked at the mention of Dean's name, and she feared she was right back in that police station, going to bat for a man she believed innocent. "We're looking for someone familiar with policing and forensics, someone who knew the area well enough to get on and off campus without raising suspicion. The forensic techs have airtight alibis for each other and the campus police officers we thought could be involved are both new to the area."

The marshal's brows met at the bridge of his nose. "So who do you have in mind?"

"The one person who knew Teshia Elborne better than anyone else," Leigh said. "The boyfriend from high school."

THIRTY

Durham, New Hampshire

Thursday, October 10
5:47 p.m.

They had a nothing but a single mention in the investigating detective's notes from eighteen years ago.

"This is some shitty police work." Ford flipped through individual papers stuffed into Teshia Elborne's case file. Witness statements, background information on the victim, incident report, canvassing reports from the dorms—none of it had done them a damn bit of good in the time they'd sequestered themselves in the too-small study room at the back of the building. Away from the chaos of aggravated students, admin, and piling bodies. "All it says is they interviewed and dismissed the victim's high school boyfriend as a suspect in her death. No name. No contact information. Bastard didn't even include the actual interview in the file."

"There's nothing here either." Leigh closed the ME's autopsy report on Teshia Elborne's remains. They were getting nowhere. The little progress they'd made turned up one obstacle after the other. And now her focus was lodged on the fact she hadn't eaten anything but two candy bars in the past twenty-four hours. Hanger was very real. "The medical examiner never found any hint of sexual assault or intercourse. There were no fluids left on the body to analyze or ID the killer, and if there had been, he ensured they were destroyed when he washed and bleached her from head to toe."

Ford scrubbed a hand down his face and closed his own file. "All right. So how do we find a metaphorical name in a haystack if it's not in the original investigation files?"

"The investigating detective who conducted the interview passed away last year. So that's a dead end." She tossed the autopsy report onto the table between them, careful not to let her attention linger on the unidentified body covered in Ford's windbreaker a few feet away. "The high school boyfriend obviously had access to the victim, not solely at school but in her personal life. They'd been on again and off again for years according to Dean Groves's statement, so she trusted him at some level. Allowed him to come visit her on campus. Are her phone records in that file?"

"Yeah." Ford handed the stack of papers off. "If he regretted her death, why make such a spectacle out of disposing the body? She was left in front of Thompson Hall, same as Alice Dietz. Seems kind of callous to me."

It was a good question. If the killer had cared for Teshia Elborne as she believed, one would assume there would've been some kind of covering to keep her protected from the elements. "You're right. He didn't hide her out of shame or try to bury her remains. He'd wanted to make a statement. They'd been together since high school. Something must've made him snap when he killed her. It's possible he was still angry enough afterward not to give her body much consideration."

"Too bad we can't get a hold of Teshia Elborne's high school yearbook. That would make this a whole lot easier. Damn storm." The marshal leaned back in his chair. "This place is starting to feel like a prison."

"You been in a lot of prisons?" They'd been shoved together for the past forty-plus hours, but in all actuality, Leigh didn't know a thing about the man across from her. Other than he certainly knew how to perform under pressure in the kissing department.

He regarded her for a moment. Like he was trying to figure out a puzzle. "A few. You?"

"I'm usually the one to send them there, but no. I've only been inside a prison once." She scanned through Teshia Elborne's phone records from eighteen years ago. None of the numbers lined up in neat little columns made any sense to her, but she was able to identify one number that called the victim multiple times a day. All incoming. There was no indication Teshia Elborne had ever been the one to initiate. The high school boyfriend's? She circled the number and made a note to look up the area code once power and internet were restored. It wasn't much, but it could get them one step closer to identifying the victim's ex. "I visited my father a few days before his sentence was overturned. Can't say I'm a fan. Though I'd even go for prison food at this point."

"Gruel. My favorite." He shifted his elbows to the table, meeting her gaze head on. "I'll keep your lack of expectations in mind for our date."

She couldn't fight the laugh charging through her chest. In an investigation of dead ends, multiple bodies, and emotional havoc, Ford had somehow managed to keep her on course. A light at the end of a suffocating tunnel. The overpowering odor of caked deodorant drove into her nostrils. The shirt she'd borrowed from the locker room wasn't holding up as well as she'd hoped. "Not sure you're going to want to get anywhere near me when this is finished. Between whatever was in that basement water, the sludge from the mason jars, and my own personal brand of disgustingness, I'm smelling ripe."

It was his turn to laugh. Deep and full and warm. The effect chased back the aches in her bones and around her neck. She didn't want to think about what she looked like from his vantage point. This case had not been kind physically, mentally, or emotionally, but the way Ford settled those dark eyes on her robbed her of some of that self-consciousness. "Considering my last date ended up with me in a hospital emergency room with a stab wound, you don't have anything to worry about."

"Your date stabbed you?" Leigh almost choked on the minuscule amount of saliva in her mouth.

"To be fair, he was a fugitive I'd been assigned to apprehend here in New Hampshire." Ford raised his hands in surrender. "We shared a bag of chips in the front seat of my car. I thought we had something special, but I realize now he was using me."

"Wow." How was it possible he'd gotten under her skin so quickly? How had he mesmerized her with sarcasm and jokes and concern when she wasn't even sure she still had a func-tioning heart? Leigh turned her attention back to the autopsy report, but there wasn't anything in there that would give her an answer. "Tell me something real."

"Real?" he asked.

"Yeah. Something that would come up on a real date and not in an investigation." Because this wasn't reality. This was a multiple homicide investigation that only ended with one result: them going back to their respective agencies and cities when it was over. The banter and laughs wouldn't be enough outside these walls, and they both knew it.

"All right." Ford sat forward in his seat. "I have a cat waiting for me at home. His name is Edgar Allan Paw."

Why did that not surprise her? Leigh's smile hiked higher. "You're not serious. What color is he?"

"Black, of course." He made a sweeping motion with one

hand. "The damn thing wandered into my apartment when I was moving in and refused to leave. My mistake was feeding it. I realized that three years too late. But I mostly work alone, so it's nice to have someone waiting for me to come home."

That space she rarely acknowledged in her chest pulsed. Loneliness had become a close friend over the years, one she hadn't been able to shake. Even after Ava had come into her life. But things were looking up.

"Your turn," he said. "Tell me something real."

"I take it you haven't gone through my life history currently sitting with the forensic techs." The killer—whoever he was— had done a good job in collating her life in bits and pieces. Too good of a job. Leigh slipped her hand into her sweats pocket and removed the sliver of newspaper she'd taken from the board before flood waters destroyed it. The edges were curling from the dampness of her clothing, and the print had smeared in places between all the changes of clothes. There was no grainy photograph. Only simple text that shouldn't have been connected back to her in any way, bleeding across the page. The unsub had somehow made the connection. "My brother was abducted twenty years ago. I didn't have any proof, but I knew who was responsible. He managed to stay off law enforcement's radar all that time. Like he'd one day decided he wasn't going to be a murdering piece of shit. I knew better. People like him... They don't change. They just get better at hiding their crimes."

She slid the newspaper across the table. "After solving my brother's case, I made a promise to find all the other kids the son of a bitch hurt. Starting with the one I found underneath my childhood home."

Ford stared at the headline of the thin article. "I don't understand. According to the media coverage, your brother's body was found underneath your house."

"My brother survived. I made sure of it." The admission shook her straight to her core. She'd never told another soul. But

Ford had earned her trust faster and more deeply than any other partner she'd taken on. "His abductor used another set of remains to keep police distracted from the truth. I've been working to identify those remains, but it seems our unsub, in his quest to get to know me better, already figured that out."

"Holy shit." Ford scanned through the newspaper article. "How?"

"I don't know. I've never made my intentions concerning that case public. Apart from you, there are two people in the world who know what I've been working on, and neither my director nor the other members of my team would say a word." While she'd been studying the behaviors and patterns of serial offenders these past few years, it turned out one had been studying her just as thoroughly. The realization cut her thoughts to Ava. What lengths would a killer go to, to get to Leigh? She nodded toward the newspaper clipping. "That article details the disappearance of a twelve-year-old homeless boy who lived on the outskirts of my hometown around the same time my brother was taken. It's possible he's the one I've been looking for these past few months."

Ford leaned away from the table, as though the article would burn him if he held on to it too long. "Well, I think it's safe to say you win the 'tell me something real' game."

"Nobody can know, Max." She hadn't meant the words to sound so... desperate. But that was what she was. Had she made a mistake in trusting him? She didn't think so, but she'd tasted betrayal in so many ways. "If the authorities learned my brother is still alive, if they found out who he is—"

"Hey." He reached for her then, set his hand over hers with a slight squeeze. It was a sliver of contact compared to the full-on make-out session they'd conducted in the corridor but just as impactful on her body temperature. "Nobody will find out from me. I give you my word."

"Thank you." The chill still clinging to her skin after what

THE KILLER SHE KNEW 237

happened down in that basement eased. Her body couldn't get enough. Of his touch, his mouth. Of him. She'd felt like this once, and it'd blown up in her face. But cutting herself off from a connection she craved wasn't sustainable either.

The door swung inward over Ford's shoulder.

An outline took shape in the frame, all too familiar.

Ford twisted around at the clear panic in her face. Too late. The butt of a gun slammed into the side of the marshal's head, and he hit the floor.

Leigh shoved to her feet and unholstered her weapon. Her heart threatened to beat straight out of her chest as the past collided with the present. Same color hair. Same angled jawline. Same dark eyes.

"You." She took aim at Dean Groves.

"Hi, Leigh." He smiled at her, weapon still in hand. "I think it's time for you and me to have a talk."

THIRTY-ONE

Durham, New Hampshire

Thursday, October 10
6:15 p.m.

"Well, this is awkward." Dean Groves raised his hands in surrender. Standing there as if he hadn't just knocked a United States marshal unconscious, potentially killed eight people, and become the country's number one fugitive. "I kinda hoped you would be excited to see me after all these years."

"Awkward." Leigh motioned at him with the barrel of her weapon to move back. Away from Ford. She rounded the table at one end and crouched beside the marshal without taking her attention off Dean. Testing his pulse, she let relief hit her only for a second before straightening. "That's one way to put it."

"He's fine." Dean toed the sole of Ford's shoe. "But he might have a headache when he wakes up."

"Forgive me if I'm not in the mood to believe anything you have to say at the moment." *You might have a headache for a couple hours.* Son of a bitch. He'd been the one to drug her. "Gun on the floor. Kick it to me. Slowly."

Dean did as she instructed, assessing her from head to toe. Then straightened. He'd added a few more layers of muscle over the years, let his beard grow in thicker. Otherwise, he hadn't changed much. Well, except he'd turned into a cold-blooded killer, but she wasn't going to nitpick. "You look good, little rabbit. I knew you'd make one hell of a criminologist."

That nickname. She'd once craved to hear it. To feel... beloved. Now it grated on her every last nerve. She used the side of her borrowed tennis shoe to drag his weapon out of reach. One wrong move and she'd pull the trigger. Whatever connection he thought they had vanished the moment he'd fled murder charges. "I should be thanking you. Your disappearance after the Teshia Elborne case really motivated me to hone my skillset."

"Aw, you've been thinking about me." Dean cocked his head to one side, the same way he had back in that pathetic dorm room she'd once considered the safest place in the world. "I've been thinking about you, too."

"Is that what this is all about? Why you killed Alice Dietz and Tamra Hopkins?" She widened her stance. Ready for anything. "Some sick strategy to get my attention. Because congratulations. You've succeeded."

The humor drained from his expression, leaving nothing more than the hardened fugitive underneath. The one who wouldn't hesitate to discard her to get what he wanted. He'd done it before. There was nothing stopping him from doing it again. Dean had positioned himself between her and the only exit from the room. And if that didn't tell her everything she needed to know in this moment, nothing could. "I didn't kill them, Leigh. Didn't kill Teshia Elborne, either. You know that."

"That's funny." Her mouth had gone dry, but she wouldn't give him the satisfaction of knowing her entire nervous system had caught fire. "I seem to recall the only reason you were released from police custody all those years ago was because I gave that detective a false alibi."

"I never asked you to do that." His voice lowered to a whisper. "I didn't want you involved in any of this."

"Right." She nodded toward the newspaper article still sitting on the surface of the table. "The serial killer collection of notes, photos, and media coverage of me and my career downstairs in the basement made that real clear."

He kept his gaze on her. As though they were the only two people in the entire world and there wasn't an unconscious US marshal at their feet. "I never meant to hurt you. Even now, I'm doing everything I can to make sure you get out of this alive. To keep my promise to take care of you."

"The strangulation bruises around my neck tell a different story." Leigh held her weapon solid with one hand and reached for her cuffs with the other. Except they were currently occupied by a dead professor in the next room over. Damn it. "Oh, and let's not forget the poison used to kill all three women and Morrow was sourced from the same biomedical lab you used to conduct research in. You still remember your key code, right? Turns out, those codes never expire. Even when you leave the university."

She stepped to her right, trying to corral him into the corner. Cut off his escape route. The sooner they had him in custody, the sooner she and Ava could go home. The sooner she could put the last fractured piece of her past behind them.

"You're wasting time trying to pin these deaths on me, little rabbit." Dean wouldn't budge. He held his ground, daring her to take that step that ended with a bullet in his chest. "The son of a bitch framed me for killing Teshia, and I've been trying to clear my name ever since. Tracking the real killer across the country. I don't have a name or a face. He's too good at moving on to different identities, but I'm getting close, and he knows it. That's why he killed that girl the same way he killed Teshia. Alice, right? He wanted you on this case. He's using you to get to me, and he will not hesitate to kill you."

Her finger slipped from the trigger. No matter how much he tried to goad her into making a move, she wouldn't shoot an unarmed suspect. "Then why hasn't he?"

"You don't think he's tried?" Dean lowered his hands to his sides. Unarmed but all too dangerous. This was a game. Another way to manipulate her. While he hadn't asked her to alibi him all those years ago, he'd known she would try to protect him. The same way she'd tried to protect her father against false allegations. He'd used her trauma and heartache, used her feelings for him, to get away with murder. But she wouldn't give him the opportunity again. "He wants me to suffer. And he knows the way to do that is to hurt you."

Lies. It was all lies. She knew that. So why couldn't she force herself to do what needed to be done? Knock him out, secure him. Build the case against him.

Dean took a step forward then.

She countered, her grip on her weapon tightening. Her throat ached with an awareness she didn't want to give him. She couldn't make sense of any of this. "Don't. Move."

He didn't follow instructions this time. Dean raised one hand toward her, setting it on the end of her weapon. The weight of that touch dragged the barrel down his frame, and she couldn't convince herself to bring it back up. "You know me. You know I would never hurt you."

A thousand questions raced to the tip of her tongue, but she clung to the grip of her weapon with both hands. Willing herself to do something—anything—other than latch on to those words. Because they weren't true. "I don't know a damn thing about you."

"Then why haven't you put me under arrest?" His shoulders dropped, making himself an easy target. Waiting for her to make a choice.

"You've been on the run for eighteen years. Why come back?" She was stalling, and they both knew it. Ford would wake up. She'd have a reason not to make this choice alone. "Why now?"

"You know why," he said. "Your brain is screaming at you not to trust me, but deep down, you know I would never hurt you. You loved me once, Leigh. I know you did, and some part of you still trusts me. Otherwise, you would've already put me in cuffs."

"I'm fresh out at the moment." Probably not a great idea to let that one slip, but it was the truth. An excuse. "Though I'm sure Marshal Ford would be more than happy to lend me a pair."

A growl vibrated through Dean's chest, and a thrill shot through her at the realization she could frustrate him. "That's the kind of guy you go for these days? The kind who lets himself get distracted by a pretty face in the middle of an investigation? He can't protect you, little rabbit. I can."

Protect her? He had to be kidding.

"Stop calling me that. You lost the right to care what kind of guy I go for when you left me in your dorm room in the middle of the night after I alibied you to avoid a murder charge." Logic slammed back into place. Leigh raised her weapon level with his chest. Her arms shook from holding the weight, but she'd make sure he never hurt anyone ever again. Including her. "And I don't need protection. Now get on your knees and lace your hands behind your head."

"Leigh, you need to listen." He dared another step toward her, but she was done playing whatever game he'd recruited her into. Dean pulled up short as she grabbed his wrist and maneuvered him to the floor. He went willingly. "You're making a mistake."

"And I'm supposed to ignore the fact you happen to be here the same time four bodies drop?" Pressing her knee into his back, she held on to his wrists with one hand and holstered her weapon with the other. Leigh lowered her mouth to the shell of his ear. "I've been waiting for this moment, Dean. You manipulated me and my emotions all those years ago. You convinced me you gave a shit about me, but it won't work again." She added more than a few inches between them. Physically. Emotionally. "Dean Groves, you are under arrest for the murder of Alice Dietz, Tamra Hopkins, Pierce Morrow, and maybe an unidentified dead guy I found in the basement. You have the right—"

"I'm sorry, little rabbit. But I'll do whatever it takes to keep you safe." Dean ripped out from underneath her in a full body roll.

Her knee slammed into the floor, hands burning from where his skin rubbed into her palm. Leigh put herself between him and the exit and went for her weapon a second time. The barrel cleared the holster. Just as his foot landed square against her chest.

The doorknob cut into her lower back as she launched backward. Air crushed from her chest. Her lungs spasmed, and she overcorrected. The industrial carpet rushed to meet her face. Boots planted in her vision, and Leigh latched on before he could get away.

She pulled his balance out from under him. Dean's body thudded hard beside her, but he was already getting back to his feet. Shoving upright, Leigh rocketed her left fist at his face. Blocked. Then her right. He blocked that, too, as though he could read her mind each time she made her move.

He targeted her left shoulder. Knowing exactly where to strike.

Blinding pain speared down her arm and up into her neck, seizing on to her spine with an electrifying shock. Her scream ricocheted off the walls. Doubling over, she latched on to her shoulder in an attempt to keep it attached to her body. The barely healed knife wound she'd sustained during her last case throbbed out of control. "For claiming you don't... want to hurt me, you're doing a very bad job."

"To be fair, you're not making this easy." His shoulders heaved. Showing her she'd gotten to him as easily as he'd gotten to her. Good. She'd use that against him.

"Are you flirting with me?" Forcing herself upright, she caught sight of her weapon between them. She could make it. He had the muscle, but it would slow him down as long as her shoulder stayed in place. "Not sure if you realize it, but we broke up when you vanished. I've moved on. Easily, I might add."

Another lie for the ages, but he didn't need to know how hard it'd been to even think about getting into a relationship after he'd abandoned her. Asshole.

"You don't trust me. I get it." Dean shook his head. "But I'm not going to have your death on my hands because you're too stubborn to see the truth."

He went for the gun.

Leigh launched forward. Too late. The gun's grip slipped from her grasp. Putting her on the wrong end of her own weapon. Fear skittered through her veins. One pull of the trigger. That was all it would take to rip her life apart. And she'd given him the power to do it all over again. "If you shoot me, you'll have the entire FBI and the Marshals Service coming for you. No amount of hiding will save you this time."

"You don't have to trust me." Dean's aim remained steady as he maneuvered around her, toward the door. He pried the only exit open. Then tossed her weapon at her feet. "You just have to survive."

In an instant, he was gone.

THIRTY-TWO

Thursday, October 10
6:40 p.m.

Why hadn't he killed her?

Dean Groves had had the chance, but he'd simply walked away. Left her with her weapon and disappeared into darkened corridors as though he'd never slipped from the shadows.

The ache in her chest and shoulder said otherwise. Leigh tried to rub the soreness out, but it was no use. The force of Dean's attack may have set her recovery back by weeks.

Ford wasn't doing any better. He pressed the wet paper towel she'd gotten for him against the wound at the back of his head. Blood seeped into the floral design, but the laceration was shallow. No signs of a concussion or internal damage, but she'd make sure he got checked out as soon as possible. He flinched under the pressure of his own hand. "I can't believe Groves was here."

"I'm not exactly a fan of surprises either, but at least now we know he's involved." Though Leigh didn't understand in what capacity. Bits and pieces of her and Dean's conversation bled into focus then right back out as she tried to recall everything that'd been said in those mere minutes. It was no use. Adrenaline and her own emotional conflict had chopped his claims into broken slivers that didn't fit the box she wanted to put them in. But there was one thing that stood out among the rest. "He claims he's been hunting our unsub across the country, trying to clear his name of Teshia Elborne's murder."

"And you believed him?" Ford brought the paper towel from the back of his head, inspecting the amount of blood. The wound had stopped leaking. Score one for him. Resting his elbows on his knees, the marshal tossed the towel and finally turned those brown eyes on her. "I think Groves will say anything at this point to walk out of this in one piece."

He was right. A killer's number one goal was survival. To stay out of custody. To leave this world on their terms. Dean Groves wouldn't be any different. But she couldn't dislodge the thought that he could've killed her and Ford to ensure he met that goal.

"What else did he say to you?" Ford asked.

I'm doing everything I can to make sure you get out of this alive. Her stomach fluttered as memories ghosted into awareness. An outline leading her to the kill room in the basement. A strong set of hands that'd kept her from drowning. Leigh leaned against the table at her back, careful of the deep bruising from hitting it during the altercation with Dean. She'd cut her attacker with a shard of mason jar. And yet Dean hadn't shown any signs of injury on his hands or forearms. But he'd drugged her. Begged her to let this case go.

"Leigh?" Ford was suddenly standing in front of her. "What else did he say to you?"

She wasn't sure how long she'd been lost in thought. Leigh shook her head like she could make sense of the jumble in her brain. Without success. "Just that he's not responsible for any of the victims' murders."

"That's what they all say. Right up until they get the needle." Ford reached for her, skimming his knuckles along her jaw. The calming effect was instant and penetrating. "I'm going to do another sweep of the building. See if I can't flush him out."

"Sure. I want to check in with Ava." And make sure Dean hadn't cracked her sternum or any ribs. She'd gone over every move, every block since Dean had left her on the floor with her gun at her feet. Dean Groves wasn't just a toxicologist anymore. He'd become a weapon she hadn't been able to fight. "Watch your back."

"You worried about me, Agent Brody?" That crooked smile broke through the haze that'd settled in over the past few minutes.

"I'm worried whoever is behind this isn't finished." Leigh took a few minutes to herself once the marshal took to the corridor. She hadn't lied. She wanted to check in with Ava, but there was something else she needed to confirm. Something she needed to keep to herself for now. Leigh collected the strip of old newspaper from the floor where it'd fallen. The article had somehow managed to survive the scuffle between her and Dean, and she folded it back into her sweatpants pocket for safekeeping.

This case wasn't about making a statement.

It was closing in. On her.

She sealed the room behind her, heading back into the lobby. Ava was there. Safe. Unfazed and ignorant of the confrontation Leigh had faced. Her adopted daughter waved from her tight circle of friends, but that wasn't what held Leigh's attention.

A hooded figure was stomping through the lobby doors.

Coming inside.

Leigh shoved through the mass of students and staff to head

them off. Then pulled up short. A woman threw back her windbreaker stamped with OFFICE OF THE CHIEF MEDICAL EXAMINER across the front. Recognition flared as she approached. It was the same medicolegal investigator who'd claimed the remains at the scene yesterday morning.

"Agent Brody." The short, dark-haired woman flapped her windbreaker to dispel the water clinging to her. In vain. She thrust her hand out. Tendrils of hair clung to an oval face and emphasized big, round eyes. "Jenny Duval. We met yesterday when there was still a crime scene out front."

"I remember. How... How did you get here?" Leigh tried to gauge the storm's fury through the double glass doors. Rain still pounded the glass. "The shelter in place order is still in effect."

"We got word the storm is moving east. Durham PD was able to clear a few of the roads between my office and campus, but cell towers and electricity are still down. I almost got T-boned by a sedan on the way here." Jenny took in the crowd of students taking cover in every corner of the lobby, her smokey voice clear. "I tried reaching you over the radio, but there was no response from your end. Looks like you guys could use some supplies."

Leigh brushed her hip. She must've left the radio in the women's bathroom when she'd changed, but the emergency radio maintenance recovered should've picked something up. Hell, so much had happened between yesterday morning and today, she wasn't sure which way was up. "What do you have?"

"Not much, but I managed to pack a couple boxes full of cereal, instant oatmeal, and a few granola bars." Jenny hiked her hands to her hips. "Water bottles, too. I'll need someone to help me unload them. Durham PD will be sending officers soon to escort students and staff off campus and back to their dorms. You just have to be patient for a little while longer."

"We'll take whatever you have. Thank you." A collective sigh of relief breathed at her back, and the hunger knot in

Leigh's own stomach untwisted slightly. But that couldn't be the only reason the medicolegal investigator was here. "Do you have any updates on Alice Dietz's autopsy?"

"Yes." Jenny patted her windbreaker, pulling her phone from one pocket. The screen lit up with a report already cued. "You wouldn't believe how hard it was to hold up a flashlight for two hours while the ME conducted his examination. We'll have to wait on toxicology results since the power is still out, but he did narrow down time of death for Alice Dietz between 10:00 p.m. Tuesday night and 2:00 a.m. Wednesday morning. There are a lot of factors that could affect that window, specifically the fact that the investigator in charge wouldn't let us collect the body until closer to 10:00 a.m., but the ME is confident your vic was poisoned in that time frame. He thinks she was injected with equal amounts of cyanide and arsenic in her left eye based off blood tests we ran under one of the microscopes, which would shut down brain activity within a matter of a minute, maybe two. Most likely with a syringe."

"Wait." Leigh stepped closer to get a better view of the screen. "You're saying that by injecting the compounds into Alice Dietz's eye, she died almost immediately? No prolonged vomiting, dizziness, or other side effects?"

Up until now, Leigh had assumed the killer had wanted to cause as much pain and disorientation as possible. But the evidence said otherwise. He'd wanted his victims dead, but he hadn't wanted them to suffer? Why use the arsenic and cyanide at all then? There were much more effective murder weapons than poisoning.

"Right," Jenny said.

Leigh's breath hitched.

I didn't kill them, Leigh. Didn't kill Teshia Elborne, either. You know that. His voice was in her head again. Trying to claw through the invisible barriers she'd put between them, but there were still too many unanswered questions.

"Were there any traces of chloroform around the victim's mouth and nose?" It was the only explanation for why none of the victims had fought being stabbed in the eye with a needle.

Three distinct lines centered between Jenny's brows. "I'm not sure the ME ran a test for chloroform. If your killer used it around the victim's mouth and nose, there won't be traces now, though. Too much time has passed."

Right. And with the power still out, there was only so much the medical examiner's office could do. Toxicology would have to wait. "I know you probably weren't expecting more than to drop off supplies and update us on details from the autopsy, but we have three bodies quarantined in classrooms down the hall."

"I don't understand. Bodies? As in plural?" Jenny's voice spiked in volume on the last word.

Leigh turned her back to the gathering students hopeful for updates on their impending release and lowered her voice. "Whoever killed Alice Dietz is still here. He's killed two more victims with arsenic and cyanide presumably—a female student and a male professor—and we discovered the remains of an unidentified adult male. We're trying not to instill panic, but there's no telling who he might target next. You said Durham PD is in the process of clearing the roads now that the storm is moving east. That doesn't leave us a lot of time. If you were able to make it onto campus, then our killer may try to escape. I can't let that happen."

"Tell me what you need me to do." Jenny folded her arms across her chest, like she was trying to hold herself together. Medicolegal investigators were called after a body had been dropped. Not during. Still, she was the only resource they had at this point.

"The unidentified adult male. I need you to tell me as much about him as you can to get me an ID. He wasn't killed like the others, which I think means he wasn't part of the killer's plans."

Leigh nodded toward the west corridor branching off the

lobby and started moving. Leading them to the sealed class-room, Leigh motioned Jenny inside and closed the door behind them. In three steps, she reached for the US Marshals Service windbreaker and pulled it back to reveal the body. Decomposition had caught up, throwing a wall of odor into her face, and it took every ounce of strength she had left not to gag.

"Whoa. That body is very... juicy." Jenny crouched beside the remains, pressing the back of her wrist to her nose. "Strangulation marks tell me how he died, but since that doesn't explain the purple marbling, I'm guessing he was submerged in water."

"The basement flooded." Leigh blocked out the memories vying for release. "He was stashed in a closet for at least twelve hours."

"All right." Jenny pulled a pair of latex gloves and her phone from her windbreaker. "Give me an hour. I'll get you some answers."

THIRTY-THREE

Durham, New Hampshire

Thursday, October 10
7:02 p.m.

It was getting dark again. And, still, Durham PD had not sent word about lifting the shelter in place order. There was a reason for that.

Ford tossed the emergency radio recovered by the maintenance staff onto the table. "Found it in pieces on the third floor. Seems someone didn't like the idea we could get news from the outside world."

Shit. She scanned his belt. "Where is the radio the chief of police lent you?"

The marshal seemed to come to the same conclusion. He shook his head. "Someone must've taken it off of me when I caught a couple hours of sleep earlier."

"Mine is missing from the women's bathroom too." Had it been the killer? Dean? Were they one and the same? She didn't trust herself enough at this point to make a determination.

Someone had been isolating them from the beginning. Sabotaging the generator, destroying any chance of aid. The storm and lack of food didn't help. Ever since the medicolegal investigator had shown up, the atmosphere in the lobby had started buzzing. "The cell towers are still down, and most people's phones are dead without any way to charge them. If I wasn't trying to catch this guy, I would admire his war strategies. But Durham PD knows we're here. They sent one of the medicolegal investigators to bring supplies and updates on Alice Dietz's autopsy."

"Did she say when we can get the hell out of here?" Ford asked.

She shook her head. "It's likely Durham PD will want to keep us contained as long as the killer is still a threat."

"What about the autopsy results?" Ford took a seat, rubbing his palm over the back of his head. His flinch told her everything she needed to know. The pain hadn't lessened over the past hour. She'd actually bet it'd gotten worse. Thankfully, they had a physician of sorts in the next room with the unidentified remains. Jenny could at least take a look at the laceration. Make sure there weren't any signs of internal bleeding. "Anything that stands out?"

"No. Not yet." Leigh shook her head, more than happy to melt into a puddle on the cold floor as soon as possible. "The ME's office is still limited in what tests they can run working off nothing but a generator. But I'm thinking our theory about Teshia Elborne's high school sweetheart might be right. Turns out injecting arsenic and cyanide into someone's eye kills them within minutes. She wouldn't have suffered any of the poisons' effects after he knocked her unconscious with chloroform."

"He didn't want her to suffer." Small wrinkles set up in Ford's suit jacket. For the first time in the past forty-eight hours, he was finally starting to look how she felt. "Could her death have been an accident? Maybe a crime of passion?"

"It's possible. Regardless, the way he handled her remains makes me think he cared about her." She shrugged, circling around to her own chair. Her knee knocked into his as she sat. A small motion but big on her part. She didn't like to get personal. With anyone. Least of all fellow law enforcement officials. There was too much bad blood between her and the rest of the system, but here she'd gone and handed over her darkest secrets. To this man. "In my experience, a serial offender's first kill tells more about the killer than the victim. Modes of operation can change over time, but the signatures—the markers that killers use to make themselves known—never evolve. The arsenic and cyanide are considered part of his MO. Sooner or later, he may try to alter the compounds or try another murder weapon, but the care he puts into washing and cleaning the victims' remains is his signature. He makes an effort to ensure we know it's him, and it all started with Teshia Elborne. He took care of her after he killed her, and that simple act probably gave him a sense of closure. So he keeps doing it. It's a cycle. In reality, she changed everything for him."

"But the unsub didn't get the chance to wash Tamra Hopkins and Pierce Morrow's bodies." Ford knocked his knee against hers this time. "He must not have had the resources or the time."

They'd done what they could for Tamra Hopkins's remains, but Leigh had collapsed from Dean's drug before she'd gotten the chance to examine her former mentor's. She stood to leave. "We should take a look at Morrow's body again."

"You talk about this guy as if you understand him. Almost like you can see the world through his eyes." Ford studied her from his seat, and she couldn't help but feel completely exposed under that gaze. Like he wanted to break her open and see how she ticked. "Makes me think the sword could've gone the other way. You would've made a formidable serial killer."

She didn't know what to say to that. What to think. There

were law enforcement officials who'd refused to work with her over the years. The ones who'd made that very same observation. Not knowing what to do with someone who lived inside the minds of the very people who brutally ended lives. She couldn't lie. Her chest tightened at hearing those words come from Ford when all she wanted was to be the woman he believed her to be from the investigation files and media coverage he'd studied over the past few months. "I wouldn't be very good at my job if I didn't try to see the world from their perspective. Does that bother you?"

Standing, he closed the distance between them. Larger, more formidable than ever before, and her blood pressure spiked. Threading his hands into the hair on the back of her neck, Ford pressed his mouth to hers. This kiss wasn't the punishing, desperate desire for connection they'd shared in the corridor or the one before that. It was something sweeter. Patient and slow. Accepting. He skimmed his thumb across her cheek. "No, it doesn't."

His smile cut through the heaviness still lingering from the past two days, and the relief Leigh felt nearly knocked her on her ass. Ford let his touch drop away but kept his proximity. "We got a name for Teshia Elborne's high school boyfriend yet?"

"No." The word left her mouth as nothing more than a whisper as she tried to regain control over her body. Leigh worked to clear her throat. Didn't help. That was one thing they couldn't solve in their current situation. Even with a repeated phone number in Elborne's phone records, they had no way of tracing it back to a registered name.

"Even if the on again–off again boyfriend is a suspect, we can't overlook the fact Dean Groves is here. Not only is he sneaking into conference rooms and knocking federal agents unconscious, he pulled your weapon on you," Ford said. "That doesn't scream innocent to me."

Another good point. Except Dean had handed her weapon back. She scrubbed a hand down her face to chase back the exhaustion closing in. Well, if she was being honest, it'd never left. The second she'd set foot on this campus, eighteen years of pure heaviness had descended. Emotional trauma for the win. As much as she wanted to believe Dean had spent the last eighteen years trying to clear his name of Teshia Elborne's murder, she couldn't altogether dismiss him as a suspect. The evidence said otherwise.

Leigh grabbed for the door handle and escaped the too-hot room into the corridor. Activity buzzed from the lobby. "He's still in the building. He won't leave until he's finished what he started. Not when he's this close."

"I've done multiple rounds through the building in the past two days. There's no sign of him, and believe me, I've been looking. But he can't hide forever." Ford closed the conference room door behind him. He'd cleaned the blood from the back of his hair, but dried flecks still clung to the fabric of his shirt and suit jacket.

Leigh couldn't help herself, reaching up to swipe away the remnants from the fabric. The action brought them nearly chest to chest, and her heart rate kicked up. The last time she and Ford had found themselves in this position, someone had thrown a rock at a fluorescent tube to cause a distraction. Dean? His name was more growl than thought in her mind. Though she supposed he'd had a point. Distractions would get them killed if she wasn't careful. "You've got blood on you."

"It's not the first time." Ford stared down at her with that look again, consuming and intense and a little bit intimidating. The one that said he wanted this to happen as much as she did. "Once this shelter in place order is lifted, this place will be swarming with cops and forensic teams."

Her skin tightened, drawing a slow exhale from her chest. Right. The case. "Dean is in the tunnels. Most likely somewhere with the least amount of flooding. It would be the last place we'd want to search, and for that reason alone, the perfect hide-out. I wouldn't be surprised if he worked out a way to gain access from another building."

"You almost died the last time you went down there," Ford said. "Don't even think about it."

His concern was... cute. But flawed. This was her job. Attraction didn't change that. And as much as she wanted to argue that she could take care of her damn self, she had to agree. There wasn't anything that could make her want to go back into that hellhole.

Commotion bled from the lobby. As though someone had taken a swipe at a hornets' nest. Shouts reached her ears. She threw Ford a glance before jogging back to the front of Thompson Hall. Students were up off the floor, crowding around the glass doors. Pushing through.

The president of the university held both hands up. "Please, the police have not lifted the shelter in place order! We cannot leave until the storm passes! It's not safe." His voice failed to reach over the cacophony of rising voices.

"There's a killer on the loose! It's not safe here!"

"They want to keep us here to die!"

"You have to let us out! Please, I have to go home!"

Leigh couldn't reach the front of the crowd without going through the mass itself. A shoulder knocked into hers, shoving her to one side. Another student jostled her holster, and she clamped a hand on the butt of her weapon. Just in case.

Strong hands held her upright. Ford. He had her back as she pushed through, but there were too many of them. Every step closer antagonized the frenzy. The lack of sleep and food had triggered a primal chain reaction that there was no coming back from this time. She could feel it the air same way she could anticipate violence in crime statistics and patterns.

"I'm getting the hell out of here!"

"I was here first!"

"Back off!"

A student fell into her and hit the floor. Pain flared across her shoulder. She lost her balance trying to catch them and was taken down in a tackle. The floor rushed up to meet her. Feet caught in her ribs and sucker-punched the air from her chest. Forced to protect her face, she turned onto her belly and tried to claw through the maze of limbs toward the glass doors.

"Leigh!" Ford's voice barely reached her.

A shoe kicked into her mouth. Blood coated her tongue and teeth.

And then came the darkness.

THIRTY-FOUR

Durham, New Hampshire

Thursday, October 10
7:17 p.m.

"I think she's coming around." Bright light singed the back of her eyes. A face cleared above her. Perfectly shaped eyebrows, thin lips stretched into a smile, warm eyes. She knew that face. Jenny. Jenny Duval. The medicolegal investigator. "I'm not a medical physician, but I can't rule out a concussion. Her nose doesn't appear to be broken. Hard to tell with so much blood."

Her stomach rolled. Leigh shoved her heels into the floor to turn onto her side, but something—or someone—held her in place. How many head injuries were too many? She was asking for a friend. She brushed her hand to her hip as the last few minutes played out in her mind. Her gun. Where was her gun? "Ow."

"Welcome back to the land of the living." Ford's features took shape behind the flashlight. Pointing to the ceiling, he smiled down at her with a white, watery layer that had to come from losing consciousness too many times.

The brassy taste of blood created a thick layer on her tongue. Silence pressed into her, yet she recognized the two-story open ceiling of Thompson Hall's lobby. Leigh forced her shoulders off the floor but didn't get far. "Where is everyone?"

Ford maneuvered around the medicolegal investigator, hands threading under her back to help her sit up. "Secured in classrooms. No more than four in a group. The loudest protestors get to sit with Morrow's body."

"Ava." She scanned the empty lobby.

The marshal steadied her before removing his hold. "She's fine. She managed to stay away from most of the fighting. She sat by you for a few minutes to make sure you were okay. Then I had her go keep an eye on the others. I'm not going to lie, she was worried about you."

"I'm sorry. I must've hit my head harder than you thought. I think you just said my daughter was worried about me, and that doesn't sound right." Maybe she was getting the hang of this motherhood gig. Maybe the fifteen-year-old she'd adopted didn't hate her as much as she thought. Them being mortal enemies and all. Ultimately, it didn't matter. Ava was okay. She was safe.

"Yeah, well, that one surprised us all," Ford said. "You must be rubbing off on her."

Leigh fought against the urge to slump back to the floor. She'd rushed to assist the university president, but she didn't see him here with them. "What about the staff and administration?"

"Minor cuts and bruising. Seems you took the brunt of the mob's anger." Jenny finally got rid of the flashlight, locking those brown eyes on Leigh. "How many fingers am I holding up?"

She shook her head. "You're not holding any fingers up."

"Then we're good." Jenny slipped her flashlight into her windbreaker pocket. "Now, I can't tell you what to do and I have the feeling you'd ignore me anyway, but I recommend taking it easy over the next few hours. Just to make sure there isn't anything I missed."

Leigh took Ford's offered hand and got to her feet. Her fingertips brushed the inside of his left wrist, catching on something sticky beneath the cuff. It took her a second to realize it was a Band-Aid. Her head swam as she righted herself—with his help—and she used his chest for balance. "Were you injured in the fight?"

Lifting his forearm, he cracked a smile as he exposed a much larger bandage beneath his suit and shirt sleeve. The sticky substance hadn't been a Band-Aid but medical tape and a patch of gauze. Stained with a slim line of blood down the middle and hidden by the sleeve of his suit jacket. "Damn kids are faster than I give them credit for. I tried to get to you at the center of the mob. Next thing I know one of them was dragging a pen down my arm. Cut pretty deep, too. Fortunately, it's not lethal. We can still make our date when we get out of this place."

Her stomach hollowed. The line of blood seeping through the fabric looked more rust-colored than bright red. Older. Had Jenny patched him up? She tried for a smile, but she was just so damn tired. Her shoulder ached where Dean had slugged her old injury, and she didn't even want to think about the mess on her face. Leigh stretched her jaw to test for damage. Everything remained in one place. "Can't wait."

"You'll be fine." Jenny packed her gear in an undersized duffle bag. "Can't say the same for our dead guy, though."

"Did you get anything from the remains?" she asked. "Something we can use to identify him?"

"I collected DNA and tried to print both hands. They were swollen beyond belief, but once this storm passes, I can get him back to the morgue to get you an ID if he's in the system." The medicolegal investigator unpocketed her phone and swiped to the photos app. "Oh, but I was able to get a couple snapshots of his tattoo. It looks custom, so there's a chance you might be able to track down the artist. Nice work, too. It would've cost an arm and a leg in shading alone."

"I didn't see any tattoos on him." Ford took position over Leigh's shoulder to get a better view of Jenny's screen.

"You wouldn't have unless you were authorized to strip him." Jenny angled the phone toward them, showing off a rather detailed American flag shaded in black with a strip of blue. "See? I told you it was nice work. Would've taken a few sessions to get that detail. Don't worry. I made sure no one else was in the room when I got the dead guy naked, but I won't be showing you any of the other photos I took until the autopsy is finalized."

Tension radiated at her back as Ford straightened. "A flag with a thick blue stripe."

"He was law enforcement." This was what they'd been waiting for. Something—anything—to tell them who the unidentified remains were. So why didn't that critical piece of knowledge make her feel any better? "When will you collect the remains?"

Jenny slipped her phone into her windbreaker and collected her gear. "I'm going back to the office now. I took the liberty of documenting the other two bodies. It'll probably be a few more hours before I can get the other techs to make the trip out here to get all three of your vics, depending on conditions. The flooding was pretty bad up until a little while ago, but I'd say no more than three hours, four at the most. I'll let Durham PD know you may need a couple officers to help you with crowd control."

Probably a good idea. There was no telling how long Ford's time out would last for the students who'd been ready to escape. Leigh reached out to hold the door open for the medicolegal investigator, but her body thought better of it. "Thanks, Jenny. And thanks for the supplies."

"Don't let anyone else die. I don't have that much room in the van, Agent Brody." Jenny allowed the door to close behind her with a grin stretched across her face.

If she didn't feel as though she'd been bulldozed by a snow-plow, Leigh might've laughed. The medicolegal investigator had the ability to turn any situation into a stand-up comedy routine. Even death. She didn't realize how much she'd needed that until now. Turning back to Ford, she scanned him from head to toe in case she'd missed any other injuries. Still as handsome as ever. Damn it. "Why do you look like that?"

"Excuse me?" he asked.

She motioned at his chest. And... him in general. "Why do you look like you have your life together when I look like I just left an MMA fighting ring?"

His laugh drove into her, warming the aches and pains throbbing with every pulse. "You're the one diving headfirst into the action. I don't want to mess up this face."

"It's a pretty face. I'll give you that." Leigh tried to rub the soreness from her jaw, but experience told her it would take a few days for the swelling to abate. At least she hadn't been shot. Or stabbed. Or drowned. Those would be the three items she listed in her gratitude journal tonight. "Jenny took care of assessing Morrow's body. That leaves us with forensics. Have you heard any updates from the techs?"

"Since you were nearly trampled by a mob of undergrads? No. I haven't had the chance." He followed on her heels. Close enough to catch her if she collapsed. "You think they'll be able to salvage anything?"

"Only one way to find out." Brushing her hip, Leigh skimmed her fingers over her empty holster. "I take it I have you to thank for confiscating my service weapon from one of those undergrads?"

The riot could've gone very bad very fast if Ford hadn't been there. Hell, how many times had he saved her life now?

Twice? More? The details were a little fuzzy now. She was going to owe him more than coffee when this was over.

"Can't say I can take the credit for that one," he said.

Wait. What? She pulled up short and cocked her head back to look at him. A flare of unease took over then. "You don't have my gun?"

The marshal shook his head. "No. Just mine. I searched every student before isolating them into the classrooms. Nobody had a weapon."

Shit. Shit, shit, shit. "We have a killer on the loose and a... whatever the hell Dean is following our every move, and my weapon is gone?"

Leigh forced herself to breathe through the initial panic. All right. How much ammunition had she left in the magazine? Ten bullets? Less? Damn it. She couldn't remember. The fact there were bullets in it at all was the problem. Not to mention she could be suspended for allowing civilians to get a hold of it in the first place.

She headed for the classroom at the far end of the corridor where the forensic techs had set up. "Do you suppose anything else might go wrong in this investigation? It might be nice to have a heads-up from now on."

"Not sure I can help you there." He tagged behind. "Though I can predict fugitives' futures once I have them in custody, but they all end up in the same place so it's not that difficult."

Leigh had lost the inclination to laugh and swung into the classroom the forensic techs had taken over at the back of the building. Both techs looked up from the two elongated tables they'd lined with evidence bags. She recognized the syringe the killer had presumably used to kill Alice Dietz in one, the bottle of dish soap in another. The bleach bottle too. Then there were the six driver's licenses spread out, each sealed in its own bag.

"Have you been able to match any more licenses to the victims in this case?"

"Agent Brody, yes. We've made some progress. We managed to process the licenses with the alkali solution from the biomedical lab to stop the acid from eating the plastic, but there's still a lot of damage. The acid ate through some sections, but we saved bits of information." The closest tech to her rounded the table and grabbed a few of the smaller evidence bags. He handed them off individually, split between her and Ford. "The photos have been compromised. There's nothing we can do to restore those, but we were able to match the names and a couple birth dates and addresses on the licenses to ones listed in the case files provided by Marshal Ford by filling the groves left behind by the machine press when the licenses were created. Kind of like running a pencil over a pad of paper to figure out the last message written."

"Pierce Morrow's license was also in the collection." Leigh could barely make anything out on the licenses themselves, but she trusted the techs had done their jobs. She turned to Ford. "So we're waiting on one more license. We must have missed a victim. Someone the unsub targeted and whose identity he stole before killing Alice Dietz."

Ford handed her the two licenses. "There haven't been any other identities the killer took on as far as I know."

"Or the body hasn't been recovered," she said.

"I'm in the final stages of restoring the last license now. Give me... one minute. And, we have a result!" The second tech's victory smile faltered. His gaze cut to Ford then Leigh. "I don't... I don't understand."

Leigh cut toward the table. "Who is it?"

Bits of ink clung to the indented letters on the plastic.

Spelling out a single name.

One she knew.

Two gunshots exploded through the room.

Leigh grabbed for her service weapon on instinct and turned to face the threat. Empty handed.

Ford leveled the gun at her chest, and the blood drained from her upper body on a gutting exhale. "I really wish you wouldn't have seen that."

He slammed the butt of the weapon into her temple.

And the world went black.

THIRTY-FIVE

Durham, New Hampshire

Wednesday, September 13, 2006
7:19 p.m.

Dean had been released from custody.

Every cell in her body screamed as though it'd been put through the blender. It'd worked. The alibi she'd given Durham PD had gotten him released. He was coming home. Any minute now. It'd been a long few days. She hadn't been able to sleep alone in her too-small twin bed across from her brother's since Dean's arrest. Classwork had been shoved to the back of her mind. She'd barely managed to remember to feed her and her brother, but none of that mattered anymore.

He was coming back. To her.

Leigh pinched the end of the balloon with one hand and blew into it. Dean hated yellow. Said he had a physical reaction anytime he saw it, but that was all she'd been able to get from the bookstore on short notice. The streamers might've been a bit much, but they had reason to celebrate. She'd done her hair and makeup. She'd told her brother not to expect her back in their dorm room tonight and left him with money for pizza. She still wasn't old enough to buy alcohol, but she and Dean could get by without it. Actually, she preferred it that way. She wanted to remember this night. Every minute, every touch, every kiss.

She tied off the balloon and tossed it onto the bed with the rest. She'd even taken the initiative to clean up his space. Washed the sheets, lit a candle, tossed all the garbage. Sitting on the edge of the bed, she set her palms on her knees and studied the decorations. Then got up and fixed a streamer that'd fallen. Everything had to be perfect. And she was ready. For them to move on with their lives. To start something new. Just as she'd tried—and failed—to do for her dad. But the past wasn't going to ruin tonight. This was about the two of them and his promise to take care of her. Always.

The minutes ticked by. Too slow. Twenty. Fifty. Two hours.

Leigh checked her phone for the one hundredth—or was it the two hundredth?—time. He hadn't called or messaged her. Hers went unanswered. Straight to voicemail. Had the police found a reason to keep him in custody? The investigating detective had told her he'd be released today, and Professor Morrow hadn't emailed her about any more developments in the case. As far as Durham PD was concerned, Dean was innocent. Her alibi had saved him.

It wasn't until after midnight Leigh got off that damn bed and stumbled back to her dorm room. Knowing Dean wasn't ever going to walk through that door again.

Durham, New Hampshire

Thursday, October 10
7:36 p.m.

Her fingertips prickled with numbness.

Leigh tried to drag her chin away from her chest, but the momentum only caused her to overcorrect. The back of her head hit metal. Lightning struck down her spine. She couldn't help the groan that followed.

"What was it that gave me away, Leigh?" That voice. She knew that voice. Familiar but different. Rawer.

Churning water reached her ears. Instant dread pooled at the back of her throat. Water. The basement. Gravity pinned her in place. So... heavy. Sharp edges cut into her wrists as she tried to bring one hand up, but the bite of pain was enough to wake her up. A single emergency lantern lit up a corner of the room. Thick columns supported an exposed ceiling of piping, electrical work, and fluorescent lighting. No windows. The entire room had been painted white, but there didn't seem to be any use for it other than storage with cubby-like shelves framed against the wall in front of her.

Her shoes were soaked, under a foot of flood water. A new wave of nausea seized control as she tugged at the zip ties around her wrists and ankles. The chair swayed as she rocked from left to right. One wrong move, and she'd never get back up. "You... You killed them."

How was that possible? How hadn't she seen the signs before now?

"Was it the driver's licenses?" Movement lapped water higher up her shins. Then he was standing right in front of her. Looking the same as she remembered. The lantern cast half of his face in shadows, but he didn't resemble the monster they'd been hunting all this time. "No. You were suspicious of me before that. Had to be the tattoo that medicolegal investigator found on the marshal's body. What's her name? Jenny. Also, that's a really weird word. Medicolegal. What the hell kind of position is that? What do you think?"

The marshal. The real Max Ford. His was the body she'd recovered from the kill room. Leigh sucked in a humidity-laced breath to clear her head. People really had to stop hitting her in the head. She wasn't sure how much more her brain could take, but, she supposed, it was better than being stabbed or given a bullet wound. She summoned the energy to meet his gaze, but it cost her more than she'd thought. Her head slumped downward again. "I'm starting to think I'm a terrible judge of character."

His laugh reverberated through her. Ford—or whatever the hell his name was—straightened. "Can't argue with that. You read killers better than anyone I've ever met. Except for the one right in front of you."

"You're a real terror. You know that? Who steals their victims' identities and tries to become them?" Leigh memorized the layout of the room. Every inch, every corner, every wall. Water leaked in from the ceiling and walls, past the rubber-like sealant and paint. The entire city seemed to drain straight onto this campus. But she had time. She could get herself out of this.

"I live those lives better than they ever could." Ford pulled his glasses free, tucking them into the breast pocket of his suit jacket. He stripped that off next, tossing it. In a matter of seconds, he stood before her as an entirely different person. No longer unsure of himself or his role in this investigation, but volatile. Provoking. With a murderous edge that could surely destroy her. He shrugged, but the movement didn't feel natural. A leftover from one of his stolen identities. "And maybe one day, I'll find one that sticks."

A laugh ripped free without her permission. Most likely from a concussion, because this certainly wasn't a funny moment. "I don't think you'll ever stop. You like the challenge too much. Staying in one place or in one identity too long equates to death for you. You've gotten a taste for it, and now you're addicted. You couldn't stop if you tried."

Ford cocked his head to one side, the lantern lighting up more of that face she'd found so handsome mere hours ago. Well, more than handsome, but she wasn't going to think on her love life right now. "Does that brain of yours ever stop trying to work out the patterns?" He crouched in front of her, showcasing the gun at his hip. Along with the badge he'd taken off a dead man. "Does it ever drive you mad when you don't get the answers it craves?"

"Do you ever stop trying to be a murderous asshole?" She was kind of proud of that one. Leigh rotated her wrists to test the slack in the zip ties. There was none. If she was getting out of here, it would most likely be in a body bag when the medical examiner recovered her remains and Ford was long gone. But that wasn't going to stop her from trying.

"Come on now, Leigh." Straightening to his full height, Ford unbuttoned his shirt cuffs and rolled them back one at a time, exposing muscular forearms. And the stretch of bloodied gauze. From where she'd sliced into him with a moldy shard of mason jar. He turned his back on her, reaching for something near the lantern. She couldn't see what. If she was being honest, she didn't want to. It most likely would be bagged as evidence in her murder later. And who really wanted to see how they would die when it came right down to it? "Be honest. You would've had me undressed in a matter of seconds if we hadn't been interrupted during that last kiss."

Acid charged up her throat, and she stuck her tongue out to counter her gag reflex. She really did have the worst taste in men. "That was before I knew you'd killed nine people. Can't say murder is a turn-on, even in my line of work."

"That's too bad. Because I'm afraid our time together is just beginning." Ford approached her with a single syringe in one hand, his thumb positioned on the depressor. "No one knows you're here. Not even your daughter. I made sure she knew you'd be gone for a while so we could search the building together. No one will be able to hear you scream. And you will scream, Leigh. I'll make sure of it."

The last shred of her bravery seemed to rush out of her at

the sight of clear liquid in the syringe. Arsenic and cyanide? Leigh tried to press her toes into the floor to add distance between them, but the chair wouldn't budge. That needle was not going in her eye. "You're Teshia Elborne's high school boyfriend."

"Surprise." His voice hiked up on the last syllable, but again, it sounded so unnatural. Trying too hard to mimic someone else. "You know, I'd done a damn good job making sure Teshia's death couldn't be linked back to me. I did everything I was supposed to. I destroyed evidence, wore gloves, changed and burned my clothes after I left her in front of this building. Never once touching the body. But your buddy Dean just wouldn't let it go. Probably because I tried to frame him for murder, but then you had to go and give him an alibi. You ruined my plans."

Ford took a step closer.

Fear spiked in her veins. Raising her heart rate. Interrupting logic. Suddenly, she was all survival skills. Faced with a very real threat she couldn't run from. Sweat beaded at the back of her neck. "Why?" She wanted that question to sound more stable, but she had to give herself credit. "Why kill her at all?"

"Would you believe me if I told you it'd been an accident? That one minute she was standing right in front of me and the next I'd stabbed her with a syringe." Ford's gaze took on a glazed distance. "We had a plan. I was supposed to take over my parents' farm. We'd planned on getting married after high school graduation, having a couple of kids. All I wanted was a simple life. I thought she did, too, but then she started talking about going to college, seeing the world, finding herself, and all that bullshit people romanticize, but I knew that's not what she really wanted. Then again, Teshia had never been good about following orders. I tried to get her to come around—by force sometimes—but the last time she checked herself out of the hospital without my permission and disappeared. Didn't take me long to catch up with her, though. Never was very bright, but I never intended for her to die. I loved her. That's why I followed her to Granite State. I just wanted her to come home, but she wouldn't listen."

So he and Teshia Elborne hadn't been on again–off again. She'd been on the run from an abusive partner. The seat of the wooden chair cut into the backs of Leigh's thighs as her body tensed against his approach. "But you didn't stop there. You framed Dean Groves for her murder, used chemicals from his lab to connect him to her death."

"He really shouldn't have touched what was mine," Ford said.

The possessiveness in that single statement dried her mouth. "And the others? The men you killed, the ones whose lives you stole?"

"Do you ever find yourself wishing to be someone else? Wishing you could run away from all the problems in your life and start over? It worked for a while. Becoming those men helped with the guilt of what I'd done to Teshia, but the more lives I stole over the years, the less I could pretend someone else had killed her. After a while, nothing helped."

Faster than she thought possible, Ford was on her, pulling her head back by her hair. Pressing the tip of the needle against her left eye, he stared down at her. A stranger. Nothing of the man he'd manipulated her to see left in his features. An unrealistic sense of calm came over him. As if this was always meant to be the end between them. Like he'd planned this exact scenario. Had any of it been real?

"Until I learned Dean had caught on to my little experiment about a year ago. Color me surprised when I discovered he hadn't been charged and sentenced with Teshia's death and that you had alibied him for the night she died. Well, I couldn't think of a better way to lure him out of the shadows than by putting you right where I wanted you. But to get to you, I needed your attention."

Understanding hit. "Alice Dietz." It'd been a trap. One she'd fallen into without a second thought. "You said you researched me. You knew who I was, knew that I wouldn't be able to turn down the chance to find Teshia Elborne's killer and close the case."

"Closure. I think that's your need, Leigh. First with your brother's case, now this one, and I wanted to give it to you. For my own purposes, of course. So I did my homework on you, discovered your ties to Professor Morrow and this university. And there she was. His plaything. She really does look an awful lot like Teshia, doesn't she?" Ford backed off a few inches. "You really have a talent for understanding why killers succumb to their nasty little urges, Leigh. All this time, after all my research, I thought I'd understood you just as well, but you surprised me with that theory I needed those victims to fulfill needs I couldn't get anywhere else. It was inspired. But would you believe me if I said you've managed to show me one need I could never satisfy with them?"

Dean had been telling the truth. He'd disappeared to find the man responsible for Teshia Elborne's death. To clear his name. Leigh clutched the end of the chair's arm, fingernails digging into the soft wood. The needle was one wrong move from piercing her cornea, and it took everything in her power not to flinch.

"You made me want to be understood." Ford tugged her head back into the chair. "That's why I'm going to make this last as long as possible."

THIRTY-SIX

Durham, New Hampshire

Thursday, October 10
7:51 p.m.

"I should be thanking you." Ford positioned himself within an inch of her face, using the needle to draw a line down her cheek. The bitter odor of chocolate and citrus she'd become familiar with assaulted her now. "You were the one who taught me how killers evolve. What is it you said? They might change their modes of operation, but their signatures are what stay the same. It gave me an idea."

He released her in a jerk.

Leigh's scalp prickled as feeling rushed back into her head. The hard angle of her neck relaxed, but it wasn't enough to purge the pain from her head. Her breath came easier now that Ford had gone back to the small table he'd set up near the lantern. She had to keep him talking. Buy herself enough time to work out her escape. A darkened corridor seemed to be the only way in or out of this dead end of a room, but the tunnels beneath this campus were complicated and confusing without any kind of a map. She could just as easily get lost and drown. "You destroyed the generator and radios. You wanted us unable to get supplies or radio for help."

"Who's going to suspect a US marshal of sabotaging emergency services when he's supposed to be there to help?" Ford picked up a second syringe. "Also, you really should be more careful about where you set your things. Especially your gun. Anyone could take advantage."

Jackass.

"So what happened, Ford?" Was she supposed to call him Ford? This was all so confusing. "You killed Alice Dietz, then what? The US marshal caught up with you, and you decided to become him to keep an eye on the investigation? To keep me close?"

"Perfect, wasn't it? What better way to get close to you than to become your partner? Someone you trusted to have your back. I will say, I was afraid you'd see right through me after learning about your case history, but you have this drive about you. Nothing else but the case matters. So, I'd say it's your fault we're here." Ford dragged a chair from the corner of the room, setting it in front of her. Two syringes in hand, he took a seat. "Alice played her part well, but during my research of you, there was something about Pierce Morrow that kept drawing me in. His work—though now I realize in the end it was your work, wasn't it?—explained so much about me. For the first time, maybe ever, someone understood me. So I approached him. Not as myself, of course. No names. No specifics about my life. I changed my hair and the way I spoke, wore colored contact lenses and gained a few pounds. You understand. But from that first conversation, he showed an interest in me. About my thought processes, about how I chose my victims, what led me to start killing people. He saw the opportunity to revitalize his career and I... had a friend."

Leigh didn't know what to say to that.

Ford studied the syringes in his hand. "I spent time with him, got to know him and all his little mannerisms. We'd meet late at night when no one could put me in a room with him, but then this woman barged into Morrow's office one night. She saw me. I saw her standing there, looking just like Teshia, and I knew how I would get you to come to me. I guess it turned out okay, though I'll admit the plan wasn't perfect. After that, it was a matter of covering my bases. Tamra Hopkins had to die after she saw me destroying the emergency radio in the stairwell, and then Morrow had to die because you discovered he had a personal relationship with Teshia. And we all know the lengths I'll go to to punish those who touch what's mine. So you see, everybody wins."

She didn't. She didn't win. "You have a funny way of celebrating."

"Who needs balloons when you have dead guys who can float?" The man she'd known as Ford extracted a blade, sliding it edge-up beneath her sweatshirt sleeve. Leigh struggled to pull her arm back, but it was no use. With a strong pull, he sliced through the material and exposed her arm. "Don't worry. I'm not going to kill you yet. Consider yourself an experiment... except we already know the end results."

Setting the syringe against her inner elbow, he plunged the needle through layers of skin and straight into the nearest vein despite her fight. There was no escape. Then depressed the plunger. "There we go."

An instant rush clouded her head and intensified gravity's hold on her body. "What the hell is that?" Her tongue filled her mouth, too big.

"That would be a barbiturate." Ford's face blurred in her vision. Then the rest of him. It was getting harder for her to keep her head up. "You know what that is, don't you? I'm going to let you sleep for a couple minutes. After that is when the fun starts."

Getting drugged into unconsciousness was better than dying from arsenic and cyanide poisoning, but that didn't answer what he planned to do to her once she woke. "I don't like your fun…"

Time ceased. She didn't know how long.

Searing pain erupted as she jolted awake.

Every muscle in her body strained for freedom. The zip ties cut into her wrists as a scream filled the room. Hers. She was screaming. Blood rushed in her ears. Too fast. Out of control. Another pinch drew her attention to her other arm where Ford pulled a needle free from her skin.

"And that is an amphetamine." His words barely penetrated the hummingbird-fast sprint in her heard.

Energy unlike anything she'd experienced coursed through her. It stole her breath as easily as drowning and took just as much effort to relax back in the chair. Her insides had caught fire. Every inch of her body overheating in an instant.

"I'm interested in how long your heart is going to last. That was the first round, but I've got to be honest, Leigh. You're not looking so good. You need to start taking better care of yourself if you're going to survive torture. You never know what you're going to face during an investigation." Ford sat back in the chair across from hers. "Barbiturate, amphetamine, barbiturate, amphetamine. I like this new combination. I originally used arsenic and cyanide because that's what I imagined Dean would use to kill a woman who'd cheated on him. He had access to all those compounds. This was when I was still trying to frame him for murder, but now I'm seeing the benefits of branching out, just like you suggested."

If she survived this, she'd have to run a marathon to get whatever he'd shot her with out of her system. Holy hell. That hurt. A growl escaped her, shredding the skin along the inside of her throat. The room tilted without her permission. Drawing air shouldn't be this hard. "You got hold of Dean's old access code to the biomedical lab."

"Would you believe me if I told you it wasn't that hard?" he asked. "He took Teshia there once. I noticed the way you tensed up while we were in that lab searching for the arsenic and cyanide. Which makes me think he took you there, too, and all those memories between you two were coming back."

Ford stretched his hand for her, curling his fingers around a strand of hair dangling in front of her face.

She tried to angle her head back and away, but he'd secured her too well. The surrounding flood waters had reached new levels, now slithering around mid-calf. While he'd chosen a new kill room, there would be no escaping this storm. Not for her anyway.

"My guess is Dean wanted to show you how important you were to him. Convince you that you were more important than his research, that he would break rules and protocols for his special girl." Ford shoved to stand, heading back toward the lantern. Back to the syringes he'd left out on the table. Multiple pairs. "In the end, though, you were nothing but a tool. You know that, right? It was the same for Teshia. He got what he wanted from her then tossed her for the next prize. When she came crawling back to me, heartbroken and alone, all I had to do was ask her for the code, and voila. Framing him for her murder was even easier."

The effects of the amphetamine hadn't worn off, but they'd become more manageable as the drug spread through her whole system. Her skin tightened to the point of suffocation, head pounding too hard and too fast. She licked dry lips. Thirsty. So thirsty. "We submitted the compounds into evidence. How did you kill Tamra and Morrow without them?"

"Use that magnificent brain of yours, Leigh." He'd collected two more syringes. "You understand me, my motives, my MO.

You say I'm disciplined and intelligent and compulsive. How did I manage to continue killing without those poisons at my disposal?"

Defeat gutted her. The ability to kill Tamra Hopkins and Pierce Morrow. His unending access to food when she'd most needed it. The way he'd managed to stay put together in those damn suits. "You had another stash."

"Well, I couldn't exactly finish what I started if I didn't have the advantage, now could I?" he asked. "I admit, I went a little off book to get my hands on these compounds. Had to go back to the biomedical lab. I was there when one of those pesky researchers came in, though. He started asking me questions about what I was doing, who I was, blah, blah, blah. Long story short, I had to ditch my trophy collection in case he called security. This storm, though. I was not planning on that."

"You and me both." Leigh flinched as he set a third needle into the crook of her arm. He was going to put her under again. She didn't know how long. How long until Ava started looking for her? How long before Ford turned all that hate-filled revenge on her adopted daughter?

"Now, I'm going to need you to scream real loud when you wake up to get Dean's attention." Ford emptied the contents of the syringe into her veins. "I know he's around here somewhere. So let's make it convincing, Leigh."

The effect was instant, dragging her back into unconsciousness despite how hard she tried to stay awake. "Don't touch Ava…"

A pinch blistered along her arm. Then fire. It burned every cell in her body. Blood and sweat beaded around the zip ties as she wrenched at her wrists. Another scream tore from her chest. She couldn't stop the tears from escaping this time. Leigh jerked against the chair to counter the agony sweeping through her, but it was no use. She wasn't going anywhere, and no one was coming to save her.

"That's two rounds, and you're still here." Cold worked higher up her pant legs as Ford's outline shifted closer. It took more effort than it should have to get a good look at him. "I'm impressed."

How long had she been out this time? How much longer would she have to suffer through the extremes of what her body could handle? Her head weighed heavier than ever. A numbness had started in her toes. Whether from the flood waters or the drugs, she couldn't tell. Did it matter? Something acidic coated her tongue. Slivers of the chair's arm stabbed into her forearm. She'd pulled against the zip ties so hard, she'd managed to crack the wood. Maybe whatever amphetamine Ford had shot her with could get her out of here after all. But how many more rounds could she realistically endure? "Glad I could... exceed your expectations."

"You know, I was hoping during our time together we could figure out how to move past this, Leigh. Sure, I kill people, but humans have done far worse when it comes down to survival. It's in our nature." Ford's laugh didn't have the same effect on her as it had earlier. Once warming at the sound, she fought against the shiver spidering across her shoulders. The marshal—no, not a marshal, she had to remember that—leaned back in his chair. Relaxed. Unhurried. Like he had all the time in the world to kill her. She supposed that was true in a sense. Because he was right. Nobody, not even Ava, would come looking for her until it was too late. "Besides, it's not every day you find someone who understands you so completely that you have nothing left to hide. And I don't think I'm ready to give that up just yet."

"Are you asking me if I still want to go on a date with you?" It hurt to laugh, but she couldn't help it. This man had taken so many lives. Tried to take hers down in that kill room. And he was still interested in a relationship? Guess she hadn't made herself clear in that regard. "Because I think I'd rather die."

"That can be arranged." Ford shoved to his feet so abruptly, her brain had a hard time tracking the movement. Damn drugs. Or hypothermia. Or shock. All of the above? He caged her between his arms, hands gripped against the back of her chair. "I will destroy you so thoroughly not even Dean Groves will be able to identify your remains."

"My ears are burning." That all too familiar voice bled from the darkness a split second before Dean stepped free of the corridor. "Does that mean I get to come out and play?"

THIRTY-SEVEN

Durham, New Hampshire

Thursday, October 10
8:39 p.m.

"It's all fun and games until someone gets hurt." Dean Groves seemed to resemble an avenging devil, dressed head to toe in black. Yet he was exactly as she'd remembered him. "That's when the fun really starts."

Ford broke his attention from Leigh, turning to face the man who'd hunted him all these years. An air of familiarity and anticipation filled the room. "I can't get rid of you, Groves. You're like a bad rash."

"I've been called worse." Tension rippled up Dean's exposed forearms as his gaze shifted to her. The hardness drained from his expression. "You okay, little rabbit?"

She didn't have an answer for him. Hell, she couldn't even breathe. What had Ford given her? Straight-up adrenaline? Her meager attempts to get free left her wrists a bloody mess, and

she still couldn't control her own damn heart rate. No. She
wasn't okay. Ford was going to kill them both.

Matte black steel absorbed the lantern's dim light at Ford's
back as he reclaimed Dean's attention. His service weapon. No,
the real Marshal Ford's service weapon. "I'm afraid Leigh isn't
available at the moment. I hate to admit it, but we're in the
middle of our first fight."

"Trouble in paradise already? That's too bad, but I'm going
to have to cut your conversation short. You see, you and I have
unfinished business." Dean lunged. His fist went wide, coming
at the faux marshal from the side. He missed, but expertly
landed a strike to the bastard's chest.

Ford's uppercut connected beneath Dean's jaw. He hit the
water, going under as Ford approached.

"Dean, watch out!" It was an odd feeling, suddenly rooting
for the man she'd believed to be a murderer all these years.
Leigh's warning came just in time.

Dean rolled as the killer pulled the gun.

Her warning wasn't enough.

Hauling a heel into Dean's chest, Ford pressed her ex under
the water. "You should've taken the murder charges like a man,
Groves. All of this could've been avoided."

Hands gripped Ford's ankle, but Dean couldn't get the
advantage from his position. Ford was going to kill him. Not
with a bullet but much slower. More painful. Sputters reached
her ears.

Leigh locked her back teeth as she focused on the table Ford
had set up near the lantern. She couldn't make much out other
than the syringes lined in neat little rows, but there was a
chance he'd brought something else to cut through the zip ties at
her wrists and ankles. She put what energy she had left into
shifting the chair closer to the workbench. The water helped
take some of the weight off but also slowed her down. Every

movement sounded overly loud in her ears. Echoing off the cinderblock walls and announcing her intentions.

Ford put his weight into keeping Dean in place.

Time. She was running out of time. Pain in her wrists and muscles stripped her nerves raw, ripping a groan from her throat. There. Ford had set her service weapon near the lantern. It wouldn't get her out of these zip ties, but with any luck, she could stop Ford altogether. She had to do something. Dean wasn't struggling anymore. Her heart kicked hard in her chest. No. This wasn't over. He had to keep fighting.

"Well, that was anticlimactic. I mean eighteen years and so many close calls, and you would think there'd be... more." Ford peeled his foot from his latest victim's chest. Then turned on her. Holstering his weapon, he dragged his chair back in front of her. "Now, where were we? Right. Round three."

Ford collected another set of syringes. Utter despair leeched into Leigh's brain. She wasn't going to survive a new round. She could feel it in her bones. How achingly... tired her body had become in a matter of minutes. She thought of Ava, of how she'd be breaking her promise. She hoped Ava forgave her.

"I have to say, disruptions aside, I am really enjoying our time together, Leigh. When you spend so long planning some-one's death, you have an idea of how it will end, but this is so much better than I ever could've imagined."

The last of the warmth in her veins vacated. Leaving her empty as she stared at the still waters where Dean had disap-peared. They were deeper now. Nearly to her knees. It would take Durham PD days to drain this basement and find her remains. And then where would Ava go? Tears burned in her eyes. What was the point in holding them back? She'd buried any feelings she'd had for Dean Groves over the years, but watching him murdered brought back those few moments he'd given her permission to be herself. Where he'd accepted her for who she was—baggage and all. "I don't even know your name. How will I know who to haunt when I'm dead?"

"Still quick with that wit, I see." Ford uncapped the syringes. One an amphetamine, the other a barbiturate. It was going to hurt again. He'd make sure of it. "It took a lot to convince the detective running Teshia's murder investigation to leave my name out of the reports, but it turns out, money *can* buy happiness."

The shadows behind Ford shifted as he set the needle into the crook of her arm. Nothing but a hallucination. The last effort from her brain to make sense of the position she'd die in. Not to mention the outfit. Sweats were not fashionable, but it was too late to change now. Acceptance settled over her like a weighted blanket. Uncomfortable at first, but she'd get used to it. At least for the few minutes she had left. "You thought of everything."

"I have." He shoved the needle beneath her skin. She didn't even feel the pinch this time.

Leigh registered the wall of muscle at Ford's back. "I mean, you thought of everything except him."

Ford grabbed for her service weapon and spun. Not fast enough. Dean slammed the palm of his hand into the son of a bitch's wrist. The gun tore from Ford's grip and was lost to the inky black waters climbing up Leigh's body. Dean's fist rocked into the marshal's face. Once. Twice. Ford lost his footing, and the two men dove into the depths together.

She was out of options. Leigh bit back a scream as she pressed her knuckles into the chair's arm. Plastic cut into skin and tendon, but it had to break sooner or later. It had to. Both men struggled for the upper hand mere feet away in a brutal desperation for dominance and survival.

But a strong kick hit her chair.

Leigh was falling backwards. Water consumed her in an instant. It drove into her mouth, up her nose. Black waters fought her attempts to break free and crushed her from every side. Her lungs were emptied in a matter of seconds. Only the dim light of the lantern gave her any direction of which way was up.

Frantic churning told her Dean and Ford were still locked in their battle. Neither of them had noticed she'd gone under. She was on her own. Trapped. Alone. The zip ties seemed so much tighter than they had a moment ago, the wood of the chair soaking up as much water as possible. Leaving her with less slack.

Her screams went unheard. Her thrashing ignored.

She was going to die in the flooded basement of the university that'd helped shape her into a survivor. As a student who learned what heartbreak really entailed. As an agent who'd stood against police corruption and senseless murder. As a woman who'd taken the leap to rebuild her family and trust again. None of it had done a damn bit of good in the end.

Strong hands latched on to her arms and hauled her upright. Water choked from her nose and mouth as she grasped for a single molecule of oxygen.

"You're not getting away from me that easy, little rabbit." Dean. He'd saved her. Calluses scraped against her jawline. "Breathe, damn it."

Her lungs took the order to heart. Air rushed to replace water in her chest. Before she had a chance to blink the water from her eyes, his touch was gone. The hard thud of fists broke through the pounding of her heart between her ears. Hair clung to her face in long streaks, cutting off some of her vision.

Dean slammed his knee into Ford's jaw then rushed to lock the imposter marshal in a headlock. Ford's elbow connected with his assailant's torso. Neither gained the advantage over the other. Light and dark. Push and pull. Perfectly matched in every way.

But Leigh could tip the scales.

The flood had increased by another couple of inches, crawling across her lap. This entire section of the basement would be underwater in under thirty minutes at this rate. Blood leaked from her wrists as she twisted against the swollen chair arm. Her toes barely touched the floor, but she had to try. She pushed her toes into the floor as much as she could and kicked off. The chair swayed backwards once again. Panic had her overcorrecting, but the precarious balance had gotten her that much closer to the workbench. There had to be something—anything—she could use to get herself out of this damn chair.

Leigh tried again. And again.

The chair hit the edge of the makeshift workbench. The lantern wobbled on impact, revealing nothing but two more sets of syringes on the surface of the table.

Her fingertips barely brushed a few inches over the ledge. If she could get to the syringes, she might be able to use one for leverage between the chair arm and the zip ties. Hope fled as she stretched her hand as far to one side as possible. Rocking forward, she tried to balance on her toes, but ripples of water knocked her off course. It was no use.

A frustrated growl vibrated through her. "Come on!"

She could do this. She had to do this. She hadn't survived the loss and grief and betrayal of those she'd once trusted to give in now. She was a mother now. Not as good as her own, but a mother all the same. That was worth fighting for. Marshal Ford —or whoever the hell he really was—was just the latest in a long line of jackasses who thought they could control her. She deserved a future. With Ava and all the complications of substitute motherhood that came with it. With the BAU and maybe even a nice guy who wouldn't try to kill her one day. A girl could dream. Or she could make that dream a reality.

The brutal fistfight at her back grew louder. Closer. Neither Dean nor Ford were willing to give in. And she wouldn't either. Pressing onto her toes, Leigh forced her weight forward. Her chest hit the edge of the worktable. One of the syringes rolled toward her, and she used her chin to position it into her mouth. Careful not to bite down and expose herself to whatever drug Ford had loaded inside, she let the chair's legs hit the floor. They were stronger than they looked, but the next few minutes would prove it.

She transferred the syringe to one hand, gripping it with everything she had. One chance. That was all she had to make this work.

Water slapped her across the face as Ford dropped onto all fours at her feet. Dark eyes connected with hers. Right before he drew his service weapon from the back of his waistband.

Turning, Ford took aim. And pulled the trigger.

Dean halted mid attack. Then stumbled back. Chin dropping to his chest. His black T-shirt revealed nothing but a red hole where there should've been skin over his right pec.

The breath rushed out of her as he dropped to his knees. Eyes focused solely on her as though in apology for taking a bullet. "Dean."

THIRTY-EIGHT

Durham, New Hampshire

Thursday, October 10
9:02 p.m.

"Now that's more like it." Ford pressed a once-polished shoe into Dean's shoulder, turning her ex onto his back. "Who knew you still had so much fight in you?"

She was out of time. Leigh gripped the plunger of the syringe and jerked it to one side. The zip tie around her right wrist broke. She had a hand free and went for the left. The ties around her ankles snapped with less effort, but they were still enough to slow her down.

Ford twisted to face her, gun in hand. He raised it level with her chest. "Where do you think you're going? We haven't finished our conversation."

"Really? I thought I made my point clear." Her body temperature hit the ceiling. Too hot. Too charged with whatever amphetamine he'd injected her with. Her heart beat out of control. A raging bull in a china shop. She couldn't take a full breath. Every cell in her body on fire. "I'm canceling our date."

"And here I had such high hopes for us." Ford pulled the trigger.

The gun jammed.

She didn't have time to feel the relief as the marshal lunged. He arced the weapon down. The butt slammed into her shoulder. Then again. Agony tore at her former injury straight down to the bone, but she was still standing. Still fighting.

Leigh let him come at her again, using Ford's momentum against him. He overstepped on the next assault. Dropping his shoulder and leaving his back open for attack. She fisted that ridiculously unwrinkled button-down and thrust him into the nearest wall as hard as she could. His face planted hard against cinderblock. Ford was faster. Stronger. More brutal considering he'd managed to take down six—now seven—fully grown men, but she'd had to make up for her size all her life.

Ford's elbow slammed into her face. The crunch of bone ricocheted around her head before the pain registered. Lightning struck behind her eyes at the impact. Blood flowed down the back of her throat and into her mouth as she fell back. She coughed blood onto her sweatshirt. Giving Ford all the time he needed to attain the upper hand.

"That hurt." He tossed the gun into a far-off corner of the room.

Out of reach.

She countered his approach, wading through knee-high waters and nearly tripping over Dean's body. He'd rolled face down into the depths—unconscious—and she latched on to him, pulling him against her chest.

"But it's nothing compared to what I'm going to do to you. All those other victims, they got out of this life easy." Ford tossed one of the chairs that'd floated into his path to the side. Intimidating and terrifying and full of a brutality she hadn't seen until it'd been too late. The man was full of surprises. "You were right before. I didn't want them to suffer. They were nothing more than a means to an end, but I'm going to enjoy what I do to you."

Dean's dead weight—bad choice of words—dragged at her already tired body. "You wouldn't believe how many times I've heard the evil villain monologue. Believe me when I say, yours isn't anything special."

She wasn't sure why she was trying to piss him off other than it felt like the right thing to do in the moment. If nothing else, she would go down running her mouth until the bitter end. But Dean didn't need to suffer for that.

"Now you're just trying to hurt my feelings." Ford launched at her.

She had to drop Dean's body to dodge the collision. In an instant, Ford had closed the distance between them. He jerked her into his chest with the help of the stupid drawstrings on her hoodie, and she had no choice but to go. Those things really were choking hazards, but not the way she'd always been told. Leigh got the sense he was holding himself back. Trying to draw this out as long as possible.

Playing with her.

She wasn't going to last much longer. The drug he'd shot her with was already starting to fade, taking her confidence and ego with it. But she wasn't going to ask for another dose either. Her face pulsed in rhythm with her erratic heartbeat. He'd broken her nose. The least she could do was repay the favor. Leigh fisted the hair at the back of Ford's head and slammed her forehead into his nose. "There, now we match."

She wouldn't let him get the upper hand again. Shoving his head beneath the surface of the water, Leigh tried to use her weight to pin him. But Ford was so much bigger. He tossed her without any effort at all. He rammed his knuckles into her face. She fell back, nearly going under. Before she had a chance to get her bearings, the marshal swung one of the chairs down on her.

The leg connected with the side of her head. The seat with her ribs. Air crushed from her chest, and she sank for a second time. Hands broke into her clouding vision and wrapped around her neck. Bubbles brushed against her skin as they escaped her clothing. She latched on to Ford's wrists to break his hold.

She'd been here before. Except there were no mason jars full of moldy sludge down here. No way for her to get to her service weapon. Ford squeezed his thumbs into her throat. Killing her. Pounding against his forearms did nothing. She kicked out, catching him in the knee, but the marshal refused to go down.

This was it.

This was when he finally got what he'd wanted back in that storage room. Her fight or flight wouldn't get off its ass with the drugs still in her system. There was nothing she could do to survive this. Rushing water sounded in her ears. Or was that the last of the blood in her head?

The edges of her vision darkened with black webs as they had that first time she'd almost drowned. Her shoe grazed the side of his knee. She was fighting a losing battle. Losing the will to thrash. Maybe she'd always known this case would be the death of her. And Ava... Ava would be all alone. Would think Leigh had left her on purpose. Abandoned her like everyone else in her short life had done. Leigh tried to shake her head. To get her body to do something other than give up.

She could barely make out Ford's features through the surface of the water. But there was one thing her brain latched on to. A thin, white tube bobbing against his upper arm. One of the syringes.

It was her one shot and could blow up in her face, but she didn't see any other option. Leigh forced her hands to release his wrists—to stop fighting—and grabbed for the tube. There was no way to tell what had been loaded inside. Amphetamine or barbiturate. It didn't matter. The syringe took shape in her hand.

Leigh stabbed the needle into Ford's ribcage and depressed the plunger.

His hands left her throat.

She shoved her feet against the floor and shot to the surface. Her gasp burned more than the drugs still in her system. The influx of oxygen claimed her in a wave of dizziness, and her knees hit the floor. Water lapped at her face as she reached out to steady herself. Alive. She was alive.

"You shouldn't have done that." Ford's growl was the only warning as he closed in again. A predator with an eye on its prey. Except the marshal—she had to stop thinking of him as a marshal—swayed on his feet. He attempted another step forward. Water dripped from his jaw, every drop crystal clear in the light of the emergency lantern. Eyes heavy, Ford struggled with some internal battle. His body versus his intention to kill her. Barbiturate. She'd dosed him with a barbiturate. He wasn't going to last long, and a crushing sense of relief wedged into her veins.

"Doesn't feel good, does it? Not being in control." Hell, her voice sounded as though it'd been dragged over gravel. Along with the rest of her. Leigh pulled her feet under her, pressing to stand. Her own steadiness wouldn't last long, but she'd make sure he paid for what he'd done. "Max Ford—or whoever the hell you are—you are under arrest for the murder of... a lot of people."

"This isn't over, Leigh. You of all people should know I don't stop until I get what I want." His laugh punctured through the haze chasing her down. Ford took that step forward. "And I want you."

Every muscle down her spine clenched. She couldn't win.

Not against his size, his strength, his determination. Ford was going to get what he wanted, and there was nothing she could do about it. Fear coursed through her at the possibility the barbiturate had been measured for someone much smaller.

"She's taken." Dean fisted the bastard's shirt and rocketed his fist into Ford's face. Knocking the killer unconscious.

Seconds ticked by. A full minute?

Time had lost all meaning in this room.

Leigh studied Dean's muscled back as he released his hold on the man he'd hunted for eighteen years. Right until her legs couldn't support her any longer. She collapsed, letting the flood waters consume her lower half and earning herself Dean's full attention. Without the threat of dying, she couldn't rely on adrenaline to keep her going. It drained faster than it was supposed to. That couldn't be normal, but there was nothing she could do about it now. The push and pull of water intensified around her. Her heart rate spiked as Dean took shape mere inches away, one arm pressed against his chest.

"Shit, little rabbit." The endearment shouldn't have soothed the frantic thoughts about being alone in the same room as him rushing to the front of her mind, but she couldn't fight it either. Strong arms threaded under hers and around her back, hauling her against his chest. Body heat soaked through her clothing and drove deeper. Becoming part of her. "It's over. I've got you. You're going to be okay."

Over? Her head hit his arm. She had nothing left, and all Leigh wanted to do was succumb to the weight increasing in her body. Shot. He'd been shot. "You're bleeding."

"So are you." They were moving. Leaving this flooded, dank room and Ford behind. Her feet dragged behind her, but he kept her against his ribcage with his uninjured arm. Dean had come for her. After all these years, he'd been telling the truth. She didn't know what to do with that at the moment. "Only difference is I look good coated in blood."

Her eyes grew heavy. The amphetamine was losing its hold on her nervous system. Blurring the exposed piping and electrical above her into wavy lines. All the while Dean was there, pulling her back into consciousness with his voice and the back-and-forth rocking of his body. "You make it sound... like it happens all the time."

"This certainly isn't the first," he said.

Leigh wanted to ask what that meant. What he'd been doing all these years on the run. Where he'd been. If he'd missed her as much as she'd missed him. She wanted to know if he'd gotten married and had kids and lived a life while she'd been brought back to the past over and over by the secrets she'd kept. She wanted it all, but her body had other ideas. It was shutting down. Giving up on her. "Ford..."

Where was he? And what was it about her that drove the men around her to violence?

"Dean. Though I can see why you might be confused." He looked at her then. He picked up his pace if the rocking sensation was any indication. Becoming more desperate. Not a good sign. "We're almost there. Stay with me, Leigh."

First named. It must be serious.

She didn't have a chance to answer as darkness greeted her like a friend she couldn't shake.

THIRTY-NINE

Durham, New Hampshire

Sunday, October 13
10:17 a.m.

Everything hurt, and she was dying.

The hurricane had finally released those stuck under the campus shelter in place. Forty-eight hours. Six bodies, including the two forensic techs Ford had shot. Durham PD was still working on pumping flood waters from the campus basement, but it'd been easy for them to get to the imposter's body. The barbiturate she'd dosed him with and Dean's fist had knocked him unconscious, although that hadn't stopped Ford's autonomic nervous system from trying to breathe face down in three feet of water. But it was over. The man they'd known as Ford—soon to be identified by DNA, dental, and prints—would never hurt anyone again. The medical examiner had a hell of a few weeks ahead of him. In the end, Durham PD would be able to close eleven open murder investigations, including Teshia Elborne's.

Leigh dragged her legs over the side of the bed. Three days she'd been stuck in this hellhole with no indication of when they'd let her leave. Scratchy sheets, thin gowns, no showers, too many visitors. She couldn't take it anymore.

She'd only made it a few steps toward the door before it swung inward.

"What do you think you're doing?" Shock widened Ava's eyes. Her adopted daughter pointed over Leigh's shoulder. "Get back in that bed. Right now."

"You realize I'm the mother in this scenario, right?" As much as she hated being forced to sustain pokes, prodding, painkillers, and fake smiles from the staff, Leigh couldn't hate Ava's need to help. To stay close. With the case closed, they finally had the time together they deserved. And all the takeout they could stomach. Residual pain throbbed in her joints and wrists. And her face. Oh, and the strangulation bruises around her throat. She turned back for the bed. Making it out of this room might've been too lofty a goal, even with three days of fluids to counter the drugs Ford had dosed her with. Her hands planted on the mattress. She really didn't want to get back in the bed. "I'm supposed to be the one to tell you what to do."

"You can't take care of me if you don't take care of yourself." Ava closed the distance between them, setting the grocery bag in hand on the side table. Unpacking the small white containers, she tossed a pair of chopsticks on the bed. "Bed. Now."

"Listen here, warden. I've survived worse than torture." Though she couldn't give an example right now. And she didn't owe a fifteen-year-old anything but a roof over her head, three meals a day, clothes, an education, and unconditional love. All of which was on the verge of being taken away if Leigh didn't get out of this room.

"Don't make me get Grandpa and Uncle Chandler." Ava pointed a black plastic fork at Leigh's face.

The warning was enough to put her back in bed. She loved

her father and brother, but they wouldn't go easy on her if she fought doctor's orders. And she couldn't stand to see their faces after being locked in the same room with them since the moment they touched down in Durham. "Fine. Thank you for the food."

"You're welcome." Ava took her usual seat in the chair beside the bed, one of the white boxes and a fork in hand. It didn't look remotely comfortable, but her adopted daughter didn't mind the long hours, the talks with the physicians and nurses, and the copious amounts of MSG. "Have you given any more thought into what happens next?"

"You mean putting all this food in my mouth?" Leigh grabbed for one of the boxes. Sesame chicken, maybe? Her stomach was done with the hospital's offerings. "Yes, I've been thinking about it all morning. I don't think I can look at another Jell-O cup."

"That's too bad. I swiped some off a cart earlier. Thought we could watch reruns of *Jerry Springer* and have dessert in bed." Ava's teasing smile was new, and if Leigh was being honest with herself, the most beautiful sight after everything they'd been through. "I meant, after you get out of here."

"I guess head back to Quantico." That'd always been the plan. That was where their apartment was, where they'd started building their life. They hadn't even given it a real shot before she'd been brought back to New Hampshire. But the words hit wrong. Leigh set the white box in her lap, her body immediately holding on to all the heat, and studied Ava. She'd made a promise back on that campus. To put Ava first. To stop using her work as a coping mechanism and distraction from hard things. To give their relationship a fighting chance. The past three days quarantined to this room had been nice, but this wasn't reality. "Unless you have a better idea."

Ava's caramel-brown eyes locked on to her. "What do you mean?"

She shrugged, as if the prospect of giving up the one constant—an obsession she'd clung to her entire life—wasn't a big deal. Because, right now, it wasn't. Ava wasn't happy in Quantico. While Leigh didn't think she would keep running away now that they'd uncovered the root of Ava's turmoil in killing her abductor in cold blood, Ava deserved to be happy. And it was Leigh's job to make that happen. "I have savings. I could take a few months off from work. We could go anywhere. Just the two of us."

The fifteen-year-old sat straighter, her own white container forgotten. "You're serious."

"Why wouldn't I be?" she asked.

Ava shook her head, eyes wide in disbelief. "Because you love your job. You love working cases, and if the past three days in this room have taught me anything, it's that you go insane if you don't have something to do."

"I love you more." It was the truth. Ava was hers. State mandated or not, and there wasn't anything—*anything*—Leigh wouldn't give to keep her. "Besides, I consulted with departments all over the country before I started working for the FBI. I could do that remotely, if needed, and you could keep up with school and therapy from a laptop anywhere in the country."

"What about Uncle Chandler and Grandpa?" Tears glistened in Ava's eyes. "You just got them both back. You can't leave them. They'll kill each other if you're gone for too long."

That was true. But maybe it was time for her to let her family stand on its own legs while she stepped into this next stage of her life. Do something for herself.

"Ava." Leigh set the white box back into the collection on the side table. "I made you a promise, and I'm keeping it. This is me putting you first. This is me choosing you over my job. So where would you want to go?"

"Clarksburg." Her adopted daughter stared at her, as though waiting for Leigh to immediately shoot down the idea of going back to where Ava had once had a life. "I want to go home. And I know it won't be the same. Mom's not getting out anytime soon, and Dad is..." Dead. Her father was dead. "But it's the place I love the most."

"I think that's a great idea." Leigh couldn't fault her for that. They sat in silence for a few minutes—content in this new agreement between them—before a knock sounded at the door.

Ava jumped up to answer it, pulling the door open. To reveal Dean Groves on the other side. "If you're here to take my mom's blood again, she might kill you. And, believe me, she knows how to get away with it. She's an FBI agent."

Mom? Leigh's chest threatened to explode. She'd never been called that before, never thought Ava would be the one to speak those words. The pain in her joints drained at the rush of warmth in her veins. "It's okay, Ava. He's a..." Friend? Ex? Life saver? She had no idea what to call Dean. "Person I know."

"That sounded really convincing." Ava narrowed that brilliant gaze on her, then onto Dean as if in warning. "I guess I'll go see if I can find more Jell-O. Don't let her get out of bed. No matter how much she manipulates you into agreeing with her."

"I'm more than aware of what your mother is capable of." A nervous laugh filled the hospital room as Dean stepped inside. Ava closed the door behind him, sealing them inside together.

"Not sure I want you here." Leigh tried to focus on the food she'd set aside, but her nerves got the best of her. She wasn't hungry anymore. Though she might have to hide some of it in case Ava came to make sure she'd eaten. Maybe one day she'd be a nurse like her biological mom. Only without the killer tendencies. "The last time we were alone in a room together, you punched me in the shoulder. Set my recovery back by a few weeks."

"To be fair, we weren't alone. Your partner—or whatever he was pretending to be—was on the floor unconscious." Dean dared another step closer. His voice wavered, but damn it if that break in his confidence wasn't human. She didn't want to humanize him. She wanted him to go back to wherever he came from and stay there. "And I'm sorry about the shoulder. It was the fastest way to get you to back down."

"You knew about my previous injury." Not a question. He had to have studied her past case reports. "Seems unfair considering I know nothing about you."

Dean didn't have any argument to that. He took a seat in Ava's chair, close enough for her to get a hint of whatever soap he'd used to shower. She was close to pouting again. She wanted a shower. "What do you want to know?"

"Why did you leave?" She hadn't meant to ask. It had nothing to do with the investigation or identifying the killer he'd been chasing these past eighteen years, but it was the only question that mattered to her.

"To protect you." No hesitation. No guilt or apology. Dean Groves was still the blunt and confident man she'd fallen in love with so long ago, and she hated it. "I knew if I told you I was bring framed, you'd sacrifice your studies and opportunities to work with Morrow to help me. And if I told you I was going to find Teshia's killer, you would've wanted to go with me. That's just the kind of person you are. You fight for people. People like your dad and your brother. People like your daughter. It's who you are, and it's one of the reasons I fell in love with you."

She didn't want to believe that. That he'd felt the same for her as she had him. "You don't know anything about me."

"I know more than you think, Leigh." Why did she want him to call her "little rabbit" again? Dean leaned forward, his elbows on his knees. The gunshot wound he'd sustained had obviously been stitched and dressed, but he showed no signs of pain. Jerk. "I never wanted to drag you into helping me clear my name, but I can't say I'm not happy to see you now."

That should've raised her defenses, but she wasn't sure she had them anymore. At least, not against him. He'd saved her life down in that basement—twice—and gotten shot in the shoulder if the sling supporting his right arm was any indication. "If that's true, why come back now?"

"Ford's trail was heading east. Up into New Hampshire. He tried to hide it, but I knew he'd somehow caught on to my movements chasing him. I also knew there was only one thing in New Hampshire he could use to make me stop coming for him." Dean's gaze softened. Or was that the pain pills they had her on? "I wanted to make him answer for Teshia's murder and clear my name, but once I realized he was coming for you... I couldn't let him hurt you for the mistakes I'd made."

"He killed Alice Dietz to bring me back here, said he knew I wouldn't be able to turn down the opportunity for closure. I guess he was right." Ford—the man she'd known as Ford—recreated the one crime that would guarantee her showing up exactly where he wanted her. Where it all started. And she'd fallen straight into his trap. Oh, hell. She'd even kissed him. Agreed to a date with him. If her brother ever found out, she'd never live it down.

"He was good at reading people's weaknesses. If it wasn't obvious before now, you're one of mine." The doubt had left his voice. "I'm sorry I disappeared on you without explaining. I know what giving me an alibi cost you, and I wanted to make it clear how grateful I am for you putting your trust in me. If I could go back, I would do things differently."

Trust. Did she trust him? She had then. She wasn't so sure now, but she didn't really know him now.

"I know why you did it. Doesn't mean I'm not still mad about it." Eleven people dead. All because Dean wouldn't let a killer get away with murder. A man after her own heart. Who believed evil should be punished, and that they could do something about it. Her voice failed her. "I was in love with you."

"I was in love with you, too." Dean set those dark eyes on

her. Unwavering. "The second you rammed me with a moving box in that stairwell, you had me."

She couldn't stopper the laugh escaping up her sore throat.

"Do you think maybe we could start over?" Dean waited a beat, reaching for her hand at the edge of the bed. "I'll let you throw another box at me if it'll make you feel better."

Hope knotted tight in her gut. She had a lot to consider. Taking another sabbatical from cases. Moving back to Clarksburg. Starting fresh with Ava. But that need for connection pulsed at the idea of reaching out. She'd thought Ford—the son of a bitch—could fix the isolation she'd clung to all these years, but while she'd fulfilled his need for understanding, he'd failed to meet hers in the end.

Maybe it was the fact she'd already taken that first step. Maybe it was Dean himself and everything they'd left unfinished, but she'd already made her decision. He was offering a future. One that didn't come with so much doubt or fear. Leigh tightened her hold on his hand. "The next box I throw at you won't be packed with pillows."

EPILOGUE

Clarksburg, Virginia

Saturday, January 11
6:43 p.m.

Three months later...

She'd faced down killers, but this was so much worse.

Leigh hadn't been on a date in... too damn long. If nerves could kill, she'd already be on the medical examiner's slab. Why the hell had she agreed to this? They were still unpacking their new apartment—another two-bedroom, two-bathroom—and trying to settle back into Clarksburg. The move wasn't as life-disrupting as Quantico, but she had yet to get used to working remote for the BAU. It was temporary. She and Ava both knew that. Sooner or later, Director Livingstone's patience would run out, and Leigh would have to step back onto active scenes. Until then, they would soak up what time they had together. Which apparently included getting a life that didn't have anything to do with Ava. Ava's words.

"Stop touching your hair. You're going to ruin it." Ava swatted her hand away for the tenth time and grabbed for some flyaways. Joke was on her. Leigh's entire head was one giant flyaway. There was no saving it. "Hold still. I need to fix your eye shadow."

"If this is what it's like getting back into the dating scene, you're never allowed to date." Leigh flinched back as her daughter nearly poked her in the eye. "I'm going to sweat through my dress if he doesn't get here soon. Do I have anything in my teeth?"

"For the millionth time, he's seen you covered in blood and unconscious. I don't think food in your teeth is going to make him run for the hills." Ava added more hair oil—what the hell was hair oil?—to one side of the updo. Then stepped back with approval lining her face. "You should've just screwed him after you closed the case. Then you wouldn't have three months of nerves."

"Ava Portman, I better not hear anything more about screwing come out of your mouth until you're eighteen." But, for real, her daughter had a point. This was torture. And she would know. She'd lived through it. Leigh smoothed invisible wrinkles from her slacks. Armor in place. "Do you think I could make it far if I slipped out the window before he got here?"

It was only fair. He'd disappeared on her for eighteen years. What was one night? Three knocks at the front door sealed her fate.

"Too late." Ava flashed a saccharine smile. "I messaged him an hour ago to come early in case you tried to bail."

"You're grounded. Forever," Leigh said. "No phone. No TV. No friends. From this moment on, you're an inaccessible island."

Her daughter closed in for a tight hug. "Answer the door, Mom. It's going to be okay. I promise. And if it isn't, I learned how to get rid of a body without raising suspicion."

She still wasn't used to that. Ava calling her mom, but the fifteen-year-old had made a good point when Leigh had asked. There were thousands of people who were being raised by two moms. Why couldn't she be one of them?

"I don't like that joke." Leigh released her hold and sucked in a deep breath. She could do this. It'd been so long since she'd allowed herself to dream about the future. She was ready to leave the past—and all the secrets she'd carried—behind. Reaching for the doorknob, she swung the door open and faced off with the man who'd sacrificed so much for the chance to get to this moment. To her. And looking at Dean now, she was glad she hadn't ducked out the back. "I'm ready."

A LETTER FROM THE AUTHOR

Huge thanks for reading *The Killer She Knew*! I hope you were hooked on Leigh's latest case as much as I was. If you want to join other readers in hearing all about my new releases and bonus content, you can sign up for my newsletter.

www.stormpublishing.co/nichole-severn

And for all the bonus content you can handle about Leigh and my other series, join me here.

nicholesevern.com/newsletter

If you enjoyed this book and could spare a few moments to leave a review that would be hugely appreciated. Even a short review can make all the difference in encouraging a reader to discover my books for the first time. Thank you so much.

This book was purely driven by Leigh's need for the healing and family she's worked for since she was seventeen years old. As I sat down to write this book, I couldn't think of anything better to bring an end to that journey than testing her learned definition of family and throwing an unruly teenager at her to see how she figures out motherhood. In the end, she's come to realize, as many of us who've suffered from trauma find, that family includes those we choose, not always those we're related to by blood.

Thanks again for being part of this amazing journey with me, and I hope you'll stay in touch—I have so many more stories and ideas to entertain you with.

Nichole

nicholesevern.com

 facebook.com/nichole.severn
instagram.com/nicholesevern

ACKNOWLEDGMENTS

First and foremost, a huge thank you to Kevin, my partner in crime of twenty years. For your undying support, love, encouragement, brainstorming, and constant threats of murder. Oh, and for our two demon spawn.

Thank you to my editor, Emily, for the unbridled excitement for this series, this character, and the vision we've built together. Your enthusiasm has pushed me to bury that critical bitch voice that haunts me every time I sit down to write, and I will never forget your direction.

Thanks to my very own Agent Lady, Jill Marsal, who pushes me to try new things, get out of my comfort zone, and take charge of my career. This series wouldn't have been possible without you.

And especially thank you to you, dear reader, for spending precious time and energy with these stories in my head and giving me an outlet to share all my visions of murder.

Printed in Great Britain
by Amazon

60090608R00184